Humans are the Problem

A monster's anthology.

Edited by
Michael Cluff & Willow Becker

This book is dedicated to the monstrous readers and backers behind this project. Thank you for being champions of our cause and holding the torch alight for monsters everywhere.

Special Thanks to the Monster Moguls, including:

Mike
Jacob
Paige Lisko
Will Blosser
Spencer Finch
T.S. Finnegan
Ross Adamson
Phil Haagensen
Bridget Sullivan
Justin Rosenbaum
Daniel Hallmeyer
Kurt G. Schumacher
Edward Potter
Lew Gibb

Chris Roberts
Chase Rahilly
Joshua Hair
Hillary Clay
Frank Lewis
Ichabod Ebenezer
Naeem Khalifa
Jesse Rice
Alton W.
Michelle Woodbury
Andrew Harding
Greg Askew
Cappy loves Emika Monster
Dr. Richard Jeckyll Gorman
Marcelino C. Collando IV
Four Corners Collectibles

Simon Holland
Nikolas P. Robinson
Christopher Baxter
Cultist Dee Berlin
Shannon Chapels
Chris Padar
Valerie Gaddy
Brad Dowdy
Maxime Gregoire
Erik Mann
Connor Mason
Scott Casey
Scott D. Musch
Aaron Frodsham

...and a proud father.

CONTENTS

WHEN HUMANS ATTACK: A CONCERNING PROLOGUE

Admit it. You want to believe that humans are just good.

Consider the 12-year-old who designed a wind-powered well for his village in Ghana, or the people who created meatless burgers, or Oprah.

It wouldn't be fair to stop there, though.

The fact is, that for every time humans are the solution to the world's problems, there are nine more times we caused the problem to begin with. From overpopulation to eating Tide pods, humans keep doing dumb things that harm other people—purposefully and not. We invented war, weapons of mass destruction, and *all YouTube comments.*

That's the kind of stuff that goes on a species' permanent record.

Saying that "humans are the problem" has an air of finality to it. Almost like there needs to be some decisive action taken to create a solution. But we are not suggesting any such final solution, although the monsters we represent might disagree.

In all situations there are two variables that are often overlooked: context and perspective. Only skimming their surface can lead to some fairly nasty or even disastrous results.

The purpose of the stories contained within this tome is to provide you, the reader, with a bit of context and perspective. That way any nasty results you may experience are on you.

We present a world in which monsters have been relegated to the sidelines by the passage of time and the shifting of priorities to where we live today: a place where fame, fortune, and information have become our gods and anything beyond the veil of concrete fact is laughable.

In the minds of the monsters, gods, and other creatures in this anthology, humans (and this shifting set of human priorities) are the problem. However, as easy as it is to state a problem, the actual understanding of that problem—comprehending the root of the issue at hand (or claw or tentacle or pseudopod)—is far more difficult.

These are the stories about how monsters are adapting and finding new ways to deal with a 21st-century world that doesn't believe they exist. They are also tales of a world in which monsters coexist side-by-side with humans, learning from one another and stepping into a new kind of future where humanity and monstrosity combine to create a new way of life.

We bring you the information about these unique creatures, but it's your decision as to what to *do* with that information. Sincerely, we hope that you make some good decisions, for lack of tolerance isn't exclusive to the human race and there are things out there with far pointier teeth than the average human.

Read the stories. Enjoy them as entertainment. Then, let yourself be impacted by them.

Our goal as storytellers both human and inhuman is to come to new, better solutions to the statement "humans are the problem." And maybe it's more of a question than a statement. Maybe humans are the problem, but even the most monstrous of us make that declaration without an air of finality, but one of hope.

Maybe the deepest, darkest parts of the human race still remind us that monsters have souls, too. And maybe the monsters—the real monsters just out of sight, hiding behind the shadows when you walk alone—want us to be better for our sake and theirs.

Or, maybe they just want to eat us.

Either way, safe reading.

Michael Cluff & Willow Becker
September 2021

ROOT ROT

SARAH READ

They used to fear me. They will fear me again.

The child sleeps, hand curled on her pillow like a soft shell, a pearl hidden inside. It's so much easier if they leave the tooth under the pillow. But they can't bear to be parted from it, knowing that someone is coming to take a piece of them away forever.

So they must make me palatable, for their own sake, deck me in ribbons and curls, delicate wings dusted in sparkle. My portrait hangs on the wall—a gleaming smile, hair as long as my body in broad curls, a star clutched in my hand. The sparkle of the painting refracts the dim nightlight from the hall behind the open door.

I clench my jaw and the forest of teeth inside my mouth shifts, sending a savory wave of hot blood over my tongue. There's space in my right cheek for one more.

I reach a long fingernail between the child's sweaty fingers and scoop the tooth out of the crease of her palm. It had settled there as if rooted in her life-line. It is so small, so white, rootless, clean as a polished gem.

I push it past my raw lips and through the jumble of all the others, filling the last empty space in my mouth. My tongue presses to the back of my throat to keep them all from tumbling down my gullet. *Not yet.* It's been a long night, but there is work yet to do.

"I'd have crumbled long ago if it wasn't for the precious kernels of youth nestled in the core of children's teeth."

It is a long way home on the mirror roads and my lips are tired from holding in so many prizes.

I do not carry a wand; I don't need one. My hair is not yellow, save for where the grey has faded to white and aged to ivory. And it does not curl, save for where the fairy knots have creased it. My dress is not pink, except round the collar, where spittle and blood have dyed the flax the color of apple blossoms. I do not have wings; I have other ways to travel. I do not glitter, except for when I smile and the shine of a thousand teeth can be seen through the dark. None of them are mine. Mine wore away long ago, ground to nothing on millennia of gristle. Thistle Bristle Gristle is what I am called, where I am known. Humans long ago forgot my name, though they called me Tand Fae then, and were fickle with their offerings, keeping their cast-off teeth for themselves.

I am an ancient thing. And I'd have crumbled long ago if it wasn't for the precious kernels of youth nestled in the core of children's teeth.

Humans have trapped me in a pretty lie to soothe their young when a part of them suddenly falls away. The charming portrait strips me of my power, my ancient rite. They have turned my bristles to gossamer.

They used to fear me. They would fear me if they knew me. But they've cultivated my image as a benevolent blossom. I am loved. They look to my coming with sweet joy.

It's an impossible standard. It ends now.

I lean over the copper pot, spread my split lips wide, and pour forth my harvest. The sound of teeth falling and hitting the metal is like hailstones on a tin roof. The smell is like something long dead, lost and found again. I sweep my tongue round my mouth for the strays and spit and spit my rose water till the bright teeth are swimming. I strike a match and light the stove, revel in the ambient heat as the liquid starts to simmer.

That last tooth—the lifeline tooth—keeps bobbing and rolling into view, brighter than all the rest. As if it had never tasted candy or caramel, never bathed in cider or lemonade.

When the broth has thickened, reduced to a paste that clings to my wooden spoon, I move the pot off the flame. Steam clouds my vision as I lean over it, breathing deep, not wanting any morsel of nutrient to escape me.

The teeth have become fragile husks that shatter under the pressure of my spoon. I grind and stir and pop them all to dust that I mix to a steaming porridge.

It all slides down my throat in a thick, hot rush, rich with young life. I can taste the perfect tooth—that shining lifeline treasure. It adds vigor to the brew, but also a chemical aftertaste. Alcohol, fluoride, chlorine. Not the meaty taste of fresh pulp.

I feel the cells of my body spark. My skin tightens, firms, the sound of it like taut paper. My muscles lift and grow restless. My scalp prickles with new growth of supple locks, the dry, aged ones breaking free and falling away. The years fall away with them. I had held a few hundred teeth in my mouth, and each one dissolves a year, maybe two or even three years for the thickest molars.

I feel every fiber of cellulose spring into place, and I believe, for just a moment, that maybe I can be the pretty fairy in their storybooks. That I can be the portrait on the child's wall. That maybe, if I had enough teeth, enough porridge potion, I could sparkle.

But that cold taste of chlorine clings to the back of my tongue. Plants a throbbing ache in my head. Ties a knot in my gut that has me bent over the hedge before long, losing my precious potion, aging with every gargled heave as all my youth splatters into the grass and the shoots vanish into the dirt as seedlings unsprouted.

Whatever was done to that tooth, to make it so perfect, unmakes me.

I stagger to my bed, to rest. To try and regain a strength that only ever seems to be slipping away. To plan.

It's easy to find the house again. The scent of a fresh, empty socket lingers in the air, and that puff of chemical clean on a sleeping child's breath draws me back to that same bedside, that same child sleeping below my false countenance.

Again the child sleeps, a small spot tinged with pink staining the lace of her pillow, so like my dress. Golden curls darkened in sweat stick to her porcelain forehead. She looks more like me than I do.

I slip a careful finger into the child's mouth and press against her teeth. None move. She won't be summoning me again soon. Each tooth is perfect. Rich and unblemished. Save for some hidden toxicity, I know that this small mouthful would erase a century of my cares.

My hand, still wet from the child's mouth, moves reflexively to the sagging, sallow skin at my jowl. To the brittle hair cascading down my curtained neck.

"What have they given you that poisons the likes of me?" I whisper across her smooth cheek.

The sleeping parents' room is an opulent mess, strewn with fine things, a shrine of material wish-fulfillment. Their faces are slack and content, and their teeth perfect. Every flaw repaired, every surface scraped clean, and that same chemical breeze rolling off their tongues.

The bathroom spills their secret. Tucked away in a drawer is a set of tools, ones used by human dentists to clean mortal teeth. One of these humans is a dentist, and they have afflicted their practice on the others.

I smile and my empty mouth gapes back at me—black and red in the vanity mirror. These chemical treatments are temporary. The toxins can be washed away, leaving behind clean, perfect teeth. Teeth fit for an ambrosia of porridge that will vanish the years from my body.

All I need to do is get the teeth away from the dentist. Just for a while. Just long enough. Just till they ripen for harvest.

I cannot fit a whole child into my mouth, not even such a small one. So I empty my leather bag of dried clover and slip her inside. My leaves are strewn all across her bed. I spit and turn them to coin. It's more than the price for all her teeth, the price of a dozen children's teeth. More than fair.

The child is heavy in my satchel. The path behind the mirror is long, and by the time I reach my cottage, I have aged again. There are ice shards in my knees and my vision is fogged.

I drop my bag inside my threshold, and the child wakes with a muffled wail.

"There, there, little one, nothing to fear. Granny is here." I pull her upright and sit her on my bench. Her brown eyes rove over the inside of my cottage, to the clover hanging from the beams, to the tarnished copper pot, and my wall of tools suspended from hooks. Tools that no doubt look much like her parents', though mine are far more ancient and made of silver.

Her eyes widen at the blackened metal hooks and she begins to cry again, this time with the low moan of fear, her lips pressing and parting in a single syllable over and over "Mu-mu-mu-mu."

The child wants her mother. It's a feeling I remember, though I am too old to remember the being herself that was my mother.

I give the child warm goat's milk with honey and lavender and the ashes of a spell to cleanse the human toxins from her mouth. I wrap her in a warm blanket that I wove myself from black goat hair caught in night-blooming thistles. "Would you like Granny to sing you a song?"

She nods her golden head.

I sing her a half-remembered lullaby and watch as the firelight reflected in her eyes disappears behind heavy eyelids.

I rinse the goat's milk from her cup, and the thick poppy syrup that sticks to the bottom, and I select my tools. Lay them carefully on the table beside the copper pot.

I cannot risk waiting. Already my fingers fail to bend with the dexterity they had last night. I curse under my breath at the humans who have hoarded my offerings, kept them for themselves as mementos of their babe's early years, while my years slip further and further away. That poisoning has brought me nearly past the point of no return. I am nearly too weak to claim those offerings which might save me. Nearly.

I pray the spell works.

I kneel in front of the child and sniff the air by her lips. I taste the sour of the milk and the sweet of honey. I smell the oak that fueled the fire that burned the spell and the stream that fed its roots. It worked. She's clean.

It shocks me how hard the mouth holds onto its treasures. Or perhaps I have truly grown that weak. When the teeth come away, with much pulling and twisting, and a sound like the crackle of unseasoned firewood, they are barely enough to cross the palm of my hand, to trace the path of my long life-line. It will not be enough to make even a spoonful of porridge. But perhaps it is enough to cure me of the previous night's poison. Enough to grant me the strength to walk the mirror road and back again.

I prepare my small meal, holding my breath lest I scatter a single grain of precious enamel dust. When it is brewed, it scents the air with vitality.

The flavor is like rich colostrum. I am new again. The change comes in a rush that burns not unpleasantly but intensely. My skin is smoothed in a way that makes me feel as if it will hold me together. My hair coils rich and brown. Not gold, but there is youth in it. I feel strength in its strands and in the strands of my muscles that move freely, feel capable.

The child's head has nodded forward, blood collecting in her lap as it drops from her empty mouth—a small, raw bow of red and black, framed in golden curls. She looks like me, transposed with the image of me that hangs on her wall.

I run my tongue over the worn flagstones of my teeth. Will any amount of porridge bring them back?

I am summoned. The tug. The call of bleeding sockets, the hopes of small children promised coin.

I leave the child to sleep in my own bed, and I fill my satchel with dried clover, freshly polished tools, and with a stoppered bottle of the milk and poppy spell. I cannot risk carrying her back with me—not yet, not while my strength still wanes. But should my spell work again, I will soon harvest a copper pot full of the most potent of potions. I will return to the height of my strength, my youth, the return of Tand Fae, and all the humans shall know Thistle Bristle Gristle for the god that I am. They will not hoard their offer-ings but lay them out for me. Perhaps then, I shall trade my bristles for gossamer. Maybe then I will sparkle like their false icons. Maybe then I will return the child.

Not all offerings are equal. They never have been, but I have never before had such a preference, been so particular. I refuse nothing, as I am in no place to do so. But I am on the hunt.

Some teeth are scarred, cracked, filled, stuck fast with growth. Some cling to the flavor of their last meal. Some cling to soft strands of flesh fresh pulled from tender mouths. I take them all, press them to my gums, fill my mouth till my smile reflects the night sky. I scatter silvered clover leaves, spreading my fey fortune.

But I cannot help, now, to tally the years I'm gathering. To keep score, and find it wanting. I want. I want dentist's teeth. It's no longer enough to smell and track the trace of blood on the air. Instead I seek the scent of poisons. Toxins. I seek that chemical breath that promises death but for the spell in my bottle.

I catch my breath and chase it, knowing I flirt with my own end—and that prospect seems to give me yet more youth, as though the thought of the risk I take has granted me new life.

The very air burns my eyes. Three children, all breathing synchronous toxicity. Their mother, hands stained with the scent of latex, practically sleeps in her white coat. Her house is decorated with images of teeth and of me. I stare back at myself from fridge magnets and tasseled pillows and posters. Bright smiles stretch in a continuous line across the mantelpiece. In one photograph, the woman herself wears wings, carries a star wand, wears a large plastic tooth around her neck on a string. My jaw tightens and the teeth cupped in my cheeks squeak against each other as they grind together.

I may not be what I once was. I may not reflect the image they expect of me. I am Thistle where they want Marigolds. Bristle where they want silk. Gristle where they want butter. I may never be the pretty pixie they imagine, but they will not dare to take my place. To wear my likeness. Especially not this poisoner of teeth.

My linen smock sticks damp to my back, coarse, where wings should be.

Did I ever have wings? Have these mortals passed down a memory I've long forgotten? Will enough teeth give me wings?

The three children each sleep in separate chambers. One has not yet lost her milk teeth. One has lost a few, though I was never summoned for them. Their usurper mother took them. They no doubt lie dry and wasted in a forgotten box. The third has lost all of hers, all replaced with deep-rooted elder teeth. The thought of those rich roots makes my stomach cramp with desire.

But the smell makes me cramp with warning. So much poison fogs their breath—far more than had been fed to the sweet child I left sleeping at my cottage. I hope I've brought enough of my spell milk. I hope my hands will be strong enough to pull out those deep roots.

I begin with the eldest, while I have my strength and to ensure I have enough spell milk for her and her bounty of teeth. There will be no placating a girl of her age with lullabies. I pray the poppies work fast, and pour. The milk is thick with honey and ash and opiate, and it moves slowly down her tongue into her throat. She coughs and sits up, choking, but swallows. Then she sees me, and she screams.

I panic. I rage. I bear my stolen teeth and I spit into her eyes, turning them to silver coins. Her hands flutter at her face, then grow weak as the poppy takes over. Her second scream is muffled by her own slacking lips as her body sinks into her bed.

My heart thunders. Face heats. Am I so terrible a sight, still, to illicit screams from children? Perhaps I am. I fold the blanket over her and step into the shadows of her closet, waiting to see if her scream has summoned the others. But the dentist, it seems, is too tired to be woken, too far away in this big house, too certain of her perfect world to sense danger.

When the silence is stretched thin and the air in the room turns sweet, I step out of the dark. The astringent scent is gone from her, replaced with the natural pulp of life.

I pull my silver grips from my satchel and set to work.

There is music in the snap of periodontal ligament. There is rhythm to the rocking of the grips. The grate of the silver on enamel like an ancient song.

I keep the perfect teeth separate from the rabble in my mouth. Twenty-eight I take from the eldest. Twenty-two from the middle child. Twenty from the youngest. There is enough milk for them all, and the younger two do not fight it, but slip sweetly into dreams. I turn them all on their sides so the blood will run free of their mouths, and I shower them with clover coins.

What will their mother do, without her garden of perfect teeth to tend? She will have to plant it anew, or make do as I have. If she wants to play at being Tand Fae, I will give her a taste of the game.

When I slip back through the mirror, I cannot help but glimpse its reflection. Like another picture on the wall. One that's not like the rest.

I hear the child long before the cottage comes into view. I hurry as fast as my tired legs will go. Her cries will draw darker things to my small hut. Things I've not the strength nor the time to contend with.

I burst through the door and I scream when I see the creature perched on my bed. Its eyes blaze, face gaping purple, neck soaked in blood. The teeth I held in my mouth scatter across the packed earth floor.

Then the wail comes again, a banshee screech. I clutch at the wet front of my dress to steady my heart. It is the child. Her face has swollen, jaw misaligned and bruised, contorted with agony and angry tissue. Her hair is soaked in blood and sweat, darkened, hanging limp around her stained gown. As if I face the mirror again.

I leave my satchel by the door, leave the common teeth in the dirt, and rush to the child's side.

"Shh, Liten Tand Fae, Granny is here." I sit beside her and wrap an arm around her small shoulders. She leans into me, and her wail lowers to a pained moan. "Lie down. Granny will make your medicine."

My hands shake. I want to be brewing my porridge. I want to pull the handkerchief of precious teeth from my pocket and wash away the weariness of this night. Instead I mix more milk and honey and poppy. No spell needed this time, just sweetness and sleep. It is some time before she is settled. And though time has ceased to move for me the way it does for humans, that hour passes as a century does.

At last, with the babe asleep, I set my copper pot on the stove and empty my prizes into the bottom. I spit bloody water over them and let them boil. I am vigilant for any scent of poison, lest it ruin the batch. One tainted tooth and the porridge will end me rather than refresh me. And then what would become of the child?

But the batch is pure, unadulterated pulp, and it fills me with hope and purpose. A thousand years are ripped from me. A curtain of fog I hadn't even known was there is vanished from my thoughts. Colors I had forgotten burn bright in my retinas. Joints long frozen now flex with strength. My back has straightened, and I see, for the first time in centuries, the dust collected on the mantel shelf.

I stare at my reflection in the copper pot. I am still far from young, far from the pretty fairy in the pictures. But it is progress. This drug distilled from perfect baby faces works miracles.

The common teeth, filmed and yellow, crunch under my feet as I cross the room again to check on the sleeping child. It's like we are trading places. Her twisted, gaping mouth was mine days ago. Now my jaw stands rigid, ready for more. But rest, first. Night will fall in a moment, and the work will begin again.

I drag a spare blanket to the floor in front of the fire and lie down. Only days ago, if I had done this, I would never stand again. Now I feel as though I could leap up, if needed. I curl up in the comfort of my own plush body and I rest.

The summons come, insistent, demanding. They have teeth for me, and a desire for coin. They place their small pearls under their pillows, sleep with one eye open, hoping to catch sight of the tiny, beautiful creature who will exchange it. We are both disappointed.

The energy I gain from harvesting common teeth is hardly worth the energy I spend. Not when I can wash away centuries with the takings from a single household. This is a new era of Tand Fae. One where I am called by my own desires, and not the desires of others.

I desire only flawless teeth. Ones preserved in poisons. I've become hungry for the toxin that once repelled me. And just as they perfect their teeth, their teeth perfect me.

Only by refining these poisons can I myself be perfect. Only with the purest powder can I be what they want me to be.

I ignore the call, the offerings, and follow instead the chemical tang of dentistry.

I will not ignore them forever. When I am young again, I will be strong enough to hold back the river of time with their meager offerings. It won't be long.

On a small stone road, in an apartment above a clinic, I find my next prize. A young boy, all milk teeth save for two ridged incisors, sleeps in a pile of small sewn bears. His arms are tangled in the toys and he sleeps with his mouth gaping, perfect teeth glowing in the dim light from the bathroom across the hall.

My sleeping nectar takes him quickly into dreams, and his pearls are in my pocket in minutes. But he is only one child, and I want more. The dentist's workroom is below, and I wonder if any teeth are saved there, still fresh inside, still worth the taking.

Again I am faced with my likeness in pictures on the walls. But one catches my eye. Something about the figure's smile, the way she cups a tooth in her palm—she is more Fae than the rest. I pull the picture from the wall and place it in my bag.

I do not find any fresh teeth—only old ones, and poor replicas. I pick up the dentist's fine tools, precise hooks and drills. I smile into the tiny mouth mirror, and slip onto the roads inside.

I return to my cottage as dawn reaches the forest canopy, with enough fine teeth for a banquet.

The child does not wail but lies grey and damp-faced in my bed, breathing heavily through her twisted, meaty mouth. Her eyes are as fogged as beach marbles.

"Would you like some milk, Liten Tand Fae?"

She does not answer.

So I brew my porridge, instead. This time, my copper pot is half-filled with perfect teeth, all scented with spellwork and clear of the chemical wretchedness. I mix a potent, thick, stew of it all, and eat my fill, till I feel the thick porridge backing up my throat, too much to fit in my hollow frame. There is still some left in the pot.

I carry it to the bedside. "Here, min elskling." I pry at her crooked jaw and insert the spoon. Her own mouth-blood thins the brew, and it goes down easy. Light returns to her eyes, and she pulls the spoon closer, taking it from my hand to scrape at the film in the bottom of the pot. I run my fingers through her damp hair and let her finish it all. I step back and watch her strength return.

I go to fetch my tools from my bag and find the portrait there. I hardly remember taking it from the dentist's wall, and its fey face stares out at me as if it were a mirror I could walk through. I hang her on my own wall, a reminder of my quest, my progress. A family portrait.

The child has licked the pot clean and has, at last, the strength to stand on her own.

"Are you still hungry, Liten Tand Fae?"

She smiles as well as her broken face allows and nods her head.

"Then let us go and get some more."

She slips her hand into mine, and I lift my bag to my shoulder. We will walk the mirror roads together till we both reclaim our smiles, our pasts. Till we are the perfect storybook fairies, as they have always wanted us to be. With enough of their drugs, enough of their sacrifices, we will make their tooth fairy dreams come true.

They used to fear me. They will love me, now.

"When Kimberly came to the underpass, she knew she should turn around."

TAFFY SWEET

MICHAELBRENT COLLINGS

They gathered slowly. Some arrived in small groups: twos and threes. Most arrived solo. Funerals weren't parties. You didn't go with friends. Perhaps with family, but in this case, there were so few family members left.

The mourners around the closed casket. Some of them said small words, and left smaller touches that traced along the wood.

No one lingered beside the carved wood of the coffin.

The casket was closed. But closed or not, they all knew what was inside. They could all imagine what it looked like—and the thought was not a pleasant one.

Only one of the grieving attendants lingered. Ben Jeksel stood in front of the box for a long time, his hard fists bunched at his sides. Everyone knew what he was thinking, because a lot of them were thinking the same thing:

I'm going to kill whoever did this.

Kimberly Hendstrom had been warned.

And she'd listened for a long time. But two facts finally drove her to ignore the warnings.

Fact one was that she hated running on beautiful days like today. The only way she'd ever been able to stand it was to use it as an exploration tool: finding new places, running new routes. She still hated running, but at least if she was going somewhere different, the scenery changed.

Fact two was that nothing got her ass in shape quite like five miles a day. So run she would, because she had determined long ago that she was not going to end up like her mother, who could land small plains on the junk in her trunk.

Big booty aversion or not, when Kimberly came to the underpass, she knew she should turn around. But in that moment, everything behind her—the whole world, it seemed—represented nothing more or less than well-traveled banality. The path behind led to the job she hated, the boyfriend she was pretty sure she wasn't interested in anymore, and friends who dropped off into the oblivion of marriage or just the malaise of approaching middle age.

Though the underpass was rumored to be a hangout for drug addicts and rapists, not to mention being cracked and the constant subject of local council meetings where concerned citizens screamed about the likelihood of collapse, it was hard to square the stories with the bright space, well-lit by a morning sun that slanted at a perfect angle to leave not a single shadow.

Besides, what was the point of running five miles a day if she couldn't outrun some wino who probably couldn't even run a straight line?

Screw it.

She squared her shoulders. Pumped her feet.

Went *under*.

Ben stood at the lectern. He had said he wanted to speak at the funeral, and even if he hadn't been the biggest, meanest person in whatever room he happened to be in, they would have let him.

He deserved it, didn't he? Wasn't he the right person to speak at things like this?

And hadn't he warned them all what was going to happen? What was inevitable? They all knew what the tunnel represented—a creeping fungus brought on by poor urban planning and poorer overall funding of infrastructure—but he was the one who screamed that it would kill one of them.

More than one. Over the years, the problem had killed many of them. But no one liked to think about that. Nothing could be done. Their civilization crumbled, one brick at a time, and that was that.

Ben cleared his throat. "We know why we're here," he said. "To mourn. To grieve." He cleared his throat again, but this time he didn't grimace. He frowned. "It shouldn't have happened. None of it. But it did, and we're stuck with it. But that doesn't mean we forget. It doesn't mean we move on. That was the problem in the first place, wasn't it? That's the reason one of us is in a box."

He was silent a long time. A few of the onlookers coughed.

Then Ben slammed his fist down on the lectern so hard the first row could hear the wood groan and splinter.

"It's not fair," he said quietly.

It didn't happen all at once. If it had, she might have turned away. Might have quit five steps in and headed back to that mundane, trite, horrible existence. Better that, she might have reasoned, than no existence at all.

But it didn't happen all at once, and even when it did, it was easy to write off as just a cloud.

In L.A.? In the middle of a drought?

Kimberly's steps faltered. Not a lot, just enough to break up her rhythm; more so as she went through the last dozen or so steps and realized it had been growing steadily darker for ... how long?

She kept running as she thought, though her legs had lost the easy rhythm that made her a state-level marathon runner in high school. She lurched a bit, slid a bit.

She lurched to a stop.

She looked ahead. The sunlight had been streaming in at the other end of the big tunnel, lighting her way as she ran. And the light still existed, she could see it easily. But it almost seemed like a scrim had dropped over the brightness: a shroud wrapped around the world, or perhaps the sun itself. The universe's long-awaited heat death had come to pass in the time it had taken to run halfway through the tunnel.

And that thought gave her further pause. She thought again. How long had she been running here? How long had it been since she took the first step under the freeway?

Shouldn't she have gone through the underpass and come out the other side?

Something's wrong.

She turned. The distance between her and the moment where *under* ended and the rest of the world began seemed to expand. She'd been running forever, and forever had taken her exactly to the halfway point. To the darkest point.

The universe dilated, stretched like taffy at the pier. Taffy was something she'd always hated. Dad had liked taffy. He'd liked all kinds of sweets.

And not all sweets were candy. Some of them were alive.

Some of his favorite sweets lived in his own home.

No one knew who said it. It almost seemed like magic, the words just floating out of nowhere. "We should stop this."

Ben had warned them for years. But now, with the addition of a second voice … now it was real. It had taken one of them. *Another* one of them.

The last one of them.

So, when the words came, they were met by a murmur, a soughing sigh of assent as heads nodded, as a few of them breathed, "Yes."

Ben was nodding, too. He repeated the words, though with one important change: "We *will* stop this."

They all stood.

They all left. Not in ones or twos or threes, though. This time they left as a group.

Grief might be, in its final form, a largely solitary matter. But Rage? Murder?

That was something easier found in a mob.

"Come on over, Kimmy."

Kimberly stiffened. She hadn't let herself think of him for years. Thousands in therapy, including a long series of extremely expensive hypnotherapy sessions, had gone a long way toward wiping him from her mind.

But she had just heard his voice, and it was closer and more present than it had been in a long, long time.

For a moment she tasted taffy. The stickiness as her father pushed it into her mouth, the sweetness so heavy it was cloying, so thick it would silence her —at least long enough.

"Got something for you. Something sweet. Come on over, Kimmy. Come and *seeeeeee ...*"

She had stiffened a moment ago. Now she stumbled to the side, barely managing to stay upright as her knees buckled.

Kimberly didn't know if she'd actually heard the voice the first time. She thought it had been in her mind, but now she couldn't be sure. She was sure, though, that this second time the voice was real.

"Sweeeeeeeet."

She turned slowly toward the sound. Part of her realized that meant she was turning away from the bright light of day. Toward the darkness that hadn't been there a moment ago, but was now thick—

(as taffy)

—around her.

She had been wrong. There were shadows after all. Hidden in the light, perhaps, but now they had come out to play their dark games. Now she saw them.

And some of the shadows moved.

The point where the wall of the tunnel met the asphalt was a slim black line in the creeping darkness. But as she watched, the line thickened, then grew slim again. It ebbed and flowed, turning and turning in on itself. It should have disappeared, should have compressed to a singularity that would take the world along with it as it blipped out of existence.

But no matter how long it turned, no matter how many times the dark ouroboros consumed itself, more appeared.

Again, Kimberly thought of the taffy. Her father loved watching it in the taffy pulling machine. She did, too. But while she enjoyed it because she knew as long as they were watching they would remain out in the open, in the light, among people ... Earl Bailey liked it for different reasons. She never understood them, but he could sit and watch the metal arms swinging, turning lines into more lines, then the original lines melting into themselves again.

Eventually, it would end.

Eventually, he would buy a small packet. Just a few taffies. Just enough to put in her mouth and keep her from screaming.

"Sweeeeeeeeeeeeeeeeet."

A hand appeared at the corner of the darkness. Something was pulling its way out of the shadow, clawing its way to freedom, a monstrosity tearing its way free from the womb of darkness that had birthed it.

Run. Shouldn't I run? Shouldn't I turn—

(like taffy)

—and run and not look back?

She tried. She managed two full steps before something curled around her right ankle. She didn't have to look to know what she felt: cold fingers. Dark fingers.

Strong fingers.

The thing that had gripped her yanked, and Kimberly's leg went out from under her, jerking back so hard and fast that she felt her hip dislocate.

She screamed.

The scream, like the morning light, didn't seem to travel as far as it should. It was wrapped in the same dark, funereal shroud that had wrapped around the sun, and the sound ended only inches from her face.

She realized, too, that all other sounds had ceased. When she had entered this place, the traffic passing overhead had been a constant, steady thrum. Now?

Nothing.

Just the darkness, and her, and her screams, and the voice of her father.

"Sweeeeeet."

Ben led the charge. He was the oldest. He had loved her the most. Had loved *all* of them the most. He was the repository of the past, of the days before death came in its creeping, crumbling, rotting forms.

The inquiry into the latest death had been quick, and mostly perfunctory. No one liked to look at rot, and the people in charge of running the world (or at least, the ones who wanted to) had a vested interest in ignoring it, or even denying it outright.

There was the show, of course. Angry men and women, pounding on thick wood tables. Demanding that "there be answers"; that "the matter be investigated to the fullest!"

But everyone at the funeral knew what that meant. It was political-speech for, "We don't know what happened. Or, better said, we don't want to know. Knowing would upset people. Knowing would mean we have to get up off our asses and do something. We might even lose the next election, and after all, isn't *that* the real tragedy?"

Everyone at the funeral knew nothing would be done. Like the thousands of lost souls before her, the mangled remains of the body in the box—cooling in the sanctuary where they had left it—would disappear into history. Barely a footnote in the history books. She would be a curiosity for a few, and maybe worth following up on for even fewer.

But she would be lost. Or, worse, seen as nothing but a cautionary story to scare errant children. Who would then grow up to be politicians themselves— the monsters of neglect, the boogeymen of self-interest.

"It's all falling apart," Ben said as he walked.

He said it under his breath, in a voice meant for his ears only. But one of the other mourners—younger, more impressionable, with the potential to be even more frightening an enemy than Ben someday—said, "What is?"

"Everything. The whole world. Our world is crumbling."

No one asked what he meant. They all knew.

Kimberly hit the asphalt hard, the wind exploding out of her with a whoosh. She felt her jaw slam into the pavement at the same time, sending her teeth upward so hard that she could hear the click in her head. Searing pain erupted in her mouth—

(*My tongue. Dear God, I've bitten off my tongue.*)

—and she tasted copper and salt and warmth.

The thing that pulled her stopped. She heard a sniffing sound, like a huge dog sampling the air.

The voice spoke. More like her father than ever before. "*Sweeeet.* Come on, Kimmy. Come on and play with me."

She screamed, the blood in her mouth turning the sound frothy, ethereal, the foam of a crimson sea. Some of it went down her throat and she inhaled, gagging and coughing.

The thing that had her—

(*Daddy it's Daddy I don't wanna play don't wannnnnaaaaaa—*)

—was still pulling, a second hand now clamped over her calf, drawing her to it. She didn't turn to look; *couldn't* turn to look. If she looked, she'd see him. A shrinking part of her brain insisted that this wasn't happening. It was all a dream, or maybe she'd been out running too long and gotten heatstroke.

Anything but what was happening. Anything but this.

The world had grown silent all around. Nothing but her own gasping, gargling breathing and the wheezing sound of something laughing as it pulled her closer, into the impossible shadows.

The thrum of the engines overhead was gone. The sum of the universe was the tunnel, and her, and the thing that she knew was her father.

But Daddy's dead.

It was true. But it didn't change the fact that she heard his voice.

"*Sweet.*"

Closer now, as the hands pulled her a few inches toward him.

"*Sweet.*"

She could feel puffs of air on her leg. The breath of something long-dead, but somehow come to life once more.

"*Sweeeeeeeeeeeeet.*"

When they arrived, they didn't have to speak.

They knew whose fault this all was.

They knew who had killed one of their own.

They spread out, creating a rough circle.

A kill zone.

Kimberly tried to pull herself away. But there was nothing to grab hold of. Her fingers scrabbled at the asphalt, the nails shearing off and the pads of her fingers turning to hamburger. It looked like she was finger painting, drawing red lines like—

(Taffy)

—abstract art on the pavement.

Then she stopped her mad painting as the thing behind her grasped both her calves and, with a powerful heave, flipped her over.

Something cracked. She thought it was her head, and prayed she had fractured her skull. Prayed that her brain had shaken loose and that death would come to claim her. But she was alive.

The thing crawled up her body.

Not Daddy. Not him. Mommy killed him. Daddy's dead.

The thing was at her knees. Her pelvis. Her chest.

It heaved itself into view.

She screamed. Blood from her bitten tongue exploded up in a fountain, spraying the face that stared down at her.

The thing grinned. It was her father ... and yet not. The visage flickered, like she was looking at two monsters superimposed over each other. One face was misshapen, lumpy. Cracks ran up and down its face in horrible lines that dripped black ichor. Its lips opened wide, and the teeth beyond were serrated like those of a shark, so sharp that she could see they had chewed up the insides of the thing's own mouth. Disgusting, yet oddly feminine. Like Kimberly was looking into a ruined version of herself.

Then the face flickered. Flashed. Now Daddy stared at her.

(Please, Daddy, don't look at me. Watch the taffy turn, turn, turn like darkness in a tunnel.)

He looked like he had when she saw him last: one eye rolled back so far she couldn't see anything but white, the other focused on her but just as terrifying due to the huge hematoma that turned everything around the iris to vivid streaks of red and black. Blood dripped from his nose and mouth, drooling onto her face as he grinned down at her.

The side of his head was dented, his temple going from convex to a rough "C" where Kimberly's mother had hit him with the lead pipe on the day they finally escaped.

Her father smiled. Blood streamed down on Kimberly's face. Red, bright, but it changed to dark, thick stuff as he flickered and she was again facing the monster that had appeared from the shadows.

"Your thoughts," it rasped. "So powerful. So vivid. So ... "

Flash. It was her father again.

"... *sweeeeeeeeet.*"

Her father's face lowered toward hers. Kimberly inhaled to scream. But before she could, his face clamped down hard on her lips. No pain, and yet every true pain imaginable. He was kissing her. Breathing into her. Then inhaling, drawing her breath into itself. Pulling her living soul out of her body.

Kimberly's mind seemed to slip to the side. She was anywhere but here. Away. Gone.

Her gaze flitted around, trying to find something that wasn't obstructed by the view of her father, the monster that had plagued her for all her life, somehow come again to plague her in death.

She saw a crack in the ceiling. A long, ragged tear in the masonry that looked like one of the long, ragged tears in the face of the thing that wore her father's face.

Even as she thought it, the thing drew back.

Flick.

Her father was gone. It was the thing from the shadows, misshapen, a female grotesquerie of cracks and crevices dug out of its skin.

As she watched, some of the cracks grew. Ichor poured out.

The thing coughed, and she wondered if, perhaps, she wasn't the only thing about to die in here.

She started praying, not even realizing it was happening. Mother had always prayed. Kimberly never had, but in this moment the words tumbled out.

"Our Father—"

(Flick! *and it* was *Father. Daddy.*)

"—who art in Heaven—"

(Flick! *and it was the thing again, the monster, and she didn't know if that was better or worse or if such things as better and worse had any meaning at all in this place.*)

The thing grinned wider than before. "Christian," it said, and in the word Kimberly found such longing, such hunger and lust, that the prayer ended before it really had time to begin.

The thing inhaled.

"Your smell. Your smell is so delicious," it said.

Something far above Kimberly cracked. Dust sifted down, the only concrete evidence that the outside world existed at all.

The thing's smile widened, then widened still more. It was all maw and rows of sharp teeth.

It lowered its mouth to her face.

Kimberly kept praying, though silently. She prayed for Mommy to save her. She prayed for God to kill her.

She prayed that what she had heard was true: that the tunnel was so old and decrepit that the bridge above might crumble and fall at any moment.

The thing kissed her, as Daddy had done. Then its face lowered. She felt pain, slicing into her chest. Felt sharp teeth boring into the meat. She screamed, and wanted to look down even in her pain, to see if the thing that came from the shadows was tearing into her chest ... or if it was the real monster consuming her. If it was Daddy.

"Sweeeeeet," came the voice. It was garbled, the mouth full of—

(*Me. Full of* me!)

—blood and meat.

Kimberly wanted to look. Wanted so badly to see.

But she stared at the ceiling. At the cracking, ancient tunnel. She prayed.

"Christian," came the snuffling, curdled voice. *"Sweeeeeeeeeeeeeet."*

Her prayer came true.

The thing looked up suddenly, and the cessation of pain as it stopped feeding was so great that it would have taken her breath away had one of her lungs not already been consumed. It stared at the ceiling, and she saw the crack widening. Heard the hum of traffic return, almost instantly replaced by the screeching of brakes. The cracks on the thing's face widened as well, not just wounds but fissures, crevasses that opened so wide its flesh began to slough away in patches.

"*No, no, no,*" it whispered.

Flicker. Now it was her father again. But the cracks were still there. The wounds that went deeper and deeper. Now chunks of bone were tumbling onto her.

She felt something else hit her as well: something heavy enough to crush her foot under its weight.

My prayer.

"*Christian!* Stop what you—"

"*Kimmy!* Don't you dare—"

Both voices spoke together, both monsters alive above her.

"Our Father," she said again, the words sweet through the blood.

More masonry fell, this time snapping not her feet but the back of the thing that still lay across her. More bones fell, resting on her flesh in a way that was almost pleasant.

"Who art in heaven."

"NO!"

"Stop!"

"Thy Kingdom co—"

The next piece of brick fell on her head. It crushed her skull, then the pulped the brain beyond.

In that moment, that millisecond between trauma and oblivion, Kimberly smelled taffy. And for the first time, it didn't smell bad at all. It smelled like victory.

Ben knocked on the door.

Strange to do such a thing, considering what would follow. But it was the right thing to do. The forms should be followed.

"Let me in, let me in," he whispered.

His quiet supplication was heard. Answered. The door flew open to reveal a small, sallow looking man. He wore a stained bathrobe over boxers, one slipper on his right foot, the other bare. He obviously hadn't bathed or groomed himself in some time, either: thick whiskers covered his chin and cheeks, hair snarled and matted.

Before the door had fully opened, William Ziege was already shrieking, "Can't you all just leave me alone? I already lost my job, my family—"

He stopped speaking suddenly. Blinked. "You're not with the news?" he said.

Ben shook his head. He smiled. "No."

"It's not about the—" Ziege's voice cut off as he stopped himself from finishing his sentence. Suddenly, awkwardly, self-conscious, he patted his hair down—or at least tried to. "How can I help you?"

Ben's smile grew. "Not about the what?" he asked.

Ziege blinked again. "Huh?"

"You said 'not about the' and then stopped," Ben said. "What were you going to say?"

Ziege's expression soured. "Who are you?"

"Not about the what, Mr. Ziege?"

"You *are* from the news. Get out. Get off my—" Ziege's voice cut off again, though this time not because he was trying to choke back his words. He looked at the shadows that stood at the periphery of his porch.

"Not about the what?" Ben said softly.

"What is this?" Ziege tried again to find bravery in bluster.

Ben smiled one last time, and as he did he allowed himself to be *seen*. Not as he appeared when walking in the world, but as he looked when in his home. As he looked when waiting for prey.

Ziege started screaming. The screams grew as the others who had been at the funeral stepped closer and, like Ben, showed their true faces to the monster who had stolen their friend.

"Not about the bridge?" Ben said, his voice now gravelly and hoarse. His true voice, and the last one Ziege would hear.

Ziege's only answer was to scream louder.

"Not about the bridge that killed my friend?" he roared.

As though it had been a signal, the rest of the trolls fell on Ziege. They held his arms and legs, stretching them out so Ziege was suspended in the air. He screamed and screamed, and when he stopped for breath he whispered, "It wasn't my fault?"

Ben laughed. "Whose fault was it?"

Ziege murmured something that sounded like "infrastructure cutbacks."

Ben's lips pursed. "Maybe," he said. Then he leaned close and whispered, "You humans have ruined the world. The bridges are collapsing from lack of funding, my people are dying. It's happening *everywhere*."

"I didn't do all that," insisted Ziege.

"Maybe," agreed Ben. "But you're here. And you're the one who designed the bridge that collapsed on my friend."

Ben started tearing at Ziege then, ripping and rending the man's guts even as the other trolls pulled. For one lovely moment, the man's arms just stretched like—

(taffy)

Then, with a loud, wet *pop,* the man's right arm and left leg pulled away from his torso. The trolls holding the prizes ground at his bones, chewing them as softly as if they were bread.

Ben just kept burrowing into Ziege's chest cavity. The man might be a terrible designer, but he tasted good enough. Maybe not as good as a Christian man—he certainly didn't *smell* as good as the average Christian—but the blood was ...

Sweet.

THE DAWN WOMAN

CALVIN CLEARY

S am didn't remember his big sister. Not really. There were a few pictures here and there, sure, but most of them were on his dad's Facebook account and who the hell uses Facebook anymore? He could ask his dad about anything he might have, but that would mean leaving the attic and having a conversation with a guy who had been getting steadily more drunk since 5:15 p.m.

Sam had started going through Laura's stuff when he was fourteen. She'd died when he was eight, old enough to understand but not really old enough to understand. Then again, how old was old enough? His dad was fifty-two, and he had just parked her boxes up here like it was garbage and hadn't touched it since. Sam had tried a couple years after her death. He had broken down in tears before he even got through the packing tape.

His therapist had suggested he make a YouTube channel as he went through the stuff. That way, he could step back from the emotions of the moment and revisit them later, process them on his own time, at his own pace. Plus, then he'd also have a record of all her stuff online. It felt like a nice way to remember a sister he'd barely known, a way to piece together her life.

What Sam hadn't anticipated was that there would be an audience for this. His audience skewed young, grew up on unboxing videos just like Sam himself. And Laura was eleven years older than him—her stuff triggered just enough nostalgia for some corners of the internet. A few thousand subscribers wasn't really enough to make money, but it helped Sam feel connected to *someone*. There certainly wasn't anyone in Zanesville, Ohio he would consider a friend. It was a garbage town, and he couldn't wait to leave.

A gentle *ping* let him know that all his clips had been imported into his editing software. Time to get to work. Thankfully, there wasn't too much editing that went into these videos. He wasn't much of an actor, but his therapist told him not to worry about the performance aspect and just focus on the objects themselves, but look, adults don't know everything, okay? If the channel got bigger, he could use it on his college applications, which was important because his grades weren't amazing. Influencers have options.

He hit play. A few seconds of silence as he practiced his deep breathing. He made a note of the timestamp when he finally started talking. "Hello, my fellow archivists," his voice said from the speakers. "We're back with yet another mystery box as I continue to process the trauma of losing my sister in a healthy and normal way." Grin. Wink. Continue. "This is a lighter one, so it might be a shorter video." Heft performatively. Frown performatively. Continue. "But let's see what we've got before I answer some of your questions from the last video."

It was a good take. No real notes, just time markers when he stopped talking. The box was slim. He shook it gently near the mic, to illustrate that it was packed too tight to hear anything. Sam trimmed profusely.

The yellow boxcutter came out next. He had never figured out why, but some people just loved the sound of the knife sliding effortlessly through the tape. He shrugged. Whatever got views.

The tape was thick, far thicker than he had expected. Multiple types of tape, each stronger than the last, covered the box, making it surprisingly hard to cut. He added an audio layer, and recorded himself saying, "Pro tip for my fellow archivists: You need to be gentle with something packed like this. As you heard, this is packed tight. If I dig in too deep, I could cut the contents of the box." Make that last shot worthwhile. Tape cut, he opened the box gingerly and reached inside.

"The first thing we have is an old book," he said, lifting it into the attic's perfectly staged lighting. "Leather-bound, with no title visible. It looks old. I wonder what Laura was doing with it?" He gingerly rotated the book for the camera, letting it capture all sides of it. A perfect take.

He noted the timestamp when he stood, knowing to cut there and go to the other camera. He set the camera on a tripod looking straight down at a well-lit desk. It let him display objects easier and just record voice-over since he wasn't physically on camera. He moved that clip onto the timeline and started playing.

"Looks like … huh," he said in the recording, as he opened the book to its first page. It was a graphic illustration of a dying woman. The body was realistic, but something about the art style was heightened—the angles were too sharp, the colors too bright, a glaring light casting a stark shadow beneath her body. She had thin knives in her knees and elbows pinning her to the ground, but her back was arched, pushing her breasts into the air, and her face looked ecstatic, almost pornographic. It made him uncomfortable in ways he couldn't quite describe, the same way he always felt a little weird when his classmates started talking about sex.

"Can't show that on YouTube," he whispered to himself. He began to trim the clip, when he noticed her eyes. Had they been that piercingly yellow before? In the book they had seemed so flat and lifeless, but now Sam felt like they were following him. He stared into his screen. Had he misread her before? She looked … hungry. And when he'd first seen the image, he had thought she was a tan woman with long black hair, but that was wrong. She was light-skinned, a pale complexion not unlike his sister's. And the hair was brown, not black. And was her face moving, somehow?

"The Dawn Woman," he heard himself say. Right, the clip was still playing. That was why it looked like she was moving. He shook his head and saw his finger on the video move to the corner of the page, where his sister had written that in a slim, elegant script. Okay, he couldn't cut the section, it would be important for later. He would just have to pixelate some of the image. It was more extreme than most of what he put on his channel, but it was October—a creepy video wouldn't be too out of place.

Sam watched himself flip the page. "I don't recognize the language," he heard himself say. He trimmed extensively after that, slowing down only to catch some of the other images in the book. Thankfully, none were as gross as that first one. That made his job easier.

Still, he didn't want to focus too much on the book. It was the next set of clips that would be the meat of the video. He cut back to the clip in front of the box, when he was reaching in and pulling out the only other item inside, an old, one gig flash drive. He held it close to the camera. He had been worried that the handwriting would be too faint, but his lighting was solid. You could just barely make out the same slim script from the book. *The Dawn Woman.*

Sam pulled it back and grinned into the camera. "Wanna see what's on here?" he asked. He trimmed extensively, just including an insert of him plugging the flash drive in before switching to a screen-recording. This was more complicated, as he didn't have a green screen.

The video on the flash drive was not what he had expected. It started off with static, and then a dark room, a few scattered rays of sunlight coming in from a grate far above. The room was tight, stone, and as the camera circled slowly, Sam couldn't see an entrance or exit. The only thing in the room was an ornate wooden vanity with a beautiful built-in mirror. There was no dialogue, and the camera moved slowly, as if underwater.

Tentatively, the camera approached the mirror. There was no reflection of anything, at least not at first. It seemed to swallow light, only reluctantly giving any back when the camera got close enough to grab it. There, Sam saw not a man holding a camera, but a slim, pretty-looking man, dirty but with striking yellow eyes. The camera bobbed left; the figure followed. The camera ducked; the figure did too.

"No-no-no-nononono," he muttered, almost too quietly to hear. Sam bumped the audio up a notch there. Didn't want to lose it. But toned it back immediately as the man yelled, "I did your three days! Just let me up, please just let me up!" As he spoke, the figure in the mirror's mouth opened, mimicking the words but revealing teeth filed to sharp points.

The camera looked up, suddenly, directly into the light at the top of the dungeon. Two figures were looking down at him as he did. "Thank you!" he yelled. "Please, please, She's not here!" At that, the pair quickly scurried away. A heavy rock was pushed slowly over the grate, extinguishing the light from the room entirely.

The video continued, for a moment, with no input but the increasingly panicked whimpering from the man holding the camera. He must have been spinning, looking desperately for some source of light, because it panned by a brief glint of yellow before a crash—the man dropped the camera. There was an audible sobbing then, before a strange voice.

"You're okay," the voice said. It was feminine. Husky and resonant. The accent was ... American? Before, he would have guessed something Mediterranean. A woman, statuesque and stately, strode into frame. She was barely visible, but the light from her eyes—how had they done that?—lit everything before her in a cold yellow light. The cameraman, a handsome young man in filthy clothes with unkempt, short hair, looked up at her with a naked longing.

"You're—"

She didn't let him finish. "—here to care for you, my love." She sat cross-legged on the dirty floor next to him. He looked like a child next to her, her barely visible frame nearly twice his height and powerfully built. She scooped him up in her arms and cradled him close. "Drink deep and be quenched," she whispered, opening the top of her simple wrap dress and pulling him to her breast. The suckling sound was audible as the man apparently latched onto her nipple.

"Ahh," she said, throwing her head back in ecstasy, bathing the room above in a pale, yellow light. "As for you, my love," she said softly, the suckling noise quieting as she spoke, "I'll see you soon."

She looked directly into the camera then, and it was pulled as if by magnetism to her hand, faster than any person could move it. She crushed the camera in her pale, meaty hand, ending the video suddenly.

Even watching it a second time, Sam felt deeply uncomfortable. There was something about the way her eyes seemed to look through the screen. It felt wrong.

That was what would make it great content.

Sam wasn't much of an actor, but he didn't have to be. His whispered expletives at the mirror would have to be censored, but the hand over his mouth when the woman appeared, and his yelp when she seemed to speak right to him? That was natural, it was good content, and it would definitely add to it. And, of course, his scream when his phone rang the second the video went black. "Spam likely," he read out loud, laughing away the tension before moving on.

He wrapped up his editing with a normal outro, answering a couple quick questions and then reflecting on what he had learned about his sister. Was she a filmmaker? A researcher? Only time would tell! Come back next week for another new video, and don't forget to like, share, and subscribe to find out more.

As he wrapped up his edit, he was struck by an idea: Why not upload the 'Dawn Woman' footage on its own, too? Let people have fun with it? He'd add that video to release on its own in three days, maybe with a joke about how he, too, had survived his three days.

"I never could have predicted where that video would take me," Sam said, smiling through the bright studio lights.

Gita, a short, curvy Black girl with box braids and a dazzling smile, leaned in towards him. "So, what happened when you hit publish? Were you at all scared that ... well, you had three days to live?"

Sam smiled ruefully. "I admit it, yeah, I was a little nervous. I had been seeing things around my house since then, like eyes that followed me everywhere I went." He didn't mention the voice in his dream, at first ecstatic and then progressively more scattered and enraged. He didn't mention that the voice had never left. That he heard it every single night for years. That it was getting louder, lately. "I didn't believe it the first time I saw the video, but I guess I psyched myself up a bit. Those were the longest three days of my life," he said, laughing. "Thankfully, my therapist upped my anxiety meds. It didn't really help with my fear of the Dawn Woman, but it definitely helped when I got my first interview request a few months later."

Gita laughed. "We're scarier than the Dawn Woman?"

"Yes!" Sam said emphatically. "Look, the worst she did was make me feel like I was being watched. Now I *know* I am." He stared directly into the camera for effect.

"Fair enough," she said. "So, you publish that first video, and three days later you upload your sister's raw footage. What happens then?"

"A lot," he said frankly. "Let's see. Some 'React' channels on YouTube picked it up, Creepypasta stuff does good numbers. That must be where the indie horror film fest in Texas came across it. They asked if they could screen it as a short film. I'm still really proud that I was able to get my sister director credit on that. She was a really creative person, and I think she would have been so thrilled."

"And then TikTok," Gita said.

"Yeah," Sam replied. "I wasn't on TikTok. I was an antisocial kid from rural Ohio, it was kind of new and intimidating at the time. But also, I didn't realize how horny everyone was for busty monster women."

"But not you?" Gita asked with a laugh.

"No," Sam replied, "not me." Why did they always ask him about that? He didn't get the obsession. The Dawn Woman was a malevolent ghost. Who was horny for that?

"Did you ever get on and see how people were remixing your idea?"

"Honestly, no. But people did send me some, and they were great."

"Do you have a favorite?"

Sam thought for a moment. "Oh, the uh ... what was it, the Dawn Woman Blind Dates. I have no idea who was playing the Dawn Woman in those, but she was genuinely so funny and sharp." He made a mental note to find out who she was. Small creators appreciated the shout-out.

"Were you ever able to find out more about the Dawn Woman story? Was she your sister's creation, or a piece of something older?" Gita asked.

"You know, for a long time, I wasn't. I thought Laura had invented her whole cloth," he replied.

"It sounds like you've found something, then."

"Not me, actually. Before I moved out, I found a box full of notebooks. My dad had hidden it for some reason. It wasn't with the rest of her stuff."

"So, there *is* more?"

"There is," he confirmed. "But ..."

"But?"

Sam laughed. "Well, if I spill the beans here, my publicist will kill me."

"So, we come to your book," Gita said.

"*The Dawn Woman.* Available next week in bookstores everywhere," Sam said, holding up a copy to the camera. He hated this. It felt like begging. But this was how it worked. He checked a monitor to make sure the book jacket was clearly visible, and he saw himself. He looked clean and sharply dressed, but his skin was pale and clammy. And his eyes ...

"Sam?" Gita asked. "Do we need to take a break?"

He shook his head. Just his imagination. His eyes were still green. It must have been the lights. His skin was pale, certainly, but he had been inside for months working. He was fine. He couldn't wait to finish this book and stop talking about Her.

"What inspired you to write a book for this?" Gita asked. "After all, you made your name doing video essays."

"Well, two things," Sam said. "First, there was *so much* stuff in those notebooks, and not all of it made sense. I started taking my own notes from them on a computer, and this took years."

"And the second thing?"

Sam looked down and took a performatively deep breath. "Yeah. The second thing. While I was in the process of moving, my dad's house burned down. He didn't make it, and neither did ... well, any of our stuff. Any of Laura's stuff," he corrected.

"I'm so sorry," Gita said warmly.

"Yeah," Sam said. "And so, while *The Dawn Woman* is about, you know, a busty monster woman—please buy it—it's also about one young woman who was lost too young, and the effect it had on her family."

Gita nodded. "You're trying to finish the story you started on your channel," she said.

"I am, yeah." He wiped a tear away before it could form. This had felt so practiced when he was, well, practicing, but he really did mean it. This was the end of a years-long quest. It was the first time he'd felt any semblance of closure in Laura's story.

Gita waited a moment to see if he would elaborate. He didn't. She continued. "I'm sure you've seen some of the criticism of your book," she said softly.

Here, he was grateful for the practice; he knew better than to roll his eyes. "I'm familiar," he said drily. "People who claim that the Dawn Woman is real. That she, I don't know, speaks to them somehow."

"After the unauthorized movie came out in 2021, that teen girl killed three other students in Middleville. Someone dressed as the Dawn Woman attacked a number of transwomen. Multiple active cults dedicated to her are running in America. Are you concerned that bringing her back into the limelight risks repeating those events?" she asked.

"I think that depends," Sam said, speaking slowly to give the impression that he hadn't practiced a variation on this response for hours in the last week. "The way people talk about Her, they seem to be attributing some sort of real power to her. But I watched the video. I assume you've seen it too?" Gita nodded. "We're still here. We aren't killing anymore. Because She's not real. She can't convince anyone to do anything. Stories can't hurt you."

"You've mentioned using this story to find closure with Laura. Doesn't that imply that these kinds of stories can have actual, material power?"

Sam looked at Gita closely then. That smile—was she smirking at him? Was she making fun of him? And her eyes … her eyes were wrong. They didn't fit in her head. He looked around desperately. The set lights weren't actually on. Why was it so hot? Where was the light coming from?

Sam stood up abruptly and walked off set, stumbling repeatedly. He didn't know if Gita called after him. He could only hear Her voice. It sounded triumphant.

Sam wasn't sure how he got back to his hotel room. He must have been driven? A Lyft. He looked up and was surprised to see the publicist that had organized the interviews and book signings was in the room with him. Standing in front of him. Talking. How long? He wasn't sure. But Her voice had quieted now, enough that he could focus on what she was saying.

" … forgotten how to speak?" she asked.

"Talia, I'm so sorry," he said, trying to think quickly. The interview. He had just left, right? That probably wasn't good. That would definitely make her angry. "I must have eaten something bad. I had to get out of there immediately, or else I would have had an accident on camera."

Talia reached her hand out towards his head, and Sam jerked back instinctually. "Sorry," he said softly. She put the back of her hand against his forehead, and Sam tried not to think about it. For a couple years now, he had found the sensation of other people's skin weirdly suffocating.

Talia frowned. "You're ice cold," she said. She wiped his sweat off her hand. "Let's order you some soup and have some water sent up here. I'm going to grab a thermometer. I'll be back soon."

Sam wasn't sure how long she was gone. It felt like hours, or maybe days.

Eventually, he got up. There was no bottled water left in the minibar. How was that possible?

The room was stifling. He went to the bathroom, splashed cold water on his face, then hot water. He looked like hell in the mirror. He took his temperature. 97.1.

He wasn't sick. He just needed fresh air. He needed to get out of there.

He pulled open the door to the hotel room, pushing a bunch of empty plastic bottles out of the way, and stepped out into the cool yellow light of the hall. Just being out of the hotel room let him breathe easier. Maybe it was just a panic attack.

The lobby was bustling, full of people trying to touch him. He shoved past them on his way out of the hotel. He pushed open the front door, ignoring the glares of the other guests, and collapsed on the sidewalk. For what felt like the first time in days, he took a deep breath. The chill evening air in Pittsburgh filled his lungs.

He was already feeling better. The hotel room felt like a dungeon. This was real air. This was freedom.

He stood unevenly. He was weak, but every breath made him feel better. He checked his pockets for his phone; it must be back in the hotel room. He wasn't about to go back and get it. Eh, he'd just go for a short walk. Talia had been gone for a while; she could wait another half-hour.

Sam walked. He wasn't sure how much time passed as he did so. At first it felt random, like he was just wandering. But it was like he was an antenna. Turn this way; Her voice quieted. Turn that; She got louder. Never loud enough to make out what She was saying, but he felt so close, like he was on the verge of understanding something profound that had been hovering at the edge of his consciousness for years now.

By the time he found the group in the small wooded area north of the city, he felt stronger than ever before. Sharp, like he was seeing the world the way he had meant to. He didn't know how he knew they were here. But he knew.

The crowd parted as he approached. Sam felt safe, not crowded or overwhelmed. He felt like he belonged there. A simple sensation, but one he had been lacking for ... he wasn't sure, honestly. Maybe his whole life. Had he really never felt this good before?

He could hear the voice from his dreams, the Dawn Woman's voice, clearly now. He could hear Her. They had been lost for all those years, each of them in their own ways. Because of Sam, she had been twisted by the million little mockeries of the internet, Her story, Her very Being, wrested out of Her control. Sam had been broken by something simpler, a trick of chemistry and a touch of trauma.

Hanging from every tree branch was a mirror, hundreds of them, each reflecting a chill yellow light from an alien sky as they swayed in the wind.

"I'm sorry," he whispered.

Then the mirrors turned. They reflected nothing but him, and Her.

Her arms opened.

He crawled through a hundred broken mirrors to reach her lap. He was shivering and weak as She opened the top of Her dress to him.

"Drink deep and be quenched," the Dawn Woman whispered to the boy who nearly broke Her, "for we have work to do, my love."

Her touch provoked none of his usual anxieties. They were together again, and he knew that he was forgiven. He was loved. He was home.

WHO WE ARE

L.H. MOORE

Dos has escaped ... again.

Prime looked up when they told him, stopping in the middle of his work. He smiled as he envied Dos' freedom and missed being out there himself. There was something about roaming among the trees and woods and open spaces of the AgLands. There was something about how he felt when he was wandering. How the wilds and woods gnawed, twisted, and amplified the need he felt within.

That need to take life and watch it leave them.

The days blended one into another and another as they had for decades. Prime had no real sense of time anymore and seemed to be aging slowly himself. He couldn't really tell. The passage of time meant little down in the warren of hallways and rooms that made up the facility's lab and quarters. The building itself was an unremarkable structure that sat in the center of over 200 acres. No one thought much of it. There wasn't much to think about. To the rest of the world, it was just an agricultural research center. But to those who knew better, it was The Facility, and to Prime, his home.

He passed by Neent's room, who was not normally quiet and would usually sit there screeching, the sound reverberating through the hallways and in Prime's ears. Sedation was not an option as none worked on them. So he howled and screeched and they all became used to it. Prime stopped and peered into Dos' room and could see him sitting there sulking. This time, he had gotten pretty far and they had cornered him in an empty parking lot, where he sat holding a bucket of chicken wings, gnawing and crunching away on bones that were not chicken. Prime shook his head and kept walking.

His thoughts were interrupted by a group of techs in white uniforms rushing past him. Prime had been an ambitious scientist, thinking that his experiments would grant him fame and recognition and convinced that he was doing the right thing. All it did was turn him into what he was now—someone that needed to be hidden away, not because of what he looked like, but for what he could possibly do and had done before. He missed the days of roaming outside the facility. They had finally caught him and made him into something they could mold to their own use when they realized what he had become capable of doing. Prime knew that he had done this to himself, but anytime he saw his reflection or somehow ended up in the woods with crimson-stained hands he was reminded of it again.

"Prime, you are brilliant," they told him, using the name that they had given him. He did not remember his real one anymore. There were a lot of things that he was forgetting and starting to forget.

Prime thought about Trois sometimes. He had escaped and by the time they caught up with him two months later, enough hikers had gone missing in the nearby woods and wilds that when they did find him, they simply put him down. Too "unpredictable and unstable," they said. Prime was always sad to hear when one of them had to be terminated, but he understood. Trois, like all of them, was dangerous. But there was liberation within that danger, and even Prime missed the time when he was known as the bogeyman of an entire region.

Shida was quiet and allowed to keep Prime company in the lab. Prime was unnerved by the way Shida's large, brown eyes paid attention to everyone and everything, including him. Nothing escaped his sixth's creation's notice. "Prime," he asked. "Do you ever worry that we are wrong?"

"What do you mean?" Prime asked, finding the question an insightful one, coming from Shida. "That these experiments that I'm doing are wrong?"

"No, that *we* are both wrong. Our existence. That all of us are wrong."

Prime frowned and looked at Shida long and hard, his expression tight. "There's nothing wrong with *us*. We are who we are."

Prime hated the walls of his room and would sometimes lie there at night for hours, staring at them. Each crack familiar, each unadorned plane and angle known. He wondered how he got to this place, this point. Became whatever he was thought to be. He could not hear Neent and wondered about him being quiet again. When he was not screeching, his cries were low and mournful. Prime turned over on his bed, listening.

I'm running out of time.

Prime did not know how he got out, only that he did. He stood there, enjoying the breeze on the long hairs of his face, his arms, his body. The hunt could start. His mouth watered as he thought about it. The taste of the iron in their blood. The satisfying crunch of their bones. He was startled out of his reverie by the man on the path, but not for long. No one could hear his shrieks and Prime, unmoved, had become used to them. He didn't hear them anymore.

Prime opened his eyes and found himself kneeling by a creek deep within the AgLands with no clue as to how he got there, his blood-soaked clothes and fur the only evidence of what he had done. *Again,* he thought. *It has happened again.* It was always the same crew entrusted to retrieve them when they strayed. He was calm as the team rushed towards him. As they helped him up, he looked down and even his hooves were covered in it. He turned his hands back and forth over and over again, watching the blood as it began to dry on them.

It was all that he could do not to lick them and get every single drop. The last thing that he could remember was that there had been screams. There would be no body to find. *There never was. There never has been, not with any of us.*

"Goatman's getting worse," one of the techs muttered as Prime was led through the halls to his room. If only they knew. Prime knew that they would cover it all up, just like they always did. No one would do or say anything. His face darkened. *Why do you think they keep me there toiling? They're hoping I can clean myself up, make a version of myself that is truly what they need instead of more monsters that they have to keep telling lies about.* Prime felt his mind was slipping, but as long as he could continue his experiments and produce, they didn't care about the toll it took on him, and them, every time. *Who is* really *the monster?*

Sieben and Acht were the twins. Prime considered them his rare masterpieces and wept at their loss, their deaths at each other's hands. He took their loss personally as he had such high hopes. Perfecting them meant finding a cure for them, for him, and becoming normal again. Whatever "normal" could be.

He was given the reports, especially when one of them managed to get free. It was no accident that any of them "escaped" at all. The experimenting was always continuing, and even their escaping was a part of that. Prime was the most surprised by Cinque, who had made it all of the way to Texas. Motorists started … *disappearing* near this one bridge. There were sightings and stories and Prime loved hearing them, loving the legacy he was leaving. They'd find torn pieces of clothing. Empty cars. Traces of blood. But never the persons Cinque must have encountered. As always, they'd never find a body. Sometimes he was filled with guilt. Sometimes he was filled with pride.

I am creating myths even as I am creating monsters, he thought. *This is how legends are born.*

Who told me I could play God?

"He stares through the translucent door toward the massive, blood-red, black-veined creature waiting inside."

AQUARIUM DIVER

PHILIP FRACASSI

T he hangar is part of a vast parcel of government land that hasn't been officially inhabited since the end of World War II. Settled among the foothills of the Colorado Rocky Mountains, the unnamed base is spread over thirty thousand acres of hard terrain, winding dirt roads, and a cracked runway pitted with stubborn weeds that have spent years pushing their way through the weathered concrete. The runway (such as it is) terminates into the main base, which consists of an empty administration building and two rows of barren hangars, lettered A through F (Alfa—Foxtrot), that are large enough to house whatever military aircraft once flew in and out of the dilapidated military complex.

Unknown to anyone who may notice the base from an aerial perspective—or perhaps from a distant vista while driving the two-lane roads that snake through the foothills—is that although the base appears unoccupied (even unusable) it is, in fact, very much active.

And despite evidence to the contrary, very well-defended.

The 20-foot-high cyclone fencing that surrounds the thirty thousand acres is vigorously maintained and, in many areas, electrified; especially in areas where a man might gain a foothold without being visible from the surveillance cameras mounted every fifty yards around the perimeter. The camera feeds are monitored by a rotating team of army personnel situated in

Hangar Delta. Were visitors allowed on the compound, they would have been shocked at the modernized interior of Delta, and equally surprised at the response-readiness of the over one hundred troops deployed within.

What would certainly cause a visitor's eyes to widen, their proverbial jaw to drop, is the inside of the other occupied space, Hangar Foxtrot (standing directly adjacent to Hangar Delta), also modernized and outfitted with the most current technology and security apparatus.

Unlike Delta, however, Foxtrot is not a security complex built to support military operations. There are no offices or weapons storage, no training areas, none of the usual furnishings and amenities to comfortably house one hundred fighting men and women on a day-to-day basis: bunkhouses, bathrooms and showers, kitchens and rec areas.

No, Foxtrot has none of those things. In fact, there are only two structures of note inside the cavernous hangar: one is a control room—a free-floating box the size of a Greyhound bus, suspended, like a web-stuck fly, by foot-thick steel cables attached to the hangar's walls, ceiling, and floor—hovering thirty feet in the air, and accessible only via a metal, switchback staircase with mesh walls that rises like a tower from the concrete.

The other structure is a 50-foot high, 50-foot-wide, cube.

The cube is enclosed on all four sides by two-foot-thick translucent polycarbonate walls, fully molded—no seams, no screws, no bindings, no crevices.

Airtight.

Inside the cube, there are no vents, no air holes, no internal temperature control, and only one door, hermetically sealed and secured by an electronic mechanism accessible only from the cube's exterior. Through the door is a sealed antechamber, much like the airlock of a space station, and this *does* have vents, but not for oxygen. At the touch of a button, from either inside the chamber or within the control room, the antechamber fills instantaneously with liquid CO_2, removing the breathable oxygen and, most importantly, dropping the temperature of the small chamber to below freezing within seconds; a last fail-safe should something go horribly wrong.

At the end of the chamber is a second door, a second electronic lock.

Beyond that, nothing but the wide-open space of the hangar. And beyond that?

The world.

The scientists who work at Hangar Foxtrot, and the soldiers who occupy Delta, refer to the giant cube as the Aquarium.

As for what lives inside, they have several names.

To a majority of the scientists, it's known simply as the Specimen. The grunts in Delta glibly refer to it as Booger or, when feeling magnanimous, Big Booger.

To the general public—ever since the events that took place in a rural Pennsylvania town over fifty years previous, when dozens of innocent people died and a tight-knit community was torn apart by terror and chaos—it's known by an altogether different name.

"How's our blob today?" Bob Cronus asks, still huffing from his climb up the stairs.

Joanne tilts her head away from the monitor a few degrees, not quite giving the team leader her full attention. "Stable," she says, and shifts her focus back to the screen. "And please don't call it that."

On an average day, the control room is stationed by six occupants.

Joanne Lewis oversees the health and general biological study of the Specimen. Her monitor's current visual is a bird's eye view of the Aquarium. Inside the clear molded plastic box, a red amorphous shape pulses and ripples, shifts and, occasionally, spreads its gooey bulk against one of the polycarbonate walls ... as if testing it. As if just making *sure.*

Also in the control room are two technicians, Jim Stuart and Robbie Bell, whose jobs are to maintain the Aquarium itself, as well as the control room equipment. They also oversee the hangar's many cameras, gauges, and general habitability, keeping the two techs constantly busy with updates, installs, or repairs. Given the stakes of what could happen if they make an error, neither sleeps well at night.

Marisha Harper, the team's catch-all science nerd, is the leading voice for decisions involving chemistry, physics, mathematics, or any other tough questions that need an educated answer. She spends most of her time both devising and studying the results of a variety of tests carried out on the Specimen, which include subjecting the creature to cold, heat, or electricity. There are also "tests" involving a smorgasbord of acids, toxins, or any other chemical compound she thinks may have some effect on the Specimen, be it positive, negative, or neutral. Joanne feels many of Marisha's tests are "cruel," "barbaric," or otherwise malicious (and often excessive), and while Marisha respects Joanne's input, she rarely capitulates to her concerns. Unlike her colleague, she doesn't worry (or care) about the Specimen's emotional state or psychological well-being since, in her estimation, it has neither emotions nor a consciousness. Marisha likens the Specimen to nothing more than a dangerous, unicellular bio-organism, such as an amoeba (albeit one that consumes flesh). To her, it's as sentient as a cancerous tumor, even if it is the size of a sporting goods store.

Daniel Tessier is the software and communications expert. For the last year his primary occupation has been developing a program that will, potentially, act as a sort of *translator* for the Specimen, a task Marisha thinks a waste of time, but Joanne believes could be the breakthrough they've all been working toward.

Bob isn't sure he agrees with either of them. No, he doesn't really think the thing can communicate, but that doesn't mean it's a waste of time, either. Daniel and Marisha have a hypothesis. Fine. And it's his job to make sure it doesn't become a theory, which would mean *more* study, *more* resources, *more* time stuck out here in this warehouse. So, he's made the development of the language software a priority, second only to the Suit, which has been finished for months. As for the Suit, it's been tested and retested and over-analyzed until there is no longer any point to gathering further data.

The Suit is safe. Now it's simply waiting for the software.

"Don't even ask," Daniel whines from his station as Bob approaches. "I know what you're going to ask, so don't even bother."

Bob strolls casually to the middle of the control room, the large viewing windows filled with the eerie white light that comes off the Aquarium, the disturbing visual of the massive creature harbored within, its writhing bulk filling more than half the cube's internal space. "I was just going to say good morning, Dan," he says, eyes comically innocent.

Daniel spins away from his monitor and looks up at Bob, a twitchy smirk on his young lips, dark eyes narrowed and wary. "I don't believe you, so I'll preempt your next volley by telling you this: Yes, it's close. Yes, it needs more testing. No, of course it will never be perfect, but I need to be sure it won't misunderstand the data, either. This isn't a conversation we want to get wrong."

Bob opens his mouth to respond, but Daniel lifts a finger, stalling him. "That all said ..." His eyes brighten, and the smirk transforms into a smile, revealing the programmer's youth beneath the mask of cynical scientific genius. "I think we can move to the next stage."

Bob's eyes widen earnestly this time. He glances around the control room, sees Robbie smiling, obviously giddy with excitement. He notices Marisha's scowl of disbelief and Joanne's wary hope. Jim Stuart, grinning like a schoolboy at the beginning of summer break, types a command into his work-station and his monitor springs to life with a 3-D rendering of the Suit. He looks over his shoulder at Bob, eyebrows raised.

"Wait, did you guys ...," Bob begins, then sets his coffee down on a nearby workstation. "No way ... you didn't!"

Robbie laughs and slaps Jim on the shoulder. Daniel gets up and stands next to Bob, both of them focused on the Suit's rendering. He looks down at Jim.

"The upload finished?" he asks, and Jim nods.

"It's your lucky day, boss!" Robbie says, and then all of them—even Marisha—begin clapping. Applauding what's to come. The next phase.

"Holy shit, you guys. So, we're ready? We're really ready?"

"They wanted to surprise you," Joanne says halfheartedly. "I told them it was against protocol, that you hadn't technically approved the install ..."

But her words are drowned out by Bob's loud "whoop!" of joy as he begins hugging each team member, one-by-one. "You sly bastards!" he yells, shaking Daniel so hard the younger man wobbles unsteadily when released. "You sons of bitches!"

"Now wait a second, wait a second," Robbie says, standing up to get every-one's attention. "Before we make this official, there's one last thing we need to do."

All eyes stay on him as he walks across the room to the locker, pulls out a stack of small paper cups and a half-full bottle of whiskey. The room brews with anticipation as he hands each team member a cup, fills it with liquor. When finished, they all stand and hold up their drinks, facing their leader.

"To Bob Cronus, the world's first living aquarium diver," Joanne says.

"HEAR! HEAR!" comes the response, in unison, as Bob fights back tears.

"And here's to not getting eaten!" Jim adds, and they all laugh. Even Bob.

It takes Bob an hour, and the assistance of both engineers, to get inside the Suit.

Similar to a suit for an astronaut or a deep-sea diver, the Suit is all about protection. Unlike a spacesuit, however, there is no globular faceplate that allows an astronaut a wide view of the world around them. The Suit has only two narrow slits for eyeholes, crafted with the same polycarbonate material as the cube. In addition to its protective functions, such as armor plating and the ability to lower its external temperature to freezing, it also serves as a high-tech laboratory, able to do everything from analyze sample tissue to monitor a target's biorhythms or measure electromagnetic radiation (the same kind humans themselves emit).

Thanks to Daniel Tessier, it can also now capture vibrations from the Specimen and attempt to translate those vibrations, or waves, into speech.

It was Joanne who first offered the suggestion nearly a year ago, soon after the Specimen had been transported from the arctic (now grown too warm to reliably sedate the creature). She postulated the vibrations could possibly be a form of communication.

Or more to the point, language.

The more the team tested the theory the more it seemed (hypothetically speaking) logical. When Marisha subjected the Specimen to more ... extreme stimuli, the vibrations coming off it grew fast and—for lack of a better word —*loud.*

As if it were screaming.

Now, hunkered within the Suit (what he still thinks of more as a vessel, or a ship, something he harbors inside of versus something he wears), Bob stands in the antechamber separating the hangar space from the Aquarium. He stares through the translucent door toward the massive, blood-red, black-veined creature waiting inside.

"How big is it now, anyway?" he asks, his voice monitored by the entire team, with Joanne running point.

"Last we checked, and there's no reason for it to have grown, it was around 25 feet high, ditto for width and length, so approximately 15,000 cubic feet, with a weight of about 100 pounds per cubic foot..."

Bob runs the math in his head.

"More than a thousand tons," he murmurs, knowing the Suit can take it, but not liking the lofty heights of the number.

"That's correct. Or, if you want to be accurate: 1,125 tons. The big guy weighs the same as, oh, a couple hundred full-grown elephants, give or take a trunk."

All in one big, gelatinous, flesh-devouring blob, Bob thinks, fighting off the sparks of panic, of fear, fighting for traction in his mind.

Bob knows the creature can't get to him. It can only absorb organic material, and the Suit was built from thick steel (the same used by modern submarines) and unbreakable plastic. It's airtight and designed to absorb nearly 200 PSI without bending or cracking. An early iteration of the Suit had it tethered to a steel cable, for extraction, before they developed the more elegant solution of the temperature plates beneath the armor—if the suit gets cold enough, the Specimen will push him out, like the whale spitting Jonah onto the shores of Nineveh.

Bob had done the dive twice before. Once with the cable, once with the temperature plates. Both worked fine, but he preferred the elegance of using the cold. Part of him also liked the idea of hurting the thing, of *knowing* he could hurt the thing. Regardless, both dives had been no more than one minute of insertion. In and out. No testing other than making sure he survived. Despite all their use of scientist's logic, the reality is the creature is essentially a giant mass of liquified muscle the size of a T-Rex, and just as deadly. Bob just hopes it isn't as smart as Joanne thinks it might be.

Smart things find a way. Smart things figure shit out.

"I'm going in," he says. "What's its core temp?"

"Forty-five degrees Fahrenheit," Joanne says. "Docile, not dormant. Still, I wouldn't linger at the door."

"Copy that. I'm ready. Let me in."

After a few seconds, the lock of the inner door rotates. There's a *pop* and a gust of visible air as the chilled ventilation of the cube gusts into the antechamber. The thick door opens smoothly, slowly, and Bob—heeding Joanne's advice, and with the assistance of built-in hydraulics—lifts one heavy foot and steps forward.

Thirty seconds later he's inside the cube, the door cycling shut behind him. He stares up at the massive folds of slow-moving goo that has been their sole focus of study for these last twelve months, feels a stomach-churning combination of awe and white-hot terror.

"Let's warm it up," he says. "It looks a little stiff."

"Copy, bringing the temperature up to 65 degrees," Joanne replies, "Careful, he'll be mobile in less than a minute."

"I'm aware," Bob says, grimacing at Joanne's use of "he" versus "it." He doesn't want her, or anyone else, giving the alien creature any semblance of humanity. It's nothing but a mindless, emotionless substance. An incognizant organism that knows only to feed and feed and feed; but that doesn't make it smart, or even sentient. It simply makes it *alive*, and very dangerous. And now that he finally has the software to decipher the strange vibrations that rumble through its core, he'll prove there's no language, no emotion, no mind. Just ... *hunger.*

Then he can finally go home. Pull the scientists and the theorists, let the engineers take over and do the only thing that mattered: keep the damned thing locked safely away. Forever.

Unfortunately for Bob, the only way to cleanly acquire these vibrations is from *inside* the Specimen, ergo Joanne's crack about him being an aquarium diver, like the ones sunk to the bottom of a fish tank, opening some long-lost treasure and leaking oxygen like a bubbling fool.

He'll be diving, all right, but not into an ocean.

He'll be diving into the blob.

"Temperature now 61 degrees ... 62 ... 64 ... keeping it here, Bob. He looks nice and pink, don't you think?"

Bob doesn't feel Joanne's lightheartedness as the concrete slab (lined with pipes that, when flushed with water—hot or cold—moderate the temperature of the cube) gently warms the thick plastic floor. Standing less than ten feet away from the immense alien organism, he watches as it loses the dull gray pallor it takes on when cooled, as the black veins running throughout turn purple, then pink; as the creature's slick, gel-like flesh brightens to the color of raw meat.

"Okay, let's see if it's hungry," he says. Then, below his breath: "God, I hate this part."

Bob takes one step toward the massive organism and then—faster than he'd anticipated, than he would have thought *possible*, even after a year of study—it *charges*. He barely contains an instinctive scream as, within seconds, the alien creature slams into him, sucks him into its slimy body, engulfing the Suit and Bob with it.

"Bob! You okay? Jesus, that was fast!" Joanne's voice sounds panicked, which makes Bob even more nervous than he already is. He can sense the pressure from the creature surrounding him—as it SQUEEZES—its internal composition trying desperately to absorb his flesh, to feed on whoever has been idiotic enough to step inside its lair.

The things we do for science, Bob thinks, and forces himself to relax, to breathe deeply, in and out, in and out. His eyes flick to the monitors. The readouts are all stable. The seals are green.

He's safe.

"I'm okay," Bob says, praying his voice doesn't reveal his anxiety. "All sensors are quiet, nothing unexpected from inside here ... but yeah, I guess the Big Booger was hungrier than we thought."

"All right, yeah, we read you," Joanne says, still sounding shaken. "Uh, you're looking good on our end. Robbie says everything reads green across the board ... wait ... okay, standby ..."

Bob, using the truncated keys built into the fingers of his armored gloves, begins typing commands. He lowers the Suit's internal temperature a few degrees, but not enough to alter the exterior. *Just enough to dry the sweat on the back of my neck*, he thinks, still unnerved by the unexpected aggression of the creature.

The original plan had been to build a probe, a robot to do what could be a dangerous, even life-threatening, exercise. But with the development of the Suit, and the complexities that could arise when "engaged" with the organism, it was decided the human element was a necessary one, and the danger, ultimately, nominal.

Now that he's cocooned inside the Specimen (still desperate to absorb his tissue and coming up empty), Bob's thinking a probe might have been the way to go after all. Still, he's in it now, so he tells himself to suck it up and start doing the work he's here for. He sets aside any thoughts of claustrophobia, of fear, and forces his scientist brain to take over the reins from the ancestral ape. Now is not the time for primal emotions. Now is the time to *think.*

"Bob?" Joanne says, her voice somewhat calm once more as it comes through the small speaker. "Daniel says he's standing by to catch the data if you want to activate the translating software. Or we can do it from here. Don't want to overwhelm you ..."

"Thanks, I got it," he replies, fingers working the keys. The small monitor, built-in just above the eyeholes, flickers to life as Bob enters the commands to activate the software and open the Suit's external microphones—less audio recorders than hyper-sensitive sensors that absorb whatever physical vibrations come from the belly of the beast, then attempt a rudimentary translation. If the vibrations are even close to a patterned consistency, the software will attempt to hack the data into an alphabet, similar to the way a code breaker would have deciphered the *clicks* and *clacks* of enemy transmissions during World War II, using a repetitive dialogue of machine-made vibrations that could be transformed into words.

"Bob, I'm gonna tie Daniel into the line, if that's okay. He's driving me nuts with his questions ..."

"Yeah, okay." Bob thinks he hears a small *pop* from somewhere in the suit. He ignores it, knowing the sensors will pick up any kind of breach. He looks through the eyeholes at the red mass smeared against the other side, wonders if it can see him, if it's studying him the way he's studying it ...

"Bob?" Daniel says, sounding excited.

"Yeah, Dan, go ahead."

"I don't want to jump the gun here, but the computer is picking up some incredible readings. I mean, it's gonna take a while to break the code, and I need more data, but we're getting pattern consistencies. I want to try a response test, see if we can narrow down the data. You game?"

"Sorry, Dan, I'm not sure I follow." Bob's eyes don't leave the vein-streaked red covering his vision. "Are you saying this thing is talking?"

"Well ... no. I mean, I wouldn't make that leap. Not yet. But there's something there, boss. It's not chaotic enough to be purely biological. There's a consciousness behind it, or whatever would pass for consciousness in an alien organism ... look, we can get into all this later. Right now, I'd like you to activate your external speaker."

"Dan, I don't ..."

"He wants you to talk to it, Bob," Joanne says, cutting to the heart of it. "Dan thinks if we can focus its responses, we can translate more quickly. And by 'we', I mean the quantum computer."

Bob blows out a breath, taps some keystrokes and brings up the prompt for suit controls. He activates the external speaker, then mutes it, so only the control room can hear him. For the moment.

"All right, what do you want me to say? Other than get the hell off me."

"Ha! Okay, yeah, not that."

There's a pause, and Bob can almost visualize Dan thinking about historic first words or some such bullshit.

"Bob? Say, 'Why are you here?' Then just repeat that phrase every thirty seconds."

This is insane, Bob thinks. "Yeah okay, I copy." Bob unmutes the mic, takes a deep breath, and says: "Why are you here?"

Every thirty seconds, he says it again, using the same tone, the same volume.

"Why are you here?"

"Why are you here?"

"Why are you here?"

After a few minutes of complete silence from the control room, Daniel finally breaks in.

"Okay, okay, hold on please. We're getting some ... oh man, this is incredible. Bob, mute your mic. I'm gonna send you the computer's transcription. This is playback of the last thirty seconds. Everything prior to that is indecipherable."

"Wait, but this isn't?"

"Just, standby ... sending ... *now.*"

Bob hears a hiss of static, then what sounds like a heartbeat, albeit one with an irregular rhythm. After a few more seconds, the heartbeats elongate into sounds that alter in pitch: some high, some low. The sounds are almost animal, guttural; then whining, strained ... but not frantic, almost ... serene. Then the sounds begin to repeat and, after a few more seconds, they begin to make sense.

... am ... here ... am ... to ... feed ... to ... am ... I ... here ... feed ...

Bob feels the blood run from his face. His body goes cold all over. His scientific mind realizes he's slipping into shock. "Oh my good Christ."

The computer-regulated voice is robotic, but clear.

Terribly, terrifyingly, clear.

"I am here to feed. I am here to feed. I am here to feed."

"Jesus Christ, turn it off," Bob says. Fresh sweat runs down his temples, hot tears spring from his eyes. He begins tapping commands, but his vision is blurred, his heart slamming inside his chest. "Joanne? Turn it off. You copy? Turn it off!"

The audio clicks off and the Suit falls silent as a tomb. Bob's breathing is too loud, too fast. "I want out of here," he says, trying to sound calm but ultimately not caring if the others can hear his fear. Not caring if the Suit's sensors register that he's pissed himself.

It's one thing to be stuck inside a brainless organism, a thing that simply consumes in the same way a cell will consume other cells ... but to know the creature is *cognizant?*

That it's *talking?*

It's too much. Too much.

"Bob, are you aborting?" Joanne sounds ... what? Relieved? Disappointed?

"Hell yes," he replies. "Activating the external coolant."

"Wait! Bob, you can't bail now!" Daniel says, his voice too loud, shredding Bob's nerves. "Good lord! We're communicating with an alien ..."

"Joanne, cut his mic. Cut his mic *now.*"

A split-second later, Daniel's voice disappears.

"All right, Bob, try and relax. It's just you and me, okay? Take a breath, big guy."

Bob does as he's asked, forces himself to take three deep, steadying breaths. His pulse slows, and he nods to himself. "Okay, okay. I'm better. I just ... I need to abort, okay? I need to abort. We'll ... I'll try again ... later. But I need to abort."

"Copy that, Bob. Why don't I activate the armor coolant from here?"

"Yeah, please. Please do that, thank you."

Bob closes his eyes, alert for the sensation of being released. Of being *pushed* out.

Nothing happens.

"Joanne?"

A few seconds pass before Joanne's voice comes back. "Standby, Bob ... we're checking a few boxes here ..."

Bob's eyes spring open, wild and wide.

You've got to be kidding.

"Checking boxes? How about checking the box that gets me the hell out of this thing?"

"Yes, I, uh ... we ... standby."

Bob brings up the operations screen, frantically types in commands. A digital representation of the Suit appears on the monitor, a 3-D control panel along with a scrolling list of its current operations. Fingers working the keys, he brings up the menu for the armor coolant.

The computer thinks, then flashes: *Command Failed.*

"The hell?"

Bob closes out the menu, reloads it. Types in the command once more.

Command Failed. Command Failed. Command Failed.

"Okay, guys? What the hell's going on? I'm not ..." He taps in the command again. And again. "The suit's not activating, the suit's not ..."

"*Do not be afraid.*"

The blood pumping through Bob's veins seems to freeze ... then stop. His hands begin to shake inside the armored gloves, and his jaw clenches. Quick, hard breaths are forced through his nose as he fights off panic.

It's a computerized voice. The translation software. And it's coming through the internal speaker.

"*There will be no pain. No feeding.*"

The creature. The fucking blob ... is *talking* to him.

"*Please relax. Do not panic. This is ... difficult for me. Do you understand?*"

No! No ... it's not possible. It can't be. If this thing can think ... if it can communicate? It's far more dangerous than we could have imagined.

Bob checks his monitor, sees the communications line is open and active. The external microphones are also active. Quickly, he types in the commands to close the mic, to shut down all communications.

The Suit ignores the commands.

Come on, come on. Get me out of here.

There's a soft *beep* in Bob's ear, and he watches as one of the control panel's green integrity sensors ... turns red.

Oh no. Please God, no.

"Um, Joanne? I ... uh ... I have a breach here. Joanne, please ... please copy."

"The others are not ... hearing you. Is that correct? Hearing?"

Bob swallows as two more green sensors flick to red. The beeping in his ears gets faster, louder. Fear swarms in his chest like angry hornets, rushes to his brain. When he speaks again, his teeth chatter, his voice trembles.

"Yeah, that's correct," he says.

"Good. I'm happy you are responding. It's been ... difficult ... frustrating. But now we are speaking. Is it clear? What I am speaking ... you understand?"

"Yes," Bob says, eyes darting from the red lights to the unresponsive monitor. *It's taken control of the Suit. Somehow it's taken control and now there are several breaches and it can get inside. God help me ...*

"I have discovered ... weakness ... in you. In your shell. Do you understand?"

Bob wills himself to stop shaking, to get a *grip* on the situation. If the thing can talk, it can reason. It could kill him ... *absorb* him ... but it hasn't. He can get out of this. He can get out of this and get out of this goddamned suit and catch the first plane to Hawaii and retire and live a long, pension-fueled life on a beach. He just needs to reason with it. Convince it to let him go. Let him *out*.

He takes a steadying breath, closes his eyes. "I understand."

"Good, Bob. Good. We have much to ... talk of."

"This is insane!" Robbie yells—as much to himself as to the rest of them—for what feels like the hundredth time. "We've got to do something!"

It's been two days since Bob was consumed by the Specimen. The team inside the control room hasn't bathed, has hardly eaten or slept. They're tired, bedraggled; pushing the limits of what the body and mind can endure.

Approximately 48 hours prior, the team watched helplessly as readouts from the Suit went down, one-by-one, only minutes after the insertion of their team leader. After 48 hours of frantically trying to problem-solve, they'd exhausted every technical failure possibility, but found nothing that needed correction. Nothing that could be fixed.

They know that anything they do to the Specimen, they'd be doing to Bob.

Freeze it, and you freeze Bob. His body stuck inside the mass like a fly in a popsicle.

They also know that things like electrocution, bursts of radiation, or other "pain" stimulants do little to harm the creature, but the risk to Bob would be immense.

The only thing that keeps the team from more extreme courses of action (such entering the Aquarium with coiled tubes that blasted CO_2), and putting other lives at risk, is the fact that Bob's vitals continue to scan as having no ill effects. From what they can tell his heart rate, temperature and other biological readings are stable. Of course, by this point, he'll be dangerously dehydrated, but his regulated breathing and the Suit's ability to convert carbon dioxide to fresh oxygen keep him from any over-exertions that would expedite his body's need for fluids.

All other data had been cut off. They aren't sure if the Suit has been breached, or simply malfunctioned. It's telling them just enough to hold their ground, but not enough to know what's happening to their friend.

"I agree," Joanne says, raising her face from where it has been resting in her open hands, eyes heavy with exhaustion and worry. "I say we go ahead with the military solution. Let's get people in there with CO_2 hoses, see if we can push it back, away from … from Bob."

There is more agreement this time than previously. Even Marisha, who seemed the most resistant to exposing more people to the specimen, knows now they have to at least try. Another twelve hours could be too late, despite what the readouts tell them. "Let's call Major Millgate," she says, concurring. "Tell him to ready the soldiers."

The others nod their agreement, and Joanne has just lifted the black handset mounted into her console, the one giving her a direct line to their neighbors in Hangar Delta, when Daniel starts to yell.

"It's moving! I mean, *he's* moving! Look!"

Joanne drops the phone, not noticing when it misses the cradle, dangles like a hanged man by the stretched cord. She doesn't hear the distant voice from the other end saying: *Go ahead Foxtrot? Foxtrot? This is Delta ... do you copy? Hey, you guys okay?*

Because they're all yelling now.

From inside the bright, red-jellied texture of the Specimen, a dark human-shaped shadow moves slowly toward the edge of the great mass, as if it is being *squeezed* out. Pushed away.

"Maybe he got the Suit to freeze?" someone says, but no one responds because they're all watching, rapt, the obscene delivery of their leader.

Like the birth of a metal baby, the head of the Suit breaks free from the gelatinous body, a gooey pink film covering it like embryonic fluid. The shoulders come next and then, more quickly, the rest of Bob's suit emerges, dropping awkwardly to the floor with a heavy *clunk*, but seemingly intact.

"All readouts are coming back online!" Jim shouts as the monitors filling the control room spring to life, showing the full array of the Suit's sensors, along with an audible crackle of the comms.

Joanne depresses the button for her microphone, doing her best not to scream into the mouthpiece. "Bob, can you hear me? Do you copy?"

"Get the medical team in there," Marisha barks, and another phone is picked up, a hurried voice asking for help. Robbie is already out the door, bolting down the metal steps. Daniel, slumped in his chair, muttering to himself like a madman, stares at a swarm of data filling his screen. "Holy shit ... holy shit ...," he mumbles, eyes tracking the insane amounts of data flooding through his monitor. "It's been talking ...," he says, then sits bolt upright. He spins to face the room, his exhaustion erased by a look of terror. "It's been ... Guys! Damn it, listen to me!"

Daniel stands fast enough to knock his chair over. It clatters hard to the floor, and the general chaos of the room quiets as all eyes turn to face him.

"It's been talking! It's been talking to him this entire time!"

———

Two days later, Bob lies on a cot in the medical tent. They have removed the IV drip since he is once again eating solid foods, drinking all the fluids they give him. He begins today's tedious regiment of exercises, prescribed by the army doctor, to stretch and energize the muscles, revitalize the strained organs of his body.

Members of his team have come and gone, intermittently and without pattern. Joanne has visited the most, stayed the longest. In a way, the team needed some time to recoup as well, given their around-the-clock efforts to free him.

Daniel, oddly, has visited only once, and as part of a group. Bob noticed the communications expert looking at him warily, as if cautious. Or suspicious.

Or afraid.

Alone now, wearing white medical scrubs, he runs through his series of light stretching and strength exercises. As he huffs and sweats, he continues to replay—over and over—the things the alien had told him.

The philosophy of perspective; how humans can only see what their minds are capable of seeing. Their senses hampered by the limits of what a body of flesh-and-blood can acknowledge. Can understand.

If you could see sound, or music, as I can, your perceptions of your world would change forever. To you, my shape is amorphous, an auditory rendering of a foghorn instead of a sonata. If my shape were human, would my ability to consume energy be any less repugnant? My way of devouring nutrients and absorbing thoughts, memories, genetic code less horrifying? Would I be less of a threat if I had teeth or tentacles?

I think not.

Bob counts his knee-bends. Fifteen, sixteen, seventeen ...

Your people wonder about my existence here, in the universe. Why I came to this world to feed. The secret, Bob, is that I only come to worlds that are dying. Or, in your case, worlds that are already dead but don't yet realize it. Like the light from a distant, long-extinguished star, the fate is written, waiting for perception to catch up.

Bob, sweating freely, begins to do push-ups, his palms flat against the cool concrete floor as he counts. One, two, three ...

When I devour this world, crossing the floor of oceans, feasting on the largest cities, toppling the deepest forest, consuming all the life which exists, I will grow to such size that the planet itself will feel my weight upon its surface. And then I will burrow, Bob, crushing the core of this world, and the continents will collapse, and the seas turn to ash. The atmosphere you breathe will wither and the planet will erupt into dust and rock, flung out into space as meteoric detritus.

The same as I've done countless times, to countless other worlds such as yours.

And then I will split into countless pieces, and each part of me will nestle within these galactic travelers, these meteors of your world, and through them I will expand further across endless space, absorbing new species, new planets. I'll go on and on, until I am spread across the breadth of the cosmos, and all of it is ME, and all of those species will be part of what I AM.

It's all so glorious, Bob ... it's all so glorious.

Can't you see?

Bob finishes his push-ups. He stands, plucks a towel off the back of a nearby chair and wipes his face.

A nurse enters his room holding a tray of food. He watches as she sets it down, but makes no move toward it.

Instead he steps, silently, behind her. She turns, surprised, but does not cry out. Does not scream.

His raises his hands slowly, rests his open palms on the sides of her face, almost tenderly.

"Dr. Cronus?" she says, her gaze steady. "What is it?"

He looks deep into her eyes, and she smiles awkwardly. Prettily.

For the nurse, this is not the first time something like this has happened, and by men less handsome than this one. She knows what he wants, of course, but is happy to play the game. "Aren't you hungry, doctor?" she says, reaching behind her to rest a hand on the edge of his dinner tray.

Then her cheeks begin to burn, as if his palms have transformed into blistering-hot irons. She wants to scream now, but it's too late, and her breath catches in her throat as the searing heat eats through her cheeks.

The dinner tray clatters to the floor.

As she stares at him—her mouth hung open and filling quickly with wet, hot flesh—his bright blue eyes appear to bleed. But it is not blood that trickles out from the corners of his eyes, that runs down his cheeks in thin tendrils.

And when he grins, a fat, pink tongue pushes outward from between his gleaming white teeth, and divides.

And when he speaks, it is the voice of multitudes.

"I'm ravenous."

"The cry came again; a low mournful wail coming from the lake."

NOTHING PERSONAL

GEORGIA COOK

Foreboding.

From ages five to seven that was Charlie's favorite word: *foreboding*, like a tiny soothsayer, his eyes magnified behind those big bottle-cap lenses. Foreboding. God only knew where he picked it up; some TV show, a passing conversation, one of the endless comics he was always reading. I remember him as a funny child, three years younger than me, small and blond, with his habit of picking up words.

After *foreboding* it was *indomitable* and then on to whatever new nonsense he liked the sound of, but the word came back to me the day I met Jen.

There was nothing immediately strange about Jen. A science major, like my brother, she was small and pretty, with dark curly hair and a small pixie-pale face. She wore dark jeans and a shirt from a rock band I knew Charlie liked—a typical college girlfriend. But seeing her there on the steps of my apartment, smiling on my brother's arm, that was the only word I could ascribe to her:

Foreboding.

"*Michael,*" she extended a hand. "Charlie's told me so much about you."

Charlie grinned sheepishly. "All good stuff, I promise," he said. "Mostly."

I blinked, realized I'd been staring ever since I opened the door and moved to shake Jen's hand. "Jen," I said, forcing away the prickle of unease. "Great to meet you too."

And just like that, Jennifer McCarthy entered my life.

I saw her often after that. Charlie had moved home for the summer, bringing Jen with him. I discovered she was from Boston originally, with family in Ireland, and no desire to travel halfway across the world to visit, and so Charlie had offered a compromise. His bedroom was large enough for the two of them, and he was old enough to extend the invitation. What our parents thought of this arrangement I didn't dare ask—they lived three blocks up the road from me, but it was a distance I'd been trying to widen since graduation—but I knew Charlie was smitten, and as his big brother, it was my job to be happy for him.

And I *was*, I told myself. I *was.*

I tried to get along with Jen. I told myself she'd be gone by Christmas, that no relationship forged at university was ever serious, but I knew Charlie, and I recognized his expression whenever he looked at her. They were inseparable, those first few months of living together. I rarely saw them apart.

Jen was sweet enough—she certainly doted on Charlie—but it was as if my brother encompassed her entire world. Conversations felt decidedly one-sided, and she had a disconcerting habit of looking you straight in the face as you talked—looking, but not listening, as if she were searching for something just behind your eyes. At first, I tried to brush it off, but as the weeks drew on, Jen's behavior grew stranger and stranger. She became increasingly agitated, jumpy and distracted. I thought maybe the relationship was finally drifting apart, but if Charlie had noticed Jen's strange demeanor, he never mentioned it.

I remember thinking it was as if Jen was waiting for something—something Charlie either couldn't see, or had simply decided to ignore.

It was the last week of summer—just seven days until Charlie and Jen returned to university—when Charlie suggested we visit the cabin. We were all sitting on a bench in the park, watching the sun make its lazy journey across the sky, listening to the rustle of leaves and the distant roar of traffic. Jen was lying with her head in Charlie's lap. I was sitting beside them, trying not to feel like a horrendous third wheel, deciding how best to excuse myself and trudge home.

"The cabin?" Jen asked, lifting her head from Charlie's lap.

"Yeah!" Charlie's eyes gleamed behind his glasses. "Tell her about it, Mick!"

I pulled a face. "Jeez, do Mom and Dad still rent that place?"

"Yeah, Uncle Roger uses it in the autumn for his fishing trips. Didn't you know?"

"Why would I?"

We hadn't been to the cabin since we were kids. It was all the way up in the Colorado mountains, surrounded by high pine forests and glistening black lakes. We'd stopped going after Dad's hip replacement, but it seemed our parents had kept it out of a sense of nostalgia.

"—out in the middle of nowhere!" Charlie was explaining to Jen. "Surrounded by woods. Big old fireplace, three bedrooms. Right by the lake!"

Jen's eyes widened. "A lake?"

"Yeah! All in the middle of nowhere. There are other cabins all over, of course, but it's almost completely isolated."

I could tell Charlie was working himself into a state. Whatever happened, they were going to the cabin together, so I took the opportunity to heave myself off the bench and make myself scarce.

They were still chatting as I left, Jen's eyes as wide as Charlie's. Totally smitten.

I assumed that would be the end of it—just an excited make-believe conversation on a park bench—but Charlie approached me again later that night.

"We want you to come," he said, leaning in my apartment doorway. "We've decided to give it a shot!"

"I don't think that's a good idea—"

"C'mon Mick. Just the three of us. Jen wants to get to know my big brother! You can spare a few days for us, surely?"

I suppressed a shudder at the thought of being isolated alone with Jen. "Would Jen mind? I mean, it'll be the three of us. Surely you want the two of you—"

"She asked specifically."

I thought about Jen's odd behavior over the last few weeks. I thought about her silent moods, the way she stared across the room at me when she thought I wasn't looking.

She asked specifically.

I felt the return of that chill. I didn't want to spend the last of my summer in the wilderness with Jen. I barely wanted to spend the next few weeks at home with her. But I wanted to try, for Charlie's sake, and for the sake of my uncertainty. Jen freaked me out, but I couldn't quite place my finger on why, and that uncertainty alone was enough to make me agree.

I only had two more weeks in which to be civil. I could manage that much.

We set off three days later; me in my truck, Jen and Charlie and all our bags bundled into the back. It was a five-hour drive up into the mountains, the road narrowing from the highway to a thin dirt track, the houses slowly petering out into miles and miles of endless trees.

Despite myself, I began to enjoy the drive. The sky was lighter up here, the blue haze extending from horizon to horizon, totally free of clouds. The air buzzed with insects, the summer warmth trapped beneath a layer of trees. It was a world away from even our tiny rural town, and a universe away from Charlie and Jen's university campus.

I shot a glance in the rear-view mirror. Jen was staring out the window, her hand pressed against the glass, watching the glint of water far off between the trees, her eyes as round as marbles.

The cabin was exactly as I remembered. Older now, filled with dust and dead insects, cobwebs draped in far corners. But these were still the same rooms, the same simple wooden furniture, the smell of dry wood and loam. Weeds poked through the slats in the wide front porch, winding up from the space beneath the house.

Jen stepped down from the truck and stared around as I lugged the bags from the trunk, her eyes gleaming in the yellow sunlight. "Oh Charlie," she whispered. "It's *beautiful.*"

Charlie beamed. "Isn't it just? Mom and Dad've had it for years."

"And the lake?"

"Out that way," Charlie pointed. "We can swim later, if you like?"

Jen smiled, but said nothing. As I turned away, I caught her staring out through the trees, at the glint of sunlight far between the trees.

That night I lay in the cabin's tiny guest room, fading in and out of sleep. The bed was stiff and uncomfortable, the air stiflingly hot. My eyes shot open. Something had awoken me. What was it? A creaking board outside? A rustle of wind?

I lay still for several seconds, struggling to hear, before swinging myself out of bed and padding to the door, peering out into the hallway. My bedroom opened onto the cabin's vast living room. The front door hung ajar ahead of me, letting in a shaft of brilliant moonlight, and on the floor by the welcome mat, glimmering wetly in the silver gloom, were a set of perfect footprints.

They were small and purposeful, leading away down the porch steps and into the forest. I blinked, glancing down to the bare boards at my feet. The footprints were here too, dark in the gloom, but just about recognizable, leading out from Charlie and Jen's room. Their door was closed. Nothing stirred within.

A prickle of resentment warmed my neck. Had they gone for a midnight swim together? Was that what had woken me?

I was about to close the front door when a cry cut through the night. I froze, my hand on the lock. The cry came again, louder now; a low mournful wail, like a woman in distress, coming from the direction of the lake.

I told myself it was some night animal—a fox perhaps, or a coyote—howling in the dark. But it sounded too sharp, too human.

Far too human.

I glanced over my shoulder again, but the house was dark and silent. No sign of Jen or Charlie. I took a deep breath, adjusted my robe, and stepped out into the night.

A bulbous full moon hung overhead, tinging the world silver. Insects whirred in the undergrowth, filling the forest with their sound. The air was sticky and hot—too humid for the middle of the night.

In the distance I could just about make out the lake, glimmering black and still in the darkness. A thin white smear floated above the water, lit by the moon. I paused, hardly daring to breathe, peering through the undergrowth to see what it was.

… someone was standing in the lake, crying great howling sobs.

The silhouette was unmistakable. Jen stood with her back to me, bent to her waist in the water, her night gown flowing out around her, hair tangled from sleep.

She was too busy to notice my presence. As I crept closer, too confused to be startled, I realized she was washing something, dunking it beneath the water with great rolling movements, ringing it between her hands, twist after twist. It looked like a pillowcase, or a T-shirt. Was it one of Charlie's? One of hers? What was she doing?

The water around Jen's hands was dark with a slowly spreading stain, winding out across the lake, and as she washed, she sobbed; great sobbing, rolling wails. A sound so full of grief and longing that my chest ached. It was the strangest thing I'd ever seen, all alone up here among the trees.

Enthralled and disgusted, I stepped closer, struggling to peer through the dark. I could call out to her, ask what was happening; whether she needed help, if I should call an ambulance. Then the thought rose within me, unbidden, full of bile and spite, the lingering resentments of the last three months:

Leave her to it.

Why should I help? I didn't like Jen. I'd never liked Jen. She was the interloper in my life, and I the interloper in hers. Better to let her get on with whatever game she was playing. Let her run to Charlie for help. Leave her be.

I blinked, startled by my own nastiness, and stepped forward. Something snapped beneath my foot. Jen whipped round, her face a pale smear in the darkness, and for a fleeting moment we locked eyes.

A bolt of panic lanced through my chest. With a surge of horror, I caught myself, turned, and ran as fast as I could back towards the cabin. I stumbled up the steps, groped blindly towards my room, and collapsed into bed, my heart pounding.

Even without the lake, even without the chilling strangeness, the look on Jen's face, the desperation ...

It terrified me. It terrified me in a way I couldn't possibly articulate. And I couldn't say why.

God, I couldn't say why at all.

My dreams that night were filled with indistinct figures, dark-eyed and skeletal, tangled with pondweed, their mouths open in a ceaseless scream, clawing themselves up from the bottom of the lake—and a far off wailing, low and mournful, through the woods.

The next day dawned bright and hot—another cloudless blue sky, another horizon filled with rustling green and spiraling heat. I watched Jen carefully over breakfast, groggy and bleary-eyed, but saw no evidence of the previous night. No moss in her hair, no dirt across her face, no watery footprints across the cabin floor. Nothing.

She caught me staring and flashed me a strange little smile, and for a moment I thought I saw the wariness I'd glimpsed back home, some residual spark of that volatile oddness. Then it was gone.

Charlie sat beside her, totally oblivious, grinning from ear to ear. I told myself this proved the dream theory. If Jen had left their bed last night, surely he'd have noticed.

As I cleared away the dishes, I caught Jen standing by the window, watching Charlie struggle across the lawn with a picnic hamper.

At first, I thought she hadn't noticed me, then she dropped the curtain with a sigh. "I love him, Mick," she said, so softly I almost didn't hear her. "I really do love him. Do you understand?"

I opened my mouth to reply but found I couldn't. Something about Jen's tone stirred a discomfort deep in my stomach, silencing any retort. Jen flashed me a thin, piteous little smile, then stepped out onto the porch. I stood a moment, watching her shadow vanish down the steps, listening to her fading footfalls, before finally suppressing a shudder.

I shouldn't have come.

I shouldn't have *bloody* come.

Perhaps it was jealousy—my own bitterness weaving a plot from half-remembered dreams and unspoken resentments. After all, my baby brother had a girlfriend, and I did not. I was the third wheel to someone else's happiness, and achingly aware of it.

Just me. Just my own stupidity. My own strange dreams.

———

That evening, we sat around the tiny fire pit in the front yard, toasting marshmallows and sipping beers. The night sky rose endlessly over our heads, a network of shimmering stars.

My discomfort hadn't dissipated with the summer warmth. Instead, it sat in my gut, hard and cloying, making it difficult to breathe. Jen sat staring into the flames on the opposite side of the fire. I wanted to say something; ask her what I'd seen—finally put to rest my own madness.

As if sensing my thoughts, Jen looked up, meeting my eye across the campfire. Her eyes in the darkness were inky black. With a jolt, I felt a wave of watery oddness sweep over me, consuming the fire, consuming the forest, rising up from the lake between the trees. It grasped my chest, filled my lungs, roared through my skull in the endless ringing of the drowned. For that snapshot second the world was gone, my brother was gone. Jen and I remained, trapped in her pitch black knowing—

Charlie let out a burst of drunken laughter from the other side of the campfire, breaking the spell. "C'mon Jen, you've gotta know at least one!"

Jen turned away. I slumped, struggling for breath, blinking back the spots of brightness behind my eyes.

"One what?" Jen asked.

"*A ghost story!*" Charlie repeated.

"About what?"

"Anything! C'mon Jen, I've been telling them all evening!"

Nobody was paying me any attention. I managed a deep ragged breath, relishing the sting in the back of my throat, grounding myself. I couldn't possibly have seen what I'd just seen. I was tired and nearly drunk. It was late. Jen was getting to me. This entire *bloody* holiday was getting to me.

Finally, Jen nodded. "I do know one story," she said, slowly. "Just one."

Charlie leaned forward expectantly, his glasses shining in the firelight. Jen smiled fondly. "Have you ever heard of the *Ben side?*" she asked.

Charlie laughed. "The what?"

"The *Banshee.*"

"Those old women who scream when someone's about to die?" I asked. I was tired of Jen's games, tired of my own unease.

Jen shot me another look across the flames. Despite myself, my stomach tightened. "Sometimes," she said at last. "Yes."

"Go on," said Charlie. I sat back, fighting down the sensation that I'd just escaped a terrible reckoning.

"She's said to haunt the castles and lakes of local lords," continued Jen. "Appearing only at night on lonely stretches of water. A spirit of sorrow and remorse."

"Like a ghost?" asked Charlie.

"Something like that," said Jen. "She mourns the doomed. Washes the garments of those about to die."

"Why?" asked Charlie, enthralled.

Jen shrugged. "Some say she's a harbinger, some say her voice is deadly to all who hear it, some say she appears only to those already on the cusp of death."

I remembered the night before. Jen's wailing cry from the middle of the lake, the stained black water coiling around her waist, washing, washing.

The fear in my chest turned to comforting anger. Was this a prank? Some bizarre attempt to warn me away from my brother? What on earth was she trying to pull? Jen had always been strange, but never *demented*.

"You can't be serious." I snorted. Jen turned to look at me, her eyes wide and ink-black behind the flames.

"It's just a story, Mick," said Charlie.

"I don't think she has a choice," said Jen, and I realized I could see nothing reflected back at me in her gaze. Nothing at all.

That night I dreamed of water. I dreamed of an endless Below and Above. I dreamed of a lake without an end, and a surface I would never find, shot through with the wailing cry of the Banshee.

I opened my eyes to darkness. The screams from my dream continued into the waking world, filling my ears, drowning all other sound.

A dream. I was still dreaming. I *knew* I was dreaming—only in a dream could the screaming sound so beautiful. Stronger now, it called to me from across the lake, dragging me down into the aching black, and this time I couldn't resist.

I slipped out of the cabin and away across the yard. Leaves and twigs crunched beneath my bare feet, leaving a dark trail across the undergrowth. My shoulders prickled with goosebumps, branches snagged my hair, but I kept walking. I hadn't stopped to grab my coat or torch, but that didn't matter. I knew where I was going.

Jen was waiting for me in the lake, her hair trailing behind her like the night contained. She held out her hand to me, silvery pale in the moonlight, and in a daze I realized that I felt no surprise, no fear. I was still walking. Walking towards her.

I love him, Michael. I really do love him.

I didn't stop as I reached the water. Ice cold, it snatched my toes, rising to my ankles, my thighs, my waist. Ahead of me, Jen's face was a pale blur above the water, her eyes large and liquid-dark, her mouth hanging open in that endless scream. Beautiful, terrible, anguished.

Foreboding.

A thought broke briefly through the haze of song: what happened to all the monsters? Every myth and medieval folk tale? They'd grown up with us, adapting as we adapted, changing themselves to suit a modern world. They'd never left, not really. After all, where was there to go?

What had become of the Banshee?

The water was up to my chest now, crushing my ribcage, squeezing my lungs.

Jen smiled as I reached her. Her song carried on—wrapping itself around me, filling my mind.

"It's nothing personal, Mick," she whispered, taking my hand. "It's just what I am. You understand?" Her touch was ice cold. Colder even than the lake, cold enough to burn. Carried by the song, I stared into her eyes and realized I understood her exactly:

... I don't think she has a choice ...

When the Banshee screamed, someone had to die. Someone would always have to die. The banshee had spoken. Drawn to the water, she had no say in her nature, just as we had no say in our demise. Perhaps once it had been my brother—perhaps Jen had known even before the start of summer. Had she stood alone in my parent's bathroom, watching the water ripple and shift beneath her fingertips, foretelling Charlie's death in stained porcelain, feeling the anguish of inevitability.

And then she'd found me. The perfect alternative.

As the water rose around my neck—as Jen's hand curled around my wrist, then moved gently to grasp my skull—I realized how logical it all was.

Jen loved my brother, loved him enough to bend the nature of her own kind, and in me she'd found her chance. In me, she'd found a way out.

It really was nothing personal.

Nothing personal at all.

"He looks into the red eyes glowing from the dog house shadows. This time, Lonnie swears there's a softness there."

WOOF

PATRICK BARB

Lonnie doesn't know how much time he has. He stands inside the old coon dog kennel holding a package of pork chops snuck from the lodge's community fridge. He waves styrofoam and plastic back and forth, trying to lure the puppy from its hiding place inside the weathered doghouse at the back of the kennel. The willow trees behind the hunting camp provide protective cover from the elements, so it's hard to tell what time of day it is. Lonnie suspects it's after sunset, based on the mosquitoes taking bites from his elbows and bared knees, and the chirping cricket symphonies heard alongside the rapid-fire drumbeat of his seven-year-old heart.

"C'mon, boy."

Lonnie's attempted command comes in a whisper like he's afraid of his voice but unsure of what else to say or do. With no reply or reaction coming from the doghouse, he takes a step forward. A growl from the shadows lets him know he's overstepped whatever arbitrary boundaries the animal's established.

The boy, a newly-established first-grader at the county's elementary school, scrambles back, nearly tripping over his own feet. The pork chops drop to the concrete, sending a cloud of ground-up leaf particles and dirt into the air.

Under the displaced debris, Lonnie glimpses deep brown stains like the old spaghetti sauce always tattooed on his Mama's apron.

Another growl. The noise reminds him of someone tearing sheets of paper, one after the other. The slightly high-pitched growls are why he's figured the creature for a pup, not yet fully grown.

Regardless, Lonnie still knows enough to stay back. Red eyes, round orbs like Christmas tree baubles, glimmer despite the low light. The eyes follow Lonnie's every move with a surprising degree of patience.

That's good. Daddy oughta like this puppy more if they listen good. If they're a good puppy. Maybe he'll let me keep it.

Landon Kurtz suspects his brother Morris intentionally passed him the shook-up can of Miller right before the opening toast at the lodge. Standing in the main meeting room before the assembled gathering of hunters, Kurtz thought he was ready to share the big news—the unexpected news, the news that might change everything for their small, fading-away-to-nothing town. But his moment in the spotlight is delayed as he coughs away a white beard of foam between desperate slurps from the top of the overflowing can. Morris slaps him on the back with his too-big hands, laughs, and calls him a "lightweight."

He's not helping.

But Kurtz can't say anything back. Not in front of the others and probably not later when things settle down and it's just family at the lodge or back at home. Instead of making a scene, Kurtz wipes the beer foam from his lips and puts a fist to his pursed lips, blocking the path of a belch.

"Well, go on then," his brother says, grinning from ear-to-ear like it's his news and his news alone to share.

No. Can't think like that. Morris might do the hunting, but this is my camp. Gonna be my boys' camp too.

Kurtz's eyes sweep the meeting room, taking in the farmers' tans, camo jackets, strapped holsters with handguns and skinning knives on display. Some folks have gear like Kurtz's—freshly store-bought, almost unused—and others have older weapons displaying the scuffed and scraped, claw-marked and fang-gnawed battle scars of past hunting seasons.

"G-g-gentlemen, as you all know, we had an im-im-impromptu lycanthrope hunt last evening a-a-and ..."

"What's that, Kurtz?"

He can't say if it's one of the old-timers calling from the back of the crowded room or if it's one of Morris's buddies pulling a prank. Regardless, he hates how flustered the interruption gets him.

Before he can answer, Morris is up from his perch on a nearby window sill. He nudges Kurtz away from the "trophies" they've covered in a velvet throw. "First thing my brother's trying to say to y'all, is that we got 'em!"

Morris pulls away the lush cloth with a showman's flourish, throwing in a little bicep flex at the end. Kurtz watches the others lean forward, as much admiring his brother as they are looking at the two werewolf pelts stripped from the previous night's kill. He even notices his eldest son, William, shuffling closer on gangly teenage limbs to stand by his uncle's side. "Look at 'em, boys. Male and female. You can tell by her slimmer coat. Gorgeous, right? Ol' girl was a vicious bitch 'til the end."

He throws his head back and laughs. Everyone joins in. Kurtz smells scotch and cigars on his brother's breath. For a moment, he wonders if he's smelling the same fumes coming from his son. This is not how Kurtz imagined things going. It was supposed to be his moment.

Kurtz clears his throat. Before he can speak, Morris continues to steal the spotlight. "And that's not all. You see, boys, when we tracked 'em to their den ..."

Den? It was nothing more than a double-wide trailer parked deep in the woods over by the abandoned rail line.

"... we blasted these two to kingdom come ..."

My ears are still ringing.

"And wouldn't ya know it, but turned out these two filthy love monsters had gone and had themselves a little whelp."

Here it comes. The questions. I should say something ...

Kurtz and Morris both start talking at once. But the elder keeps going, determined to stop baby brother from taking over like he always does. He wishes Morris were more like his own second-born Lonnie. Quiet, contemplative. The kid cares more about doggies and kitties than about what his older brother is doing.

Seeing that *his* older brother wasn't about to give up, Morris backs off. "Alright then, I'll let my brother tell y'all the rest. Seeing as this is *his* camp after all. Even though he don't use it all that much ... And seeing as the pup was his ki ... well, I'll let him tell it."

Kurtz's cheeks redden at Morris's last comment. Because while Morris made direct hits to the hearts of the adult male and female, Kurtz's shot ricocheted off a rusted-out station wagon attached to the trailer and struck the pup with a glancing blow. "Well, you see, it wasn't exactly a kill. The, uh, the silver shrapnel pierced the skin. But not so ... deep."

"What's that mean, son?"

This time it really is one of the elders making a gruff, "don't give us any bull" type of query. It sounds like McCormack, one of the old men who hunted vampires in Appalachia with Kurtz's father before he'd passed.

"It ... it means ... it's still alive."

"And can't change back. Not all the way." Again, Morris must get in the last word. The whispers pass among the others, and it's Morris who will have their attention when they finish.

Outside, a cloud passes across the waning yellow face of the moon as glimpsed through the open window. The shaggy pelts of the slaughtered wolves turn back into stretched-out human skin. Then, harsh winds blow away the sickly gray clouds as fast as they appeared. The werewolves' black and silver hairs sprout back into place.

Lonnie can barely hear himself talk over the winds blowing around the kennel. The drooping willows shake like they're having a fit. Lonnie figures if he can't hear himself, then there's a good chance the puppy can't hear him either.

He looks into the red eyes glowing from the dog house shadows. This time, Lonnie swears there's a softness there. Like his reflection in the lodge's bathroom mirror earlier, wiping tears away after Daddy yelled at him.

Daddy usually yells when he's around Uncle Morris.

Lonnie decides to give the pup a second chance. After all, he snuck all the way out here after hearing Daddy and Uncle Morris whispering about the "pup back in the kennel" with another man who he didn't recognize, but guessed was a doctor. He had a syringe with a long needle on the end of it, and needles mean "doctor" as far as Lonnie is concerned.

He also figures if someone jabbed him with a needle as big as he'd seen, then he might do some growling of his own. So, he tries again. "It's okay, boy. I won't hurt you."

Lonnie puts one foot forward, sliding the tip of his sneaker across the concrete.

From the shadows, the puppy replies with a quick bark. *Woof!*

Not a growl. Lonnie figures that's a start. "Yes, boy. Woof! Woof! Woof!"

Woof!

The call-and-response routine's a surprise. A pleasant one. Lonnie slaps a hand over his mouth, hiding his gap-toothed smile. He doesn't want to jinx it. The toe of his sneaker taps the pork chops, sending the package to the edge of the dog house.

The puppy sniffs and snorts. Then, it reaches for the meat.

Except, instead of seeing plump little puppy paws with claws on the ends as expected, Lonnie's eyes go wide at the sight of hands, tiny little boy's hands like his own. Wispy hairs like dandelion seeds sprout from the knuckles. Long yellow fingernails scrape against concrete, exploding out from white flesh and pink, puffy nail beds.

The fingernails pierce the plastic coating over the meat, then press deeper into the raw meat below that. The sharp tips of the puppy's little-boy nails pierce the meat, making the same squelching sound Lonnie's rain boots do when he's walking in the mud. A scraping sound follows, as the meat and the puppy's hands retreat into the darkness.

Lonnie realizes the wind must've died down if he could hear everything that happened so easily. It's not something a seven-year-old can process just like that. The little boy steps back, whimpering and whining like he was the pup. Since Daddy won't let him have a pet, sometimes Lonnie pretends he *is* one. Except it's reached the point where pretending comes more naturally than anything else. He's breathing heavy. So heavy, he thinks he might get light-headed and fall to the ground.

Then, the puppy with little boy hands responds with an inquisitive whine of his own.

"We had Doc Cheney take a look at the, well, I guess wolf-boy is what you'd call him..."

Kurtz stands with arms crossed over his chest, watching while his bigger little brother commands the audience of monster hunters, like a maestro conducting a symphony. Doc Cheney stands between the brothers at the front of the room. Kurtz watches from the corner of his eye as the other man struggles to hold himself upright. The reformed boozehound's taken a hard fall off the wagon since they brought him back to the kennel.

"... well, tell 'em, Doc."

Morris delivers a sharp elbow into the armpit of the hammered veterinarian. Kurtz steps forward and grabs Doc's opposite elbow, trying to stop him from falling back against the werewolf pelts. Once he's steady enough to sway and wobble of his own accord, Doc pushes both men away. He looks up into the crowd with bloodshot eyes. "Wazzat?" he asks.

"Tell them what you concluded," Kurtz stage-whispers.

"About?"

"Oh, gawd dang! The werewolf cub, pup, whatever it is. Tell 'em what ya told us!"

Kurtz suppresses a smile, watching his brother lose his cool. He realizes he must be patient though. If he plays his cards right, he might still get to play the hero after all.

Finally, Doc Cheney gets with the program. "I think it's a purebred."

That's right.

Kurtz looks around the room, watching the news settles in and the implications of what it might mean following afterward.

That's right. A purebred werewolf, offspring of two lycanthropes. So it comes about its condition genetically. Not from a bite.

"Well alright then, but what's that gotta do with us?"

Old Man McCormack's question couldn't be more perfectly timed. And Kurtz isn't about to let the moment slip away.

"It means we can bring back the hunting in these parts to the levels it used to be at. Back in our Daddy's and your day."

It's Morris who answers. *Of course.* He steps forward, like an actor searching for his light on the stage. "We're gonna have ourselves a stud in a few years. And we all know about that purebred sow Nelson Lambert keeps in that shed out back of his property. Most of us menfolk know *all* about her. Don't we, William?"

Kurtz's eyes widen and he looks over at his eldest. The barely-a-teen's cheeks are twin purple bruises they're so red. But there's also a smile curling up the corners of his lips. Kurtz can't believe it.

"Whaddaya say, Nelson? Think you can keep the old gal alive long enough for this new pup to reach his wolfmanhood?"

Nelson Lambert nods.

Kurtz hates Nelson Lambert at that moment. Hates him more than anything. The pervert. The pimp.

But maybe he hates his brother that much more.

"What happens after the mating?"

Kurtz admires the persistence of McCormack's questions. He only wishes he could be the one keeping Morris on his toes.

Then again, it's not like his brother seems phased by the geriatric's interrogation. Instead, he's all smiles.

"Well, it means a litter of little werewolf pups. More purebred ones. Ones that don't gotta wait on the full moon to change. We let 'em grow into big ol' werewolves and we set 'em loose here on our property—"

"*My* property. Mine. Daddy left me this camp," Kurtz says, interrupting and hating how much of a child he sounds like when he does.

Morris laughs that off. Like he laughs off everything. Because it all comes easy to him. "Yeah, alright. Anyways, like I was sayin', we can repopulate the area with at least them furry and fanged monsters. Maybe domesticate 'em somewhat. Then we bring people, ya know, big city folk, out here and take 'em on a monster hunt. Let 'em bag a tranqed-up werewolf. Give 'em a pelt like these two that they can put up in their man caves or whatever they're callin' it these days. And the best part ..."

While his brother pauses for dramatic effect, Kurtz hears something halfway between a howl and a child's cry out in the dark. No one else seems to notice.

"We can charge 'em and make ourselves a whole ton of money acting as guides."

And then it's Old Man McCormack who starts up the applause that spreads like a row of bottle rockets lit all at once in a dry field.

Soon everyone's on their feet. Laughing, cheering, singing snippets of old country-western songs with tears in their eyes that they'll deny later if asked about them. Morris plays for the crowd, taking the female wolf's pelt off the rack and pantomiming a slow dance.

Then he stops abruptly, a savage glint in his eyes.

"Whaddaya say we head out to the kennel and see the wolf-boy who's gonna make us all rich, boys?"

When the puppy with little boy hands finishes the pork chops, Lonnie hears an inquisitive whimper from the dark. *Woof?*

"Yeah, boy, 'woof.' You like them chops?"

More shuffling in the dark. Yellow nails against concrete. Yellow nails *into* concrete, they're scratching so deep. Lonnie gets ready to step back. The kennel door is behind him. Swung out open to the forest. The lock dangles from one of the links. His Daddy's key is still in the lock.

The pup's arms appear first. Then, a wet black nose above a sleek white-furred muzzle. But above that, it's skin. Skin just like the skin on Lonnie's face, though the beads of sweat dripping down from the shaggy-haired top of the pup's head suggest a feverish condition in the strange-looking animal.

Faced with this bizarre sight, Lonnie stands firm. His mind races the way only children's minds can race, arms waving and screaming for no reason, bouncing from conclusion to conclusion with the faultiest of logic.

If I can love this puppy, if I can show Daddy I can do it, maybe he'll let me keep it. Maybe he'll let me take it home and let me let it sleep in my bed and ...

Those wild thoughts stop when the pup's fully out of the doghouse and Lonnie sees the torn and blood-splattered superhero t-shirt stretched across the pup's furry chest. Striations of silver glitter in the moonlight, mesmerizing the little boy. Lonnie can feel the darkness all around them. The long willow branches shake like the puppy's tail extending from a bare dimpled bottom.

Something pushes against Lonnie's hand. A gentle nudge. Then harder. The spell finally breaks and Lonnie looks down at the pup. Its red eyes pulse, like blood seeping from a wound. Lonnie catches sight of his reflection in those shimmering pools.

Then, twigs crack, and leaves crunch.

Lonnie looks down as the pup's black lips curl back from its muzzle. The growl travels up the creature's throat and out between flat white teeth. Not fangs, but little white pebbles spaced apart like churchyard gravestones.

It's too late to pull his hand back and run away. Lonnie can only scream when the puppy's hands grab onto his and its teeth sink into his skin.

Even though it's Morris who makes it through to the willow grove and the empty kennel first, Kurtz is the one who voices the outrage of the masses. "No! No! No! What have you done?!" he yells at Lonnie, standing beside the open door.

That's the second of his sons he's yelled at in less than ten minutes. William had already received his wrath on the way from the lodge. When Morris had called for the key to the kennel lock, Kurtz's eldest mumbled a confession about seeing his baby brother playing with them earlier in the evening. "How could you be so stupid?" Kurtz had asked. He thought that'd make him seem tough, thought that might impress the old-timers like McCormack.

But when he notices the damp spots on Lonnie's cheeks, something breaks inside and the play-acted tough monster hunter façade crumples like cardboard cut-outs in the rain. Kurtz pulls the still and nearly silent boy to him. He presses his child against his red-and-black flannel.

Already Morris is shouting orders to the others, breaking them up into smaller parties. "C'mon, y'all. The little runt's still got the silver in 'im. Couldn't have got too far. C'mon!"

Kurtz can't see too well by the obscured starlight and moonglow melting down from the canopy of the willows. He checks the ground for blood, but can't be sure what might be new and what was there before.

Lonnie lets Daddy hold him tight. The boy's holding back the overwhelming urge to whimper. He knows he can't make his Daddy mad. Not with all those men with their guns and knives around. He won't embarrass his Daddy by whining and whimpering like the pup.

Instead, he looks at his hand. The marks from where the pup's tiny teeth broke his skin and pulled back, taking a little piece of Lonnie with them so the animal could chew and chew, are gone. He can't tell he was even bitten in the first place.

But that's not the strangest part. Lonnie gets one arm free from his Daddy's embrace and touches fingertips to wet cheeks. Those spots are where the puppy licked him, all friendly and affectionate after it bit him. Acting like a good boy. And that was all Lonnie ever wanted.

Then, it pulled back and padded out on all fours through the open kennel door. It had looked back, tilting its head, and offering an inquiring "Woof?"

Lonnie wonders if he should've followed. He wonders if maybe there's still time.

IF WISHES WERE

JOHN LANGAN

Once the road passed under the old rail bridge
(which Marla called the fairy portal—except she insisted it be
spelled "Faerie, like in Tolkien"—and whose twelve foot height
and rough stone columns did lend it the appearance of a portal into another
dimension)

and dead-ended in the turn-around which doubled as a parking lot for
anyone who wanted to walk the rail trail that had replaced the rods and ties,

(reached by a precarious scramble up the rise on her right)

Diane put in the clutch, tapped the brake, and downshifted into first,
bringing the Subaru, already crawling along this final unlit stretch of the road,
to a virtual halt as she scanned the maples, birch, and oak lining the tarmac for
the pair of brick pillars marking the entrance to the farm road.

("A portal within a portal," Marla had said. "Wouldn't that lead you back
to our world?" Diane said. "Oh, no," Marla said.)

She must have looked past them half a dozen times, panic rising within
her as she thought, *Are they gone? Has the road been closed?* She flicked the
high beams on and there they were, standing where they had always been, the
hand-carved wooden sign, *Myrddin's Farm*, hung on the pillar to the right.

("Who's Myrddin?" Diane had asked, the first time Marla had brought her
here, when their relationship was in the brand new, let-me-show-you-every-

thing-about-me phase. "He's like an early version of Merlin," Marla said. "You know, from King Arthur. I think he was Welsh? Lived in the forest, was kind of a madman.")

A chain stretched from one pillar to the other, hung from the middle of it a sign reading NO TRESPASSING. Diane shifted into neutral, set the parking brake, and opened her door. In the fifteen minutes it had taken to drive here, the temperature had dropped from cool to cold. She crossed to the chain, which she hadn't anticipated. Now that the farm had been purchased by the state nature preserve next door, she had assumed it would be bustling, full of workers preparing it for whatever new identity it was going to assume.

Avoiding such people was the reason she had not pulled out of her driveway until two in the morning.

From the looks of things, her concern had been misplaced. There was no guard, no night watchman standing with a flashlight and cell phone, ready to turn back anyone intending to pay the old farm a visit or call the police on those who would not heed his demands. Even the chain was attached to the rings set in the pillars by simple clasps.

Diane unclipped the end on the right and walked it over to the pillar on the left, the links clinking and clacking. She deposited it in a pile on the ground and returned to the car, imagining as she did the non-existent watchman strolling up to the Subaru, his oversized flashlight in hand, sweeping its strong beam across its pitted and dented green exterior before directing it through the windows. He would have seen the undersized dream catcher dangling from the rearview mirror; depending on the kind of guy he was, he might have commented on the decoration, advised Diane she wasn't really supposed to have anything on the mirror. Whether he remarked on the dreamcatcher or not, he would have noticed the back seats folded down, the figure lying wrapped in a white sheet in the cargo space. "Is that ...?" he would have started, and before he could finish, Diane would have answered, "A body, yes. It's my partner. Her name is Marla. We were together twenty-one years. She died of cancer. Of the pancreas. Right at the end, she made me promise to bury her on the farm. I didn't want to, but she was persistent. Told me it was her dying request, so I had to honor it. 'Bury me with my horse,' she said. Marcel. He's here, obviously. Died a couple of years ago. Anyway, I gave in."

There was no need for explanations, though. Diane returned to the car walking through tunnels of light in which clouds of insects fluttered and spun. She pulled her door shut, put the car in gear, released the brake, let out the clutch, and steered through the entrance to the farm.

The dirt road beyond was as pitted and potholed as ever. Driving here had always been a test of patience and skill, a slow motion passage through an obstacle course whose challenges, such as the big rock jutting from the road a mile or so ahead, could tear the hell out of a car's undercarriage if you weren't paying attention to your speed or what was in front of you. Not to mention, the animals you might encounter at any point along the dirt ribbon's two and a quarter miles, a sampler of the Mid-Hudson Valley's fauna. There were deer everywhere, small groups of a couple of does and their fawns, as well as at least one larger herd of around a dozen mothers and children roaming the farm's 500 acres. It was rarer to see a buck, decades of hunters' sites having made them almost preternaturally cautious, and the couple of times Diane had seen one—bounding into the fields to the left as her car rounded the first of the road's three bends, and standing in those same fields as she and Diane were on their way home—the vision had felt like a gift, a glimpse into Marla's world of Faerie.

Once in a while, people would wander over from the rail trail to indulge their curiosity about the farm, five decades after Tim and Dana Melbries had taken it over and transformed it into a center for what they called mythopoeic studies, still a source of interest and some degree of hostility for the locals. It was probably too late now for such investigations, but Diane left the high beams on, anyway. Their brightness flooded the potholes with shadow. After a moderate to heavy rain, the holes would fill with water, which tiny birds would use as baths.

(Marla seemed to know the names of all the local aviary: black birds, redwing black birds, blue birds, blue jays, cardinals, chickadees, crows, goldfinches, purple finches, grackles, hummingbirds, nuthatches, orioles, robins, pileated woodpeckers, red bellied woodpeckers—a catalogue Diane never was able to master. To the end, Marla had held onto her memory for such lists. Lying in the hospital bed they had moved into the downstairs office, her brain swimming in the morphine which only partially dulled the pain, Marla would lift her hand to point at and name the bird perched on the rhododendron outside the window. Sometimes, when Diane was especially tired, she fancied the birds were coming to bid their farewells.)

There was a flock of wild turkeys, too, who wandered the fields and the woods at their edges, and whose lean members, so unlike their domesticated brethren, stalked across the road, heads bobbing, unconcerned for whatever vehicle was approaching.

("They look so *different*," Diane had said, the first time they had come upon the flock. Growing up in Queens, the only turkeys she had seen were the cartoon images appearing at Thanksgiving, the fat bird wearing a pilgrim hat and costume, holding a blunderbuss with one wing/hand, a platter of its family members in the other, an idiot expression on its face. These creatures, on the other hand: "They look like dinosaurs," Diane said. "Ben Franklin wanted them as the national bird," Marla said. "When you see them like this, you understand." "Yeah.")

And there were Canada geese, more seasonal guests than year-round inhabitants. They favored the stretch of road around the next, sharp bend to the left, past the arts center at the top of the short, steep hill on the right.

("Arts center?" Diane had said. "What kind of arts?" "The dark ones," Marla answered. "So: yoga?" Diane said. Marla laughed. "And jazzercise.")

Here, the shoulder fell sharply on both sides, dropping a couple of feet to a marsh whose water was deep enough to sustain schools of small fish, mostly bluegill, and crayfish, and frogs, and a family of fishers whose members Diane glimpsed out of the corner of the eye, a sudden movement followed by a splash. Her headlights spread across the surface of the water in a white glow. If you weren't careful, you could hook a wheel over the edge of the road and bang the axle, which made meeting anyone driving the opposite way an exercise in nerves, as you eased your vehicle alongside and past one another. Now, Diane drove straight down the center of the road. The marsh was also home to a massive snapping turtle whose craggy shell was a foot and a half in diameter, a venerable beast who preferred to remain submerged, but whom Diane had watched cross from one side of the road to the other, lifting his limbs in a straight-legged gait almost puppet-like, dragging his spiny tail behind him.

("I call him Old Goliath," Marla had said. "How do you know it's a him?" Diane said. "Would you like to check?" Marla said. "Old Goliath it is." "The resident dragon," Marla said, which, looking at his blunt head with its horned beak, his broad shell with its rows of raised points, his thick legs with their long claws, Diane supposed was as apt a metaphor as any.)

Once, when evening was on the verge of being swallowed by night, Diane's headlights had picked out a four foot black snake lying in the middle of the road, soaking up its heat.

("Hail, grandmother," Marla had said, then turned to Diane, waiting for her response. "What?" Diane said, her hands tight on the wheel. "It's Faulkner, sort of," Marla said, "'The Bear.'" "Oh. Okay." "Honestly," Marla said and opened the door to step out and hurry the snake out of their way.)

According to Marla, plenty of different kinds of snakes called the farm home: black rat snakes, garter snakes, milk snakes, ribbon snakes, water snakes, and a small family of timber rattlesnakes who dwelled in the rocky hill line which defined the farm's western border. The rattlers tended to keep to the vicinity of their stony demesne, and were only a concern for anyone hiking or riding in that stretch of the property. All the same, Diane, who shuddered with primordial revulsion at the sight of any snake, no matter how small, no matter how harmless, was made deeply uneasy by the idea of the snakes and refused to venture very far in the direction of the hills.

("Besides," Diane had said, "wasn't there something about a mountain lion over there?" "Years ago," Marla had said. "We hadn't been together very long. I think we were still in the house on Springgrown. Remember the garden?" "I remember the soil was a pain in the ass to dig," Diane said, "all clay. I also remember the print you showed me near the pony's field. What was his name? Napoleon?" "Napoleon, yes," Marla said, "all of us were worried for him. But," she added, "he was fine." "Which doesn't mean there wasn't—isn't a mountain lion there." "According to DEC, the eastern mountain lion is extinct." "So this is a western mountain lion," Diane said, "taking advantage of an opening in the local ecology. Or extinct doesn't mean what it used to. Either way, it's another reason to steer clear of that side of the farm." "There's nothing to worry about," Marla said. "I'm glad to hear it," Diane said, "and I'll do my not-worrying over here." Marla responded with a sigh.)

As the road took another sharp turn to the left, the marsh surrendered to dry ground. In the field to the right, the remains of the trapeze school shone at the edge of the car's brights, a trio of tall metal frames held in place by a spider web of cables. The safety net was gone, packed away with the trapezes, themselves.

("A trapeze school?" Diane had said, watching the slender poles rise. "Yeah," Marla had said. "It's for troubled kids. From the city, mostly. They'll come up for a week in the summer, learn the basics of the trapeze, and help around the farm." "Who's going to run the trapeze part?" Diane asked. "The Folk of the Air. They're friends of the Melbries. Tim and Dana know them through the Renaissance fair down in Tuxedo.")

For the better part of a decade, the school had been a tremendous success, drawing kids from as far away as Oregon every July and August. It had been featured first in the *Wiltwyck Freeman*, then in an article in the weekend *Times*, then in a segment on the CBS Sunday morning show. Already driving slowly, Diane had had to drop her speed even further because of the knots of teenagers crossing the road between the trapezes on the right and the rambling yellow farmhouse on the left, several of whose additions had been converted into makeshift dormitories for the students.

The house, which occupied the left hand side of the bend in the road, was home to a trio of long-term enters with whom Diane had exchanged what must have amounted to thousands of friendly waves and perhaps ten words in total. They came and went at odd hours. One, a woman who favored ankle-length floral dresses, worked at the arts center—in what capacity, Diane column't remember—while the pair of skinny brothers in overalls and tie-dyed shorts never seemed done repairing the rust-riddled VW van whose front wheels remained parked on a pair of metal ramps, making it appear caught in a perpetual wheelie. The house was home or at least, home base to an indeterminate number of cats at various removes from feral. They sprawled in the dirt parking area in front of the house, prowled under its porches, and sat attentively on its assorted roofs. They were capable of sudden bursts of speed, especially when either of the two rescue dogs living at the house decided it was time for a game of chase. Diane didn't know the long-term renters' opinion of their summer visitors. The cats avoided the kids, while the dogs barked ferociously at them for a couple of seconds, then collapsed at their feet and rolled over to show their bellies.

When the trapeze school failed, it did so all at once. The couple who had spent nine years buckling the kids into their safety harnesses, standing beside them at the top of the frames, demonstrating how to swing out and back on a single trapeze, coaching the kids and cheering them on as they pendulumed out and back, progressing from there to more complicated maneuvers, transitions from one trapeze to another, had announced their departure for Iceland two weeks prior to the first day of classes. The scramble to secure replacements at so late a date had yielded nothing, and the school was shut down for the season. Afterwards, it never recovered. There had been plans to take down the frames, so Marla had said, but they had remained in place, transformed into enormous perches for larger birds—red-tailed hawks, Cooper's hawks, and turkey vultures. Although bald eagles had been spotted flying over the farm, none had lighted on the frames, nor had the blue heron and his mate, who preferred to stand at the edge of the marsh.

The farmhouse was dark, its yard empty of dogs and cars alike. Cats, too, from the look of it; though a few could be hiding somewhere. When had its tenants departed? She was sure Marla had told her, but in the thick of dealing with her partner's cancer, the detail had been one more piece of information her memory didn't have room for, so she had dropped it. She had the impression the woman and the two brothers had relocated west, some time toward the very end of the farm's long decline.

Owls were supposed to nest among the woods that lined the road for its last and longest stretch, making it a place of perpetual twilight no matter how high the sun, and a place of darkness no matter how bright the moon. But Diane had never heard, let alone seen, any among the dense mix of what Marla had identified as white ash, yellow beech, cedar, hemlock, and sugar maple standing to either side. What she had seen were more gray squirrels, who darted out in front of the car as if in the grip of a species-wide death wish. More foxes, too, as well as a pair of wolf-like creatures who had flashed in front of her headlights one night and caused her to stand on the brakes. Coyotes, Marla had said, members of a larger pack who roamed the area and whose mournful cries could be heard sometimes in the wee small hours of the night.

("Are you sure those weren't wolves?" Diane had asked, her hands tight on the wheel, her heart thwacking against her chest, "because they looked an awful lot like wolves to me." "Actual wolves would have been much bigger,"

Marla said. "You would know if you had seen a wolf. Those were their little cousins." "Jesus," Diane said. "They looked plenty big enough to me.")

There were racoons, too, hurrying across the road as if fleeing the crime they had put on their masks for, and possums, smiling their hideous, toothy grins, moving less quickly. This section of the road climbed in a succession of rises and falls. Diane took the crest of each at a slow roll, her brights running up and down the trunks of the trees, careful for what might be waiting in the decline. Once, this had been a black bear, plodding from left to right no more than ten yards in front of them.

("Holy shit!" Diane had shouted. "Holy shit! Do you see this? Do you? Look at that! Look! Right there!" Her voice was loud with surprise and excitement. It was late afternoon. The bear was huge, unconcerned with the car and the screaming woman at its wheel. Marla was calmer than Diane would have imagined possible. "That's Arthur," she said, the incongruity of the name enough to distract Diane. "Arthur?" she said. "Like the children's show?" "More like the king." There was no arguing the majesty of the creature, which despite its slow gait was already stepping off the road. "Where's he going?" Diane said. "He's making his rounds," Marla said. "Black bears have a pretty sizable territory." "What about the stables?" "He avoids them," Marla said. "As a rule, he stays away from people and their places." "Doesn't Konrad have his house around here?" Konrad, last name unknown, was the older handyman who lived in a small cabin in the woods in exchange for helping around the farm. "He's fine," Marla said. "Konrad and Arthur have an understanding." At the time, Diane had let the remark go, more focused on the bear moving between the trees. Later, she wished she hadn't.)

The biggest concern, though, on this or any part of the way, were the horses and their riders. There were nine stalls in the big barn at the far end of the road, plus an outside spot with a small roof for cover next to it. You could stable your horse(s) in the barn and pay full price for room and board—which was not as much as what the other local places charged—or you could knock the price down by helping with their care and feeding. Marla had chosen the second option to lower the cost of keeping her horse, Marcel, on the farm.

In addition to the trails in the woods, the farm road was a favorite route for riders to take their horses for a leisurely stroll, especially those newer to the saddle. There were a couple of places where the road widened enough to allow you to pass the horses (slowly), but for much of it, the only option was to follow behind at a safe distance and try not to drive through the piles of shit that tumbled from their rears. For Diane, those times were an exercise in the patience she said she was trying to develop. Depending on how long they were stuck following a rider or riders, even Marla could become irritated, muttering an assortment of curses as the car inched forward, her brow cloudy.

However, her irritation dropped away the instant their destination came into view. The road swung down and to the right, past the sprawling log house on the left where Dana and Tim Melbries had lived, the broad pond with the tiny island in the center behind it, the sawmill also on the left, and to the barn at the end of the road, big and red as every picture of one Diane had seen in a childhood book. The moment Marla opened the door and stepped out of the car, Marcel, who resided in the outdoor stall, would begin to whinny and to trot back and forth.

("See?" Marla had said the first time she took Diane to meet her horse. "He's a sweet boy." "So why is he out here?" Diane said. "Well, he can be a bit of a pig," Marla said, reaching into the pocket of her sweatshirt for the apple she had tucked there. "Define 'pig,'" Diane said. "I wouldn't stand behind him," Marla said, "or he's likely to try to kick you." She held the apple cupped in her palm to Marcel, who reached his head over the fence to nibble the fruit with surprising delicateness. She rubbed his neck with her other hand. He was a rich color somewhere between brown and red, his mane and tail darker brown. "Also," Marla said, "if you're in the stall with him, he'll crowd you against the boards. You just have to give him an elbow to the ribs and he'll back off. Oh, and if you're carrying his feed bucket in, he'll do his best to shove his snout in there before you have it hung up. You'd think he was starving. Honestly, though, he's most likely to misbehave when we're out for a ride." "What does he do?" "It depends. Mostly, he just wants to stop and eat grass. He's tried to throw me a couple of times. And he hates running water. There's a little stream that crosses one of the trails and he wants nothing to do with it. Yes," Marla said to the horse, who had finished the apple and was standing as she continued to rub his neck, "you don't like the stream, do you?" "He doesn't look big enough to hold so much trouble," Diane said. "That's because he's a quarter horse," Marla said, "bred to be nimble and fast. He comes from a long line of champion barrel-racers." "What happened? I mean, how come he isn't racing?" "I don't know," Marla said. "I mean, not really. I don't think he was properly trained. Whether that was because of his bad bad behavior, or was the cause of his wicked ways, I can't say. Most likely, it's a little bit of both. Or maybe a lot of both. He tyrannized the woman who had him before me. When she sold him to me, she made me sign a note saying I wouldn't return him. Not that there was any danger of that happening. It was love at first sight. Well, for me, at least. Once I realized what a handful he was, I reached out to the previous owner, but she refused to return my calls. She was probably afraid I was going to give him back, note or no note, or at least yell at her for selling me such a difficult horse. My guess is, she got him from one of the less scrupulous horse dealers, who emphasized his lineage and passed off any bad behavior as high-spiritedness. The poor woman probably thought she was getting a bargain. But I was the one who got the bargain," Marla said to the horse, who pushed his head against her, "wasn't I?")

There were no horses at the barn anymore. Diane wasn't certain when the last one had departed. After Marcel's sudden death last year from a heart attack, they had driven to the farm less and less, despite offers from the owners of the other horses, including Dana Melbries, for her to come spend time with their animals. Not too long after, Marla had started to feel unwell, complaining of fatigue Diane at first attributed to depression over the loss of Marcel, for whom Marla grieved as fully and deeply as any human. The extent of her grief was not a surprise. Not only had she loved the horse in all his wilfulness and recalcitrance, her relationship with Marcel had fulfilled her in a way nothing else did.

"I see him," Marla had said, "and I feel like this is where I'm supposed to be, where I'm most … present."

Diane, who felt much the same onstage with her guitar, understood (or understood enough) to allow Marla whatever time she required to mourn. She did not say so to her partner, but she imagined another horse lay in their future, one she hoped would have better manners.

After Marla was diagnosed with the cancer, she and her oncologist both reassured Diane there was no need to blame herself for not having urged Marla to make an appointment with her regular doctor sooner. But Diane knew better: she had done the research, quietly, online at reputable websites, and confirmed what she had already suspected, namely, that your best chance with pancreatic cancer was early detection. The later you discovered it, the worse the outlook. There had not been time to wallow in self-recrimination, as Marla had required a great deal of care in short order, the oncologist beginning an aggressive course of chemotherapy which burned through her like a wildfire through a forest.

No doubt, however, her acquiescence to Marla's burial request had been fueled in part by regret. The emotion fueled her drive out here in the deep dark with the body of the woman she had loved with such completeness it had continued to astound her, decades after the two of them had met at a mutual friend's dinner party in Joppenbergh. Sometimes, she would remember driving back to her apartment after sitting across Virgil's table from the remarkable librarian with the clear green eyes and panic would surge through her as she thought, *What if I never see her again?* And she would have to remind herself, *It's okay, you did see her again, it's okay.*

While technically the farm road ended at the barn, it connected to a rougher track leading into the stand of trees beyond. Really a pair of ruts studded with rocks of varying sizes, it passed through the ash, cedar, and oak to the long meadow on the other side. Trees loomed out of the darkness, their branches spread wide, as if forbidding her forward; Diane fancied they were Tolkien's Ents, guarding the way. *That's something Marla would have said,* she thought, and had to sniff back a sudden onslaught of tears.

Clearing the trees, the track curved left, in the direction of the farm's western edge and the border it (had) shared with the state preserve (though still a safe distance from that stony place and its rattlesnakes). Here, a broad, grassy circle marked the place where the farm's horses were buried, six of them in six mounds of earth arranged in a rough crescent. The newest, Marcel's grave still showed patches of soil, where the others were thickly overgrown with wildflowers, Beardtongue, Blueflag, and Milkweed, as well as clumps of Buttonbush, and on the older pair, diminutive apple trees. At the center of the space, five ash logs all the same approximate size had been stood upright in the ground. Once upon a time, they had been roughly carved into some sort of figures, but the seasons' onslaught had weathered them practically featureless.

("What are they?" Diane had asked, their first hike out here, when there were only five mounds. "Gods," Marla answered. "Which gods?" "Old ones."

"Like, Zeus and Hera?" "Older than the gods of the Greeks," Marla said. "Older than the gods of the Egyptians." "What are their names?" "Forgotten," Marla said. "Then why are they here?" "To consecrate the place." "Okay," Diane said, "if you say so." "They are older than the rocks among which they sit," Marla said, "like the vampire, they have been dead many times, and learned the secrets of the grave; and have been divers in deep seas, and keep their fallen day about them." Diane stared at her. "Walter Pater?" Marla said. "Talking about the Mona Lisa?" "If you say so." "God, you are such a peasant sometimes." "Fuck you," Diane said. "Finally. Something we can agree on," Marla said, her fingers already at the hem of her t-shirt. Surprise had not dampened Diane's arousal. Afterward, Diane would think there had been more to their lovemaking than she had understood, an aspect to it she had not grasped, but she could not find the words to ask Marla about it.)

Diane pulled up facing Marcel's grave. She left the engine running, for the headlights. In the high beams, the rounded earth stood forth with supernatural clarity, every flower petal, every stalk of grass, every rock visible. She walked to the back of the car and reached inside for the work gloves, shovel, and pickax she had laid beside Marla's shrouded form. Before pulling on the gloves, she placed her right hand on Marla's leg. She might have been touching her sleeping form on the way out the door to catch an early flight. "The things I do for you," she said.

The soil on top of Marcel's grave was not as loose as she had hoped. Diane used the pick to break up the earth, then switched to the shovel and set to work excavating Marla's final resting place. The dirt was dense, threaded with worms surprised at this sudden intrusion. No time at all seemed to elapse before Diane's lungs were heaving, her shoulders and back burning, sweat trickling through her eyebrows and onto her eyelids. At least her heart, whose rhythms had been of concern the last few years, felt fine. *Wouldn't that be great?* She thought. If she had a heart attack, dropped dead, and some random hiker stumbled on the scene a day or two from now, what would they think? What would they find, if the animals visited her and Marla's remains first? What narrative would the police construct, after they were called in? The situation was clear enough to Diane, but of course it would be, wouldn't it? Professionally suspicious, the cops would incline toward foul play, which in this case would mean what? Her murdering Marla and attempting to hide the body here, until irony in the form of a faulty heart both delivered a capital sentence for the crime and left it exposed to the world? Something along those lines, which shared enough real estate with the truth for the cops to entertain it, until one of them undertook a modicum of investigation and the criminal explanation burned away in the light of a sentimental one.

She dragged her forearm across her eyes. The grave was taking shape: she was about three feet down at the deepest part of a trench a couple of feet wide by maybe four long. Fatigue weighted her arms, tightened her lower back. Her head felt full of helium, detached from the rest of her, which she attributed to a combination of her present exertions and the ordeal of Marla's long last days. She had not gone easily; though her death was a foregone conclusion, had been for months, she had refused to embrace the fact, had wrestled the reaper as his bony embrace tightened relentlessly. Throughout, Diane had been at her bedside, holding her hand when there was nothing else left to do, when the most the pain drugs could do was render the pain merely unbearable. None of it felt real. Not that it felt unreal: Diane had come to terms with the awful truth of Marla's end not long after the oncologist had said there was nothing more to be done to delay the inevitable. Rather, it was as if Marla's death had admitted Diane to an enormous space, a room whose dimensions were unclear and whose rules were unknown, possibly nonexistent. In this expanse, sneaking onto an abandoned farm to bury her partner with her beloved horse was no less outrageous an idea than anything else.

It would be nice to have Tim Melbries's backhoe to help with her task. He had employed the machine to dig Marcel's grave, scooping a large pit out of the ground with the rear bucket, then to bring the horse to it, carrying his remains in the front loader. Diane and Marla had walked behind Tim in the snorting and snarling backhoe, at the head of a procession consisting of everyone else on the farm: Dana Melbries, Konrad, the trio from the yellow farmhouse, and at least a dozen other people Diane vaguely recognized from coming and going on the place but could not name. All of them were wearing white shirts and jeans, Marla's requested attire for Marcel's funeral. The sleeves of her shirt, its front, were stained dark red with Marcel's blood.

("You did what?" Diane had said. "I removed his heart," Marla said. "Poor thing, he wasn't using it anymore." "He—*why?*" "It's all right," Marla said.

"Dana was there. She talked me through it." "I don't—" "Come on," Marla said, "the funeral's starting.")

Later, after they had stood watching as Tim pushed the dirt piled next to Marcel's grave back into it, Marla carried a drawstring leather bag with her to the car. Diane knew what it contained. It was on the tip of her tongue to ask Marla what the hell was going on, but she decided to let the question remain in her mouth. This wasn't the strangest thing her partner had ever done, and in a bizarre way, she understood the impulse behind wanting a memento of so beloved an animal—her dear friend, as Marla had so often called him.)

Climbing out of the grave required more effort than she was anticipating; no doubt, Marla would have a quotation ready for her. Would have *had*, she corrected herself, the revision a pinprick reminding her of Marla's absence anew—one of a thousand, of ten thousand such wounds every day.

Leaving the shovel with its blade stuck in the ground, she returned to the car, whose rear bumper she sat against with a groan. "All right," she said. "All right." She stood, turned, and reached for Marla.

Dead, her partner weighed no less than she had at the end of her life; it was more that she weighed *differently*. Carrying Marla in her arms like a groom hoisting his bride, Diane crossed to the grave on legs trembling, knees ready to buckle. At the edge of the hole, she clutched Marla against her and lowered to sitting before sliding down into it to lay Marla on its floor. The rustling of the cotton sheet in which she had shrouded Marla was astoundingly loud; tears hovered in her eyes.

Diane crawled out of the hole again and walked to the car, from whose cargo bay she removed the leather satchel inside which was tied Marcel's heart, no doubt dried and tough. The bag was bound with strips of white cloth stained with old blood, the remains of the shirt Marla had been wearing when she cut the horse's lifeless heart from him. She had scissored the shirt into long strands, which she had wrapped around the bag in an intricate weave, tying each strip in an elaborate knot.

At the edge of the grave, Diane knelt and leaned forward, positioning the satchel over Marla's chest before letting it fall onto her with a soft *wump*.

Her next trip to the car was for the dozen large pieces of slate tucked into the footwells behind the driver and front passenger seats. "They'll help keep the animals away," Marla had said. Diane had selected them from the pile she had stacked next to the garden, in which they seemed to grow as plentifully as any of her other crops, and washed the dirt from them with the hose. Marla had passed the early afternoons of a week last month decorating them, painting all manner of fanciful designs and figures on them. Diane carried the stones one at a time to the graveside.

All of them transported, she knelt, picked up a piece of slate, leaned into the grave, and began to cover Marla. Her back screamed with the effort, her arms shook, but she succeeded in layering the stones two deep.

Finished, she rolled onto her back and lay there panting, gazing at the sky. It must be extremely late: she did not recognize any of the constellations overhead. The prospect of dawn's appearance pushed her to standing. For the final time, she reached for the shovel. The remainder of her task, she completed in a daze, pushing the last of the soil onto the grave with the insteps of her boots when she could no longer lift the shovel.

Her original plan had been to throw her tools into the car and leave as soon as Marla was buried, an overly optimistic plan. The best she could do was to drag the shovel and pickax to the Subaru, fumble them into the cargo bay with hands half numb, close the hatchback, and stumble to the driver's seat. She did not bother removing her gloves. With an arm heavy as lead, she turned off the headlights, the dome light, and the engine, but left the keys in the ignition. She reclined the seat and closed her eyes.

To open them four quick heartbeats later. She struggled to sitting, pushed open the car door, and half-fell out the Subaru. She raised herself to her feet and walked stiff-legged to what was now Marla and Marcel's final resting place. Diane looked up at the stars burning in their unfamiliar arrangements. Eyes still on them, she said, "I feel like I should say something. It's not like we didn't say everything there was to say, already. But. It's tradition, isn't it? So. You asked how I would remember you. I think I said something like, 'In bed.' Which, you know, is not untrue. I'll remember you in bed, and I'll remember you at Virgil's dinner party, and I'll remember you on the beach at Wellfleet. But. How I'll most remember you—my best memory of you—it's of you and Marcel. The morning after the hurricane—was it Irene? I think it was Rita. We drove out here first thing, because you wanted to check on the farm—to be honest, the horses. The phones were out. Cell service was out. No internet. We made it most of the way. The marsh was up over the road, but we chanced it and got across. It was a tree on the last bit that stopped us, a huge evergreen the storm had knocked down. Konrad was there with his chainsaw, getting ready to cut it up. You didn't want to wait for him, so we left the car and walked the rest of the way. The trees were still dripping with rain. Every time a breeze blew through, there was another shower. When we reached the farm, we saw the oak that had fallen on Tim and Dana's house; I remember, he was trying to start his chainsaw and not having much luck. She was moving stuff out onto the porch from inside. Boxes of manuscripts—from the exposed room, I assumed. Dana saw us—saw you, really, and asked if you would help take a look at the rest of the farm, survey the storm's damage. Yes you could, you said. You went to the barn, where they'd let Marcel shelter in an empty stall. You threw a bridle on him, climbed on bareback, and off the two of you went. If anyone had asked me, I would have predicted he'd buck you off and gallop away. He didn't. You said it afterward: it was like he knew this was not a normal situation. I watched the two of you ride around the outbuildings, pick your way through the trees behind the sawmill, inspect the wire fence out there. I remember thinking, for all the times I had seen you on Marcel, never had I seen the two of you so perfectly in sync. It was as if you were halves of the same creature. Long past what I thought was his limit, the horse kept going. When you dismounted, he let you lead him back to his stall without protest. I felt like I had seen something profound, a moment it was a privilege to have witnessed. So. There's my memory. There's how I'll remember you."

She looked down at the earth beneath which the woman she had loved lay. As she did, sleep rushed upon her with such speed, she barely had time to sit. She leaned on her right side, falling into unconsciousness as she went. Her dreams were distant, glimpsed through a heavy gray fog. She sensed time passing, the night spinning above her, rotating its weird constellations in and out of view. A meteor dragged its fiery tail across the sky. Naked, Marla stood in front of her, the shroud puddled at her feet, her body still bearing the marks of the cancer's assault. Her lips were moving, murmuring, "The strange horses came ... We saw the heads like a wild wave charging." "I'm sorry," Diane said, "I don't understand." "It's Edwin Muir," Marla said. "'The Horses.' No? Honestly."

A thunderclap hurled Diane from sleep, sent her tumbling across the soil and into the grass, earth and stones raining on and around her. A cloud of dirt engulfed her, dawn's first rays lighting it peach and orange. Soil coated her face, clotted her hair; the stones pattering around her were so hot they sizzled on the grass. She rolled onto her belly and curled into a ball, rocks bouncing and thudding off her back.

After a moment, the hiss of the dirt dropping on the ground subsided and Diane heard a new sound, the thump of hooves on the earth. Through the fingers covering her eyes, she saw a form rising out of the hole where she had buried Marla, where Marcel had lain beneath her.

It was an impossible shape, one whose halves refused to cohere in her mind, even as they did in her eyes. She saw the horse's flowing tail, the muscled haunches, the slender forelimbs, and where the neck should have risen to a long head, a woman's torso leading to a pair of strong arms, to the head whose hair continued in a mane down the center of her back.

Diane dropped her hands from her face and pushed herself to kneeling. The horse's legs and flank were a rich color between brown and red, which blended into the deep bronze of the woman's skin. She peered through the settling dirt at Diane, and her eyes were Marla's eyes, her long nose and narrow cheeks Marla's.

There was no way this was not impossible; all the same, the scene was far too vital, too vibrant, for a dream or hallucination.

Marla stumbled slightly on her hooves, as if not yet accustomed to them, and the motion produced a slight smile on her face, along with a whinny. A wave of something like vertigo swept through Diane, giving her the momentary impression she might hurtle into space. The sun's rim was lifting over the trees, casting gold light over everything, picking out the sinews on Marla's legs and arms. She extended her right hand in Diane's direction.

"Oh," Diane said. "Oh, baby." She stood.

Marla smiled.

For a long time, there was the curve of Marla's lips and the reach of her fingers. Diane felt herself trembling on the brink of an interior precipice, of plummeting away from the life in which everyone who had known Marla— her parents, Diane's mother, her sisters, their friends—had been dumped into the grief Diane had been swimming in for months. In just the last couple of days, Marla's father had been on the phone constantly, for hours at a time, sharing rambling anecdotes of his daughter's younger years, as if reciting them might lead him back to her. What would he—would all of them do if she disappeared, as well? At last, Diane said, "Oh. Baby. I don't think I can. Not yet, baby, not yet."

The smile did not leave Marla's face, but she lowered her hand.

"Not yet," Diane said. "There's too much I still have to do."

With a nod, Marla spun away from Diane and leapt over the exploded grave, landing on the opposite side in a gallop. Her gait was unsteady, but quickly improved. She ran west out of the horse cemetery, across the grass, and into the tree line. The sight of her running—shining, sheathed in gold, into the trees, ranked like pillars of flame—made something lift inside Diane. At first, she was able to follow Marla as she swerved amongst the maple and birch, the cedar and ash, and then the woods closed around her. The thud of her hooves faded soon thereafter.

"Not yet," Diane said. She realized she had been crying for some time. She turned toward the car. On the way, she stooped to pick up a fragment of slate. Still warm, it bore Marla's drawing of a horse on its cracked surface. Where was this new Marla headed, what kingdom was she running toward along the sun's morning rays?

Diane tucked the rock in her pocket.

ON THIS SIDE OF THE VEIL

GABINO IGLESIAS

The man sitting across from Sandra had seen something. She could tell. People came to her for different reasons, and many of them had no business looking her up and taking up her time. These people with no real stories to tell were folks who had heard about her and came with fake narratives about ghosts and spirits just to satiate their curiosity. Others came to her because they didn't want or couldn't afford to go to a doctor, but whatever was haunting them was entirely in their head. This man was different. The truth was in the desperation in his eyes, the way his hands shook, and the way his voice cracked.

"Tell me again about the figure in the kitchen," said Sandra, her voice an invisible balm she hoped would put the man at ease and get him to slow down and explain things better.

"Like I said, it was around 2:00 a.m. when I heard the noise," the man said, fear turning his bloodshot eyes into jumpy animals. "It sounded like someone was dragging a chair across the tiles. I thought it was a burglar or something, you know? I've been living on the East Side since my divorce … you know, it's not the best part of town. Anyway, I keep a baseball bat by my bed. Been doing that since college. I grabbed the bat and slowly made my way to the kitchen and—"

"This is the most important part," Sandra interrupted. "Slow down and describe it as well as you can. Your description can help me know what we're dealing with."

The man took a deep breath and went on. "There was a man—a figure—standing next to the table. It was ... it was all black. Really tall. Its head came up almost all the way up to the ceiling. It was skinny, like an afternoon shadow, you know? I walked into the kitchen ready to swing and the thing's head turned to me. It had no eyes or mouth or nose that I could see, but I knew—I felt—that it was looking at me. I've never felt fear like that. It was like someone had injected me with one of those snake venoms that paralyze you or something. I didn't swing or scream or anything. The black thing turned around and walked away from me in the direction of the fridge. Then it went through the wall and that was it."

"You mean that was it for that night, right? You mentioned some other ... occurrences in your apartment," said Sandra.

"Yeah, yeah, that was it for that night, but more stuff happened," said the man.

"Like?"

"Well, I've heard the chairs a few more times. I've seen things, too. You know like, out of the corner of my eye. Sometimes it's a shadow, a dark thing that vanishes into a room or that I'm sure is there but there's nothing there when I look at it directly. And I've found stuff in my living room moved around."

"Moved around?"

"Yeah," said the man. "You know, like my keys will be on the floor in the hallway instead of on the little table where I put them, or I'll wake up and everything on my coffee table will be on the floor as if someone had picked it all up and placed it down carefully to wipe down the table ... you know, things like that."

The ability to move things around and pull chairs across the kitchen floor worried Sandra. It meant whatever the man was seeing, whatever was haunting his apartment, could hurt him. It could hurt anyone. She had to go there and figure things out quickly. Sandra looked at the man sitting across from her and spoke in the same calm voice she'd had during their entire meeting.

"The black thing turned around and walked away from me in the direction of the fridge. Then it went through the wall and that was it."

"I believe you, Mr. Gunnels. What I need from you now is your address. You can text it to me at the same phone you called to set up the appointment. I need to go there and ... feel around. This might take a few days, but if whatever's bothering you is still there, I will take care of it for you."

"Thank you, Sandra," said the man as he texted her his address. "I really appreciate that. The lack of sleep is killing me and the noises at night ... I mean, I lock myself in my room every night, but I saw that thing go through a wall, so my wooden door doesn't give me any peace, you know?"

Sandra nodded.

"How do I pay you?"

"You don't pay me now. When this is all over and you're sure the place is clean and you can sleep again, then we'll talk about that."

The man stood up and looked at the photos of women hanging on the walls. He nodded and moved toward the door. Sandra followed him, opened the door, and wished the man a nice day. Then she went back to the kitchen and stared at the same old photos the man had been looking at: Sandra's grandmother, mother, and two aunts. They were all gone now, but Sandra knew they watched over her as she carried on their work. She wanted to make them proud. She wanted to let them know that their knowledge wasn't being wasted.

Mr. Gunnells' apartment complex was a decrepit box lined with windows trapped between two new, shiny monsters of steel and glass that perfectly embodied the look of East Austin's cancerous gentrification. Sandra sat in her car half a block away and looked at the building.

The thing about old buildings is that people can see things in them that aren't dangerous. Sometimes a violent death, a traumatic event, or years of abuse leave a dark imprint on the walls that never goes away. Movies often show priests or witches cleaning a house and vanishing a ghost forever, but that's not how it works. Some energy is so powerful it causes something like a scar between this world and the one behind the veil, and those scars can't be erased.

But an imprint, that darkness that can seep into the floor or the walls and stain a place forever, doesn't interact with whoever lives in the place now. Scars don't have an agenda. They don't move things around. Whatever was messing around Mr. Gunnells' apartment was something else.

For the next two hours, Sandra watched people go in and out of the building. She'd been doing this so long that sometimes just looking at someone was all she needed to identify the source of the problem. In the half decade that preceded her living in Austin, she'd lived in Orlando, Biloxi, Mobile, New Orleans, Baton Rouge, Beaumont, and Houston. In every place, she'd encountered the same thing: people who, for one reason or another, wanted to contact the dead—to offer a spirit something in exchange for a favor. The problem was that the internet gave them that access without the responsibility that came with it. Evil ghosts, mean spirits, haunted haints; whatever you want to call them, they have been around forever. However, knowing how to get in touch with them was something only a few people knew. People like her mother and aunts. The internet changed all that.

In New Orleans Sandra had met a young woman who asked a ghost to possess her because she thought recording the ritual would help her YouTube channel gain subscribers. In Orlando she had dealt with a woman who wanted to write a book about séances and had paid dearly for it. Each case was different and yet each one was the same, and many of them had happened because technology had turned arcane knowledge into something akin to a game, something that people could acquire online along with candles to Santa Muerte, a tarot deck, healing crystals, or a book of love spells. The commodification of the spiritual world had dire consequences those selling it were not willing to discuss or simply ignored.

Having access to a scalpel doesn't make a person a surgeon. The same thing applies to evil spirits. That's why so many people came to Sandra despite the fact that she had never advertised her services and only posted a phone number in the classifieds of whichever city she moved to. All it took was one case and word of mouth always did the rest. And she took on as many jobs as she could. For her, saving people was a calling, and keeping the space between worlds safe was in her blood.

Mr. Gunnells' apartment was on the fourth floor. Apartment 4-C was the second one on the left side of the hallway. This meant he had neighbors to the right and left. That made Sandra's work a bit harder. If he hadn't done anything—and he certainly didn't sound like he had—and the entity in his apartment wasn't a leftover from something awful some previous resident had done, then it meant whatever was going on had its roots in one of the nearby apartments.

Before leaving the car, Sandra had grabbed a brown paper takeout bag she kept in the car for times like this. She pulled out her phone and knocked on the door of apartment 4-A. No one came to the door or called from inside. She rang the doorbell and waited a bit before knocking again. She got no answer, so she turned around and moved to 4-B. An older woman with glasses opened the door with a confused smile on her face. She wore a beige cardigan, and the smell of too many cats wafted out of the apartment.

"Afternoon, ma'am," said Sandra, holding up the brown paper bag and looking at her phone. "Did you order Tom Yum from Madam Mam's?"

"Oh, no, I'm sorry. You have the wrong place," said the woman.

"Sorry to bother you," replied Sandra, while stepping back and looking at the number on top of the door. "Have a nice day."

The woman smiled and closed the door. Sandra walked up to 4-D and knocked. She heard shuffling and then the door opened just a bit. In the few inches of space between the door and the doorframe, a haunted brown eye peeked out at Sandra. The bloodshot eye sat over a dark half moon that spoke of sleepless nights and the kind of stress that pushes people to make bad decisions. Sandra knew she'd found the person she was looking for.

"Did you order Madam Mam's?" Sandra asked while holding up the bag.

The woman said no and closed the door. Sandra lowered the paper bag and looked at the door. Single lock. Old and cheap. Sandra took one last look at the hallway—no security cameras. This was the type of building where people live because they can't afford a better place, and no one cares much for those who can't afford to be cared about. She walked back to her car. She needed to get home and rest. The work she'd have to do that night would require a lot of energy.

It was almost 1:00 a.m. when Mr. Gunnells texted Sandra. She'd called and asked him to let her know as soon as he heard the noises that night, but to stay in his room no matter what he heard.

Sandra grabbed her kit, which was black and looked like a small purse, and slowly made her way to the fourth floor.

She stood close to the door of apartment 4-D, closed her eyes, and concentrated on listening. There was no one walking around inside the apartment, no water running or toilets flushing, and she couldn't hear voices or a TV. Sandra pulled out her favorite tool from her kit and slowly inserted it into the lock. She carefully turned the tool clockwise, feeling each and every pin inside the lock as it tensed and then fell into place. The lock was timeworn and low-cost, and in less than three minutes, Sandra had the door open. She quietly slid into the apartment and focused on her breathing while allowing her eyes to adjust to the darkness.

There was a small kitchen to the left of the door and a living room to the right. A dark futon took up a third of the living room. Next to it was the entrance to what Sandra guessed was the apartment's only hallway. Sandra moved to it, her senses hyperaware, her steps slow and careful in case the old floor decided to play tricks on her and moan under her weight.

Sandra passed a small bathroom on the left side of the hallway and then entered the apartment's only room. A queen-sized bed took up almost the entire room. A tiny bedside table with an old lamp, inherited probably, stood to the left of the big mattress and right below the room's only window. A minuscule closet was open, and shoes were spilling out of it, leaving even less room to maneuver.

The woman Sandra had seen at the door was lying on the left side of the mattress. She wore a yellow shirt and white shorts. Her left leg was bent and her right arm was across her belly. Her mouth was open, her breathing deep and steady. The parasitic entity that was draining this woman's energy was somewhere else, and Sandra knew that meant she wouldn't wake up easily.

Every job was different, but the sadness was always the same. Sometimes it came early on. Sandra recalled the poor young woman who wanted more YouTube subscribers. She had beautiful green eyes and her smile had been bright enough to burn itself into Sandra's memory. She'd made the sadness hit fast and hard. Other times, the sadness seemed to wait like a predator and only jumped out at Sandra and clamped down on her heart at the last moment. Regardless of when it came or how much of it she felt, Sandra knew she had to ignore it. Ignoring it was the only way to do the work, and if she didn't do the work, ghosts would eventually hurt people, drive them insane, or force them to hurt others. Her mother had learned that the hard way and that's why she was a smiling face in a photograph hanging in Sandra's kitchen wall and not here doing the work with her.

It bothered Sandra that ghosts were now responsible for so much heartache and pain. It bothered her that the only reason so many evil spirits were allowed into this side of the veil was because people thought calling on the spirit world, opening doors, and offering themselves as hosts—willingly or unknowingly—was just a joke, a challenge to post on Instagram, a weird way to get a job or a partner, or a way to get more views and subscribers on social media. Evil spirits had always been around and at one point they had been an occasional problem, but now they were all around and they weren't the problem; the problem was people like the woman in front of Sandra, people who called to them, who pulled them into the world of the living.

Before the sadness morphed into anger, Sandra pulled out the knife she carried with her at all times, the knife that had been blessed in New Orleans, and approached the bed. She hated this part. The sight of blood made her dizzy, and the sounds people made as they struggled to stay in this realm always turned into emotional scars that haunted her. She hated killing people, but she'd learned that ghosts weren't demons; they couldn't be exorcised. Once an evil spirit found a host, they were like an aggressive cancer that spread to everything and everyone around their host. Killing the host was the only solution.

A single cut had to do the trick; fast and hard, from one side to the other so she could get the jugular veins on both sides. She'd always heard the carotid was the quickest way, but she lacked the strength to pull that off, so Sandra limited herself to a line across the neck.

The woman jumped. They all jump. Or scream. Or gargle. Sandra didn't want to stick around or look at the woman, but she had to stay.

A few seconds later, the black figure emerged from the wall. It was long and thin, its face a shifting maelstrom of pained expressions framed by bones that appeared to constantly break and settle briefly before breaking again. The mouth was a dark hole that never closed. It was one of the ugliest ghosts Sandra had seen. Its movements were jerky in a way that made Sandra think of a strobe light. It turned its head to her and Sandra knew it had bad intentions, but it knew time was running out. Its host was dying.

Sandra had dealt with ghosts that wanted to jump into her in those desperate moments, but she had protection and it was really hard for them to do so without being called, without the host performing a ritual to lift the veil and open their inner doors. Sandra performed rituals to do the exact opposite.

The ghost began to shake violently, its lanky body twitching as if it'd been electrocuted. It was taking a little too long to vanish, which meant it was a strong ghost.

The ghost launched itself at Sandra. For a second, she saw a tall white man carrying the body of a kid into a swamp. The kid's face was bloated as the man placed the kid in the water, walked to the edge of the swamp, and started collecting rocks. Before Sandra could see the man putting the rocks on top of the kid's body to keep it submerged, the vision vanished. The ghost was gone, and with it the darkness of the deeds it had done and carried with it into the other realm.

Sandra took one last look at the woman on the bed and was thankful for the darkness in the room that made her blood look like very dark shadows. The same questions that always came to her came then, and she, once again, couldn't answer any of them. Why would this young woman contact an evil spirit? Where had she found the ritual? How many people had she shared the information with? Sandra hated that the sacred knowledge, the knowledge held by women like her grandmother, mother, and aunts, was now available to anyone. She wasn't angry because she thought the women in her family, like many women like them across the world, were special; she was angry because people played around with things they should know enough to leave alone and the internet was like an uncontrollable river of information that claimed too many lives and couldn't be stopped.

There was empty space where the ghost had been. Sandra knew it was gone. She felt it in an ineffable way that few others were capable of feeling.

Sandra walked out of the woman's apartment and texted Mr. Gunnells.

When Mr. Gunnells opened the door, Sandra spoke quickly and with a tone of voice she knew would crawl into the man's throat and kill the questions that were there, eager to explode out of his mouth.

"Your house is clean," said Sandra. "I took care of the problem. Now you pay me. I don't want your money; I want your silence. No matter what happens, you've never met me. You have no idea what happened to your neighbor. You will keep your mouth shut and be thankful for every night from now on because you will sleep and not be disturbed. Is that clear?"

It was late and her voice had done its job. She looked at Mr. Gunnells' eyes and allowed the pain and anger inside her to flow out of her and into him so that he understood that what she was saying simply had to be done. The man nodded, his eyes filling up with tears that Sandra knew were a combination of relief, fear, and confusion. Sandra walked away from him and went back to her car.

Sandra sat in front of her photographs and asked them if it was time to leave. None of the faces nodded, so she knew there was more important work to be done. There was always work to be done. She didn't mind. The work fed her, gave her energy, gave her a reason to wake up in the morning.

She sat there and imagined thousands of people online, looking for a thrill, finding ways of opening doors to the other side of the veil. A shiver ran down her spine. The work would never be over. There were too many people, and people were now the problem. Deep inside her, the need to protect others—a thing she knew was buried deep in her DNA—stirred. Sandra took a deep breath and steadied herself. The four women on her wall were smiling. She could see pride in the faces and yearned for the day when they would all meet again, but that day was not here yet.

Ding!

A text. Sandra could feel another bad night coming, so she ignored it and instead looked out the window. She would turn her phone off and go to bed soon, but first she would watch the birth of a new day. A new day, her grandmother had told her, is a promise and a new opportunity.

As the first rays of the new sun made their way into Sandra's tiny kitchen, she felt the sadness leave her body. She felt strong and ready. She would sleep and then read the text. If it was someone who was just curious, she would send them packing. If it was someone in trouble, she would do the work. She always did the work to keep people—the problem—safe on this side of the veil.

"The troll shook him. "Quit screamin,' kid. Take it like a man, dammit!"

EPIC TROLL

AUSTON HABERSHAW

Corey Marsh knew Donnie Caputo was going to jump him on the
way home, so instead of going past the 7-11 on Dime Street, he
decided to cut through Gravel Park and avoid the main streets
altogether.

Because of this, he was about to be eaten by a troll.

The troll had him by the ankle and was suspending him upside down so
that Corey's book bag and windbreaker had slipped down over his shoulders,
making it hard for him to move. He still thrashed and kicked out with his free
leg, but it didn't make a difference. He was caught. A true goner.

"Please don't! Please, please! Oh God!" Mom had always told him not to
cut through the park for just this reason. Gravel Park was five hundred acres
of paved jogging trails through dense forest and poison ivy—*perfect* troll habitat. Corey should have known better, but here he was, his young life about to
be cut short.

The troll shook him. "Quit screamin,' kid. Take it like a man, dammit!"

Tears were blinding Corey now. His voice cracked. "I don't wanna die!
Please don't eat me! *Please!*"

The troll scratched behind one long, pointy ear and grumbled something
under its breath. It dropped him on the ground. "Shit."

Corey scrambled to his feet and backed away, wiping his tears from his face. The troll watched him, its big yellow eyes blazing in the gathering twilight.

It had to be about eight feet tall, with bulky, stooped shoulders and thick skin like a rhinoceros, but green. It was wearing a T-shirt and boxer shorts. On the T-shirt were printed the words "TROLLS DO IT UNDER BRIDGES" with a picture of a covered wooden bridge and a quartet of troll-like feet sticking out.

Corey was shaking too much to run; his legs felt like jelly. "You ... you aren't gonna eat me?"

The troll shrugged. "I hate it when they cry, you know? Makes me feel like a monster."

Corey blinked. "But ... you *are* a ..."

The troll pointed a black-nailed finger at him. "Don't you say it! I'm starvin'! Could always change my mind!"

Corey pulled himself to his feet and backed away a few more paces. "So ... I can go?"

The troll scratched an armpit, "Well ... if I let you go, then you'll tell your mom, and then she'll call the cops, and then the cop'll call the Rangers ..." The troll trailed off and shrugged again. "Then I'm screwed." It picked up a head-sized boulder. "So maybe I should just kill you and call it a day, huh?"

Corey put up his hands. "I won't tell! I won't tell—honest! Don't kill me!"

The troll raised the rock as though ready to throw, but never let it fly. Its ears drooped. "Dammit. And I'm so hungry, too. You got some good meat on you, kid. Hey, maybe I can just have a leg or something—ain't doctors got robot legs they can fix ya with these days?"

Corey flinched. "What? No!"

The troll dropped the rock and ran a huge hand across its warty, hairless scalp. "Never was much good at eating nice people. Pops was right."

"Nice people?"

The troll pointed at his backpack. "Gotcher homework in there. Over there's where you dropped a clarinet or somethin'. Mom wrote your name inside your windbreaker. Hell, you probably only came this way so bigger kids didn't beat you up, right?"

Corey gaped at the hulking, mythological monster.

"Don't fix my problem, though—how'm I supposed to know if you snitched on me or not?" The troll sighed, watching Corey as he edged himself towards his backpack and clarinet. If Corey could just reach them, he could take off and *maybe* outrun the troll in the woods.

The troll's ears perked up suddenly. It clapped its giant hands. "Hey, I got an idea!"

"Uhhh ... what?"

The troll produced a cell phone. "You on social media?"

Nobody noticed that Corey had a new follower online. It was weird, but was a pretty small price to pay in exchange for his life.

He could have told his mom, he supposed. Or the cops. But, well, he'd seen enough videos of what Federal Rangers did to troll dens and goblin nests— flamethrowers, poison gas, cattle prods, and so on—that he'd feel kinda bad if he got the troll killed or hurt. It *did* spare his life. His biology teacher, Mr. Whatley, had spent one class explaining to them how many of the Reawakened creatures deserved the same rights and considerations we gave people. It wasn't a *troll's* fault that it was a large carnivore whose natural prey was humans. Extinction of a sentient species wasn't the proper solution, Whatley said. For the time being, Corey sort of agreed. The troll had, in the end, been pretty nice to him.

And besides, informing the world that he had met—and survived—an encounter with a troll would have drawn attention to himself, and drawing attention to himself went against every survival instinct Corey had. It had long been his goal to merely survive high school and then leave and never see any of these people again. The only way a geeky kid with a clarinet was likely to do that was by being ignored by the apex predators of high school society. Predators like Donnie Caputo.

On that front, Corey's fortunes were flagging. Donnie, some other guys on the hockey team, and their girlfriends had decided to make Corey the target of some nasty fun at his expense. They had been sending pictures of rotten bananas to each other and tagging him in the captions:

@ballerdonnie41: *Look, its @cMarshWiz's dick*

@stickmanUber: *No, this 1 looks more like @cMarshWiz's mom's dick*

@cheerchick11: *Ohmygod, is that @cMarshWiz's penis? Nope.* *#mybad lol*

The joke caught on and had been circulating for a few days. When the cafeteria served banana pudding one lunch period, Donnie spent the whole time pretending to jerk off into Corey's dish. A lot of people laughed. Corey got up and ate his lunch in the hall. Because of that, he got detention when a hall monitor reported him to the principal.

That afternoon, after an hour of writing an essay on personal responsibility in the detention room, Corey was walking home when Donnie pulled up next to him in his dad's Camaro. He rolled down the window. "Hey homo!"

Corey just put his head down and kept walking, his thumbs looped through his backpack straps.

Donnie let the car roll with him. He had gleaming white teeth and hard black eyes. "Hey, homo—I'm talking to you!" His girlfriend, Blake, giggled from the passenger seat.

Corey sighed. "What?"

"Sarah Creamer really wants to date you." Donnie said, grinning. "She thinks you're hot."

Sarah was a cute girl in his bio class, but he hadn't said anything to anybody about her. Corey felt his cheeks flush and instantly wished they hadn't.

Blake caught on instantly. "Awwww! Wittle Corey's in wuv!"

Donnie leaned out of the car window. "You wanna do her, Corey? You wanna whip out your banana?"

"Screw you, Donnie." Corey said, but the words were too weak. Too wavery.

Donnie laughed while Blake took a picture of him with her phone. "Later, dick!" he said, and they sped off.

That night, pictures made the rounds. Corey's face photoshopped on a banana leaning over a photo of Sarah Creamer while moaning sounds played on loop. The caption read "Banana-Cream!"

It got 413 likes and 147 shares. An instant sensation.

School the next day was harsh. Somebody left a rotten banana in front of his locker. He started getting bombarded by texts from kids all over school, all parroting Donnie's stupid joke. In bio class, Sarah sat as far away from him as possible and didn't look at him at all. Everybody watched Corey's every move; he felt like he was being dissected, like a frog under magnification. He seemed unable to keep from blushing.

When Mr. Whatley asked him if everything was all right, the whole class laughed. Even those kids like him—the bottom feeders, the perennial dorks— put on a brave smile and chuckled along. He knew what they were feeling— he'd felt it too. Like him, not being noticed was an instinct deeply ingrained. If you broke through the fragile surface tension of conformity and flopped out into the open, nobody could help you. They could only watch the wolves circle.

The day was too much. At lunch, Corey slipped out a side exit and went home. His mom was at work, so he had the house to himself. He crawled into his bed and pulled the quilt over his head. In the semi-darkness, he contemplated his own powerlessness. *I just won't go online again,* he told himself. *They'll get tired of it. Move on to somebody else. Maybe Paula Finkel—she had an eye-patch on today.*

But thinking of Paula Finkel getting mocked for her eye-patch didn't make him feel any better. Nothing seemed to. Inexorably, he was drawn to his computer to see how egregious the damage was going to be. His feed displayed his humiliation in the form of hastily constructed GIFs and badly photoshopped jokes. Endless copies of the "Banana-Cream" picture littered his feed, each with a small raft of likes, all wallowing in his discomfort. There was a picture of him in bio class, taken surreptitiously, as he was blushing from ears to nose. They'd made it into a meme: "When the Girl U Like H8s Bananas." Under some morbid compulsion, Corey read all the comments. About a third of them explained how he would be better off dead. The "lol" they tacked on the end of such statements somehow made them sting all the more. His death —whether social or actual—was the subject of popular amusement.

Then came the coup de grace. It was a tweet from Donnie. It read:

@ballerdonnie41: *Just talked 2 @sarahcreamer01: @cMarshWiz showed his 8=> to her little brother in 8th grade. She h8s him. @cMarshWiz is a pedo. Truth. :(lollollol rotflol*

The comments went on for a while. Corey's heart sank from a rapid beat of terror into a cold, empty thump of despair. Kid after kid—most of them upperclassmen—piled on the stories about him, calling him "pedo" and "perv" and "creep." The thread was like examining his own corpse. He just kept refreshing it to see who posted next: a teacher, maybe? His own sister? How low could he sink?

Then something strange happened:

@epictroll88: *hey, @ballerdonnie41, heard yr girlfriend made out w/ @cMarshWiz. Got pictures. Hot.*

@ballerdonnie41: *lol*

Corey sat forward in his desk chair. Was that ... no. That would be crazy.

@epictroll88: *heard he did her harder than Brentonville did yr stupid hockey team last Sunday except she begged for more lol*

Somebody Corey didn't know chimed in with: *rotflol #shotsfired*

@ballerdonnie41: *who the fk r u @epictroll88? Need an ass-kicking?*

@epictroll88: *im the guy who's gonna make u my bitch #come@mebro*

@ballerdonnie41: *place and time*

@epictroll88: *gravel park, sunset. Bring tp—gonna rip off ur head and shit down ur neck*

@ballerdonnie41: *gonna bring friends. want an audience for ur beatdown*

@epictroll88: *more the merrier #chickenshit*

And that was pretty much it. The conversation moved on and Corey sat back, staring at the screen. Did a troll just stick up for him? Really?

The next day, Corey convinced his mom he was sick and stayed home from school. The internet was thankfully quiet—no sign of Donnie at all—and it did, indeed, seem as though Corey's turn in the scathing spotlight was over, at least for a bit. Oh, there were still a few posts on him and the whole banana cream thing, but it was on the wane. The embarrassment still hurt—fresh as it had been the day before—but at least it wasn't getting worse. He spent the day in his pajamas watching superhero movies and tried to assess if he could live with the shame of this latest attack. He determined, ultimately, that he could carry on. The next day he put on his windbreaker, pulled up the hood, and kept his head low on the walk to school.

Nobody had any interest in him that day, though. The only thing on everybody's lips was "what had happened to Donnie?" He was missing—hadn't been to school, hadn't been home, nobody had seen him. He had vanished. Blake was gone, too, as well as two other members of the hockey team—Cameron O'Shea and Dave Wittick. The police showed up that afternoon and started interviewing kids in the principal's office. Corey's turn was just before dismissal.

The principal's office smelled like pencils and had faux wood paneling. The officer was a huge, musclebound man who introduced himself as Tyler and offered Corey a seat while he perched himself on the corner of the big desk. Dr. Washington, the principal, sat behind his desk, his face fixed in its perpetual frown. Corey sat with his knees pushed together and his palms sweating.

"When was the last time you saw Donnie, Corey?"

Corey shrugged. "Tuesday, maybe. He was in his car … his dad's car, I guess."

"Did you see him on Wednesday?"

"No."

Officer Tyler referred to a notebook. "You aren't friendly with Donnie, are you?"

Corey shrugged and looked at the poster on the wall. It was of hot air balloons, rising into the autumn sky; "REACH HIGHER," it read. He cleared his throat. "Donnie's okay, I guess."

Officer Tyler was watching Corey carefully. "Do you know anybody who'd want to hurt Donnie? Make him disappear?"

The entire chess team, maybe? Every single freshman? Corey shrugged again. "I dunno. He wasn't always so nice to people, you know?"

Officer Tyler nodded and kept asking questions, Dr. Washington kept glaring. Corey didn't think anything much was illuminated, for either of them. Donnie was missing, anyway. For Corey's part, it wasn't too hard to imagine what had happened to him.

On the way home, after band practice, Corey cut through Gravel Park again. He found the troll sitting on a log right around where they had first "met." The troll was wearing another giant T-shirt. This one read "CAUCASIANS: THE OTHER OTHER WHITE MEAT."

"S'up," the troll said, putting away its cell phone.

Corey's throat went dry looking at the troll—every instinct was telling him to run—but he planted himself. His stomach did flips as he asked the question, "Did you ... did you eat Donnie?"

The troll smiled a snaggle-toothed smile. "Yup. His friends, too." It patted its stomach, which looked unusually distended. "Good eating, lemme tell you. Nice and lean meat."

Corey's hands grabbed his hair. "Oh my God! Holy ... holy *shit!* I knew it! You *killed* them!"

The troll laughed. "That's usually how it works, yeah. Look, you should give a shit, right? Those punks were real assholes to you."

"But ... but they're *dead!* I ... I thought you felt *bad* about eating people!"

"Eating *nice* people. They weren't that." The troll picked between its teeth with a long black nail. "That Donnie creep tried to trade his girlfriend for his own life. What a crappy thing to do," it shrugged. "Ate 'em both anyway."

Corey felt dizzy. He backed away from the troll, head reeling. "I didn't want them all *dead!*"

"Wasn't about you—told you I was hungry, and now I ain't." The troll stretched, swinging its huge, tree-like arms back and forth as though it were about to go for a jog. "Look, kid, I just improved your life. Stop complaining and have the manners to say thanks, okay?"

"Th ... thanks?" Corey steadied himself against a tree. He wanted to puke.

"Welcome! Look, I gotta work off some of these calories, okay? A fat troll's a dead troll, as my pops used to say. Later!" And with that, the troll jogged off into the dark of the woods. Its massive footfalls, cushioned by wide, scaly footpads, barely made a sound.

Corey stumbled home. When he got there, he actually did puke.

The cops, National Guard, and a team of volunteers searched for the missing kids for three months before finally calling it off. They found Donnie's car under a bridge deep in Gravel Park. The news said it looked like he had driven it along the bike paths. There were no other obvious clues, but all the usual theories were floated: runaways, kidnapping, serial killer, wild griffon attack, *trolls.* The cops investigated a rumor of a fight that was supposed to go down in the park that night, but nobody knew with whom—@epictroll88 was evidently a joke account. The leads dried up. The "Gravel Park Four" were gone.

The troll had been right about one thing—Corey's life did get easier, in a way. The disappearance and presumed deaths of three members of the hockey team overrode all other social activities at his school. The popular kids sought to outdo one another in shows of grief and concern and Corey and all his ilk were mercifully forgotten. The only thing he had to do was wear a black armband every day and the whole school seemed to act as though he had always been part of their collective community. When they announced they had found the missing car, he was hugged in the hall by Janice Peters, the hottest girl in school. She acted like she hadn't called him a pedophile on Twitter. It was like that life—Corey's daily life for a year before he met the troll— had never happened.

But it was wearing in other ways. He had to go to candlelight vigils every Friday for the missing kids. He had to volunteer on weekends to distribute flyers at the bus station. After they had been declared dead, he had to go to all the memorial services and listen to all the eulogies and read the articles in the newspaper about them. Donnie had been a good kid, they said. Helped his grandma go grocery shopping. Cameron O'Shea had made honor roll. Dave Wittick had been applying to veterinary school. Blake was a Big Sister.

Nobody once mentioned what jerks they had all been. To him. To everybody he knew. Even his friends—all of them regular targets for Donnie's bullying—had stopped complaining about him. If the topic came up, they shook their heads and muttered about tragedies and how "it really makes you think, you know?" Corey felt like he was going crazy.

He knew that he should have felt guilty, but every time somebody did something "in honor" of Donnie or Blake, he felt his heart harden just a little more. When they established the college scholarship fund that spring, he couldn't take it anymore. He posted online:

@cMarshWiz: *the closest the Gravel Park Four would ever have gotten to college in real life would be when they changed the oil in my car #sorrynotsorry*

No likes, twenty retweets, and an invitation to the principal's office. Officer Tyler was there.

Dr. Washington shook his head slowly. "This isn't the kind of conduct we expect from our students, Corey."

Corey didn't say anything. He kept his arms folded and stared at the stupid balloon poster.

Officer Tyler smiled at him. "Look, I know it's difficult to talk about it. People process grief in different ways—"

Corey laughed out loud.

Dr. Washington exchanged a look with Officer Tyler. "Is something funny, young man?"

Corey felt like something hot and bitter was welling up from his stomach. He'd felt that feeling so many times—so *many* times—and he always pushed it down. *It's not worth it* he'd tell himself, over and over and over. *Just sit down and take it, move on, forget it.*

This time, though—this time he let it out. "They all sucked and I'm glad they're dead. They deserved it, all of them. They were mean to me, mean to my friends, mean to *everybody,* and nobody cared about us, then. I don't understand why I need to care about *them* now. Good riddance."

Dr. Washington raised one finger, his face severe. "Watch your tone, young man."

Corey found himself rolling. "Nobody called *them* into the principal's office and had *them* talk to a cop or a counsellor or whatever! You know once Donnie slipped an actual shit into my jockstrap at gym? Actual shit, from the toilet. You know what happened to him? *Nothing.* Absolutely nothing. And now they're saints? To hell with them!" Corey noticed he was standing, the two men in the room looking at him with grave expressions. His bravado crumbled, he folded his arms, and he sank back into the chair. Quietly, he added one last thought, as much to himself as anything: "I hope they rot."

Four day suspension. His mom had to sign him up for "aggression counseling" with a shrink. So much nonsense.

Over the summer, Corey thought long and hard about defense mechanisms in nature; he thought about how camouflage hadn't worked for him and never would work—it would only kill him slowly from the inside. There were other ways to warn off predators, though. A lot of creatures chose bright, bold colors—chose to stick out instead of blend in. The colors were supposed to send a message: *warning,* they said, *poison.*

The next fall, Corey took up wearing black. He pierced his nose, dyed his hair green, started smoking. His mother, always harried by her job, threw up her hands and called it a phase. He knew better—it was armor; it was a message to those who wanted to screw with him. The plaque they'd placed out by the flagpole to commemorate Donnie and his asshole friends was evidence of its truth, if only in Corey's mind.

One day, he was sitting out by the dumpsters, smoking a butt, when he heard a kid crying. He rounded the corner to see a freshman, his blue polo shirt smeared with ketchup, his eyes red. "Go away!" the boy growled, and wiped his eyes.

Corey only smiled. "Who did it?"

The kid scowled. "What's it to you?"

Corey blew smoke out his nose, like a dragon. "You ever been through Gravel Park?"

THE MAN OF SEAWEED AND REEDS

COREY FARRENKOPF

The Man of Seaweed and Reeds attempted to blend with the invasive phragmites growing beneath the bridge. His gangly arms draped into the water, bulbous head tucked between backwards-jointed knees. The Phragmites resembled cattails, something like an aquatic wheat field brushed by the current. His coloration was off. The vines and ferns sprouting from his body were a dull, burnt brown where they needed to be pale. He failed to adapt to new flora, sticking out like a colored illustration in a black and white world.

Fred hated pointing him out on his tours; camouflage was camouflage for a reason. But it was what the people wanted, what paid the bills at the bird sanctuary. They couldn't afford to lose donations with the most recent land-grab under way. One hundred and fifty acres of brackish wetland would be on the market at the end of the month, and their fundraising goals were abysmal.

"What does the marsh man eat?" a young boy asked from the back of the group, binoculars pressed to his eyes.

There were twelve people huddled close on the nature trail, all carrying bird watching equipment. Some wore wide-brimmed hats. Others smelled of sunscreen. They'd passed a glossy informative plaque minutes before. All the basic biological information on Reeds, as he was affectionately known, was spelled out in simple terms. But the boy must have missed it or was too young to read about the species' thousands of years in the same marsh or their once prominent role as apex predators.

"A little meat. A little vegetation. He's omnivorous. Usually we see him catching fish, pulling reed grass from the riverbank," Fred replied.

"Why's he so skinny?" the boy asked.

"There aren't as many fish in the river as there once were and the Phragmites pushed all the reed grass out. Phragmites just don't taste as good. Too much fiber."

The crowd laughed at Fred's joke even as the words soured in his throat. He hated making light of Reeds' predicament, but humor brought in more money than the dour reality of diminishing habitat. No one wanted to hear about apex predators reduced to skeletal remains, all the wolves and bears and cougars, their trail to the end nearly identical. Only the time and place varied.

"He's a protected species, right?" the boy's mother asked.

"Well, yes. Technically he's functionally extinct, but you never know," Fred said.

The boy lowered his binoculars.

"So, he's going to ...."

"Like I said. You never know," Fred replied.

"Did you see the trail cam footage?" Beth, Fred's supervisor, asked the next day as they punched their timecards. The central education building was two miles downstream from where they'd seen Reeds on the last tour. It was a modern, glass-walled structure composed of classrooms, office space, rehab tanks, and lecture halls.

"I didn't, why?" Fred asked. "Is he eating the turtles again?"

The turtles in question were Diamondback Terrapins, an endangered species with a glimmer of hope at a comeback.

"No, it's not that," she replied. "He was up here, walking around the building, knocking on windows, trying doorknobs."

"That doesn't sound like him."

"No, it doesn't, and it's a little concerning."

"Should we cancel the tours?"

"Oh god no. We can't afford to lose the revenue."

Fred knew that. He had three tours scheduled for the day and a potential fourth if enough phone calls came in. With the neighboring land getting bought up, more and more people were taking their last chance to see Reeds. Word had gotten out that if the land was developed, there wasn't much chance for survival.

"But what if he ..." Fred began.

"Keep your distance. They have binoculars for a reason," Beth replied.

A belted kingfisher peered into shallow water searching for minnows. A pair of white ibis panned about the reeds. An osprey nest sang with the squall of fledglings above the walking path. Fred pointed to each as they passed, noting identification details, behaviors common to the species. He prayed it would be mostly birds that morning, that Reeds was tucked away somewhere, maybe eating his first decent meal in months.

Two twenty-somethings at the back of the tour wore matching Reeds t-shirts, the marsh man's face done in tie-dye. Fred knew there wasn't much chance at avoiding the subject.

He'd spotted Reeds' tracks earlier, leading down to the muddy banks of the river, away from the education center. He hadn't pointed them out. It was important to avoid false hopes.

They didn't see Reeds every day. Sometimes he slept in the nest that they had never been able to locate. Sometimes he managed to find a stand of native plants he could actually blend with. Sometimes he was passed out asleep in the middle of a path. Fred never knew what they were going to get.

Fred didn't think of himself as fatherly, but maybe more of a concerned uncle—a godfather waiting for the phone call after an ill-fated plane crash. He loved the creature from a distance. Like he said the day before, Reeds was omnivorous.

For a while, he'd left food out, deli meat and watercress salads, until Beth caught him and said he had to stop. It was one of the tenants of conservation: not introducing another unsustainable means of survival. Fred wouldn't always be there to share a sandwich and some sushi, so it was better for Reeds to not get accustomed.

Since then, Fred had been thinking of other, less noticeable, ways to help, but he'd been drawing a blank.

"Is that the marsh man?" one of the two t-shirt-clad enthusiasts shouted, drawing Fred from daydreams.

He squinted, covering his eyes from the sun.

There was no doubting it. Reeds hunched by a small pool on the side of the river where the current was weak. A number of turtles swam around him, the silver scales of fish sparkling about his ankles. His own vegetation drifted into the water, casting shadows across the surface. Fred couldn't tell what he was eating, but Reeds had his hands by his mouth, the faint sound of chewing reaching them.

"Yup, that's the Man of Seaweed and Reeds. Now, if we're real quiet and keep our distance, we'll be able to observe him for a bit before we move on," Fred said.

"Move on?" one of the enthusiasts said. "Why don't we just camp out here all day? You're kidding yourself if you think any of us came for the birds."

An elderly man with a birding guide to North America in hand moved to correct them, but stopped mid-gesture, tucking his book into his backpack.

"Well, we can stay for a while, but not too long. We don't want to disturb him more than necessary," Fred said.

"Whatever you say, man," the twenty-something replied.

Reeds continued to eat with the fish surfacing around him, fighting the current's pull, nipping at scraps of food dropped into the water. It almost looked like Reeds was feeding them—his own open-borders aquarium. The group watched in silence, binoculars raised, some jotting lines in notebooks or doing quick sketches of the creature. Whispers circulated in pods. Some thrilled at the noises. Others were moved to tears.

Then someone gasped, "What's he eating?"

Fred hadn't focused on the meal itself, just the muscular figure hunched in the shallows. He brought his own binoculars up, training them on what Reeds held.

Fred gagged, bile climbing his throat.

It was a human arm, wrist to shoulder, pale and decayed.

"It was a human arm, wrist to shoulder, pale and decayed."

"Is that a …" a young girl began.

Her question was cut off by Reeds turning, black eyes narrowing in their direction, almost waving the arm in a twisted gesture of welcome.

The little girl, and half of the group, screamed in unison before running down the path they'd just taken. Fred had to grab both the enthusiasts by the shoulders to force them to follow. They were too busy snapping photos, eyes wide, some dream fulfillment flashing before them.

Fred couldn't let them linger. He didn't know what Reeds would do, especially with his meal interrupted and a newly discovered food source.

"Run," Fred yelled, pushing them towards the education center.

They tripped over themselves, stumbling up the path, casting glances over their shoulders in an attempt to see if the marsh man was going to follow, if he was still hungry.

"I'll write up the report," Beth said, sitting across from Fred in the break room, twin microwavable burritos steaming between them. "It's traumatizing enough having to see that, let alone write about it."

"Shouldn't we call someone? Like the police?" Fred asked.

"You know what they do to Tigers in India when they start eating people, right?"

Fred nodded. He read about the shooting of the endangered big cats, the way quick concern morphed into violence in seconds.

"Yeah, but whose arm was it?" Fred asked, the beef and bean scent of the burrito turning his stomach.

"Who knows? Could have been something washed in from the sea. You never know these days, with ships going down and all the sharks along the coast. He probably just picked it out of the water."

"So you think he didn't kill someone for it?"

"No way. He's pretty peaceful. More of a scavenger than anything else, right?"

"I guess," Fred replied.

"Just bring the gun with you on your next tour. He's like a grizzly. Fire into the air and he'll run away."

"We're not canceling the other tours?"

"Nope. You'll be fine. Like I said, he's just a scavenger."

———

Fred didn't find Reeds on his third or fourth tour of the day. The marsh man had melted back into the marsh or returned to his nest to enjoy the rest of his meal in peace. The weight of the pocketed revolver was a terrible reminder of potential—a forked reality Fred wanted nothing to do with. Each of the tour groups lamented the lack of the main attraction, but they had seen a number of herons and a bald eagle, so a portion of the discontent was alleviated. Part of Fred would be glad when all there was to see would be birds, simple and nonthreatening. Part of him dreaded it.

———

"I can wait if you'd like," Fred asked Beth as she sat in her office, computer screen laden with emails and word documents.

"Naw, I'm backlogged. You'd be here all night," she replied with a smile. "I'm taking a half day Friday, so don't feel bad."

"Are you sure?" Fred asked.

"One hundred percent. I'll grab some takeout and wine on the way home as a treat. It all balances out."

———

Albert, Fred's half chihuahua, half pit bull, greeted him at the door to his apartment. Fred was thankful Beth hadn't made him wait. Albert didn't have the best bladder control and it was almost feeding time.

The apartment was small: a bedroom, a kitchen, a bathroom. He'd tried to fill it with as many terrariums as he could, recreating habitats he saw throughout his day, or ones he glimpsed in nature documentaries. Fred wanted to understand the world around him, how he could help, where the pieces fit together. With Reeds, he'd felt like a failure for the past year, his tours never able to bring in enough money. The op-eds he wrote to local newspapers changed no one's mind. If the money wasn't there, the owners of the land weren't going to reconsider. The calendar hanging on his wall had a large red circle on the day of the land auction. Those few weeks between seemed too scant to count—an inevitability approaching too quick.

Albert licked at his hand, then sniffed at his food dish.

"Don't worry, I didn't forget," Fred said, retrieving the bag of kibble from the cabinet. "We all need to eat."

Fred was early for work the next morning.

The legs jutting from beneath the bushes that greeted him wore black heels.

Torn stockings disappeared into the undergrowth.

Fred traced a line of blood leading from the path between the education center and the parking lot. His heart quickened. A viscous lump pooled in his throat. He walked towards the shrubbery, leaning forward, before the crack and snap of branches tore his attention away. In the distance, a shape plowed through the forest. Fred's eyes shifted from the body to the front door, fight or flight flickering in his veins.

The body was still. There wasn't anything he could do, so he sprinted to the front door, hurrying with his keycard, palms sweaty as the knob finally turned. The air-conditioned breath of the center surrounded him—that filtered scent, the splash of rehab pools drifting from deep inside the building. In the distance, the crash of tree limbs grew louder. The entire building wasn't much more than one continuous window bisected by steel girders. It felt as if he were still in the woods, leaves pressing against his face.

Fred watched Reeds approach, indifferent to what lay in his path, tearing pine and oak limbs, uprooting small saplings. In moments, they were face to face, Reeds' large black eyes peering in at him, his face wrapped in algae and vines and the reeds for which he was named. His hollow mouth chewed the air, a nearly toothless cavern opening and closing.

Fred pulled his cell phone from his pocket. He dialed 911, but hesitated before pressing send. He knew what the cops and animal control officers would do if they showed up, the tigers flashing through his head. Fred didn't know if he'd blame them after seeing Beth's body in the bushes. She didn't deserve what had happened, but pressing send meant the death of an entire species. He could blame the other factors leading to this moment—the lack of food, the lack of habitat—but the final nail would belong to him if he made the call.

Reeds ran a finger over the glass, breath fogging the pane, searching for an ingress to get to Fred. The smooth surface led to nothing, so the creature slammed his palm against the barricade. The glass shivered, barely holding. Something at the edge whined. The sound of a thin splinter ran through the surface.

Fractals spread, obscuring Reeds' mouth, his eyes, his grasping hands that kept slamming into the window.

Fred couldn't bring himself to press send as he ran into the interior of the building, assessing which door would be the thickest, which locks the sturdiest. Beth had told him he wasn't allowed to tamper with Reeds' diet. They weren't permitted to interfere. It was part of conservation.

Maybe the right door/lock combination would hold. Maybe Reeds would wander deeper into the building to feed from the turtle rehab tanks. Maybe he'd get bored and leave.

Regardless, Fred couldn't make the call.

Nature had to play itself out.

THE SOUND

LEAH CLAIRE KAMINSKI

My hands run a brush through my hair and stop, startled. I ignore them. What do hands know. But they feel their way back.

The hair feels thicker. Longer? Cottony. Like hers must have been, after days in salt water. My hands hold hanks of hair, weighing it against memory. I look in the mirror. It looks like my hair. It comes from my head. It's fine. But my hands protest, fretting.

My previous life was made of voices. Murmuring, racketing, needing voices that became nothing but horrible noise once her small voice was hushed for good. And then the voice of the ocean, rushing and falling, always calling me back, always calling me to join her. In the woods, I imagined, the only sound would be humus settling.

At first, just skittering leaves, animals trading places at dawn. Or crows circled. Caws tearing the canopy in purple dusk. Noises that did not desire me. But then yesterday—I turned and there it was. It was. A medium-high white noise. No, not a noise. It was too intentional for that. A sound.

But even saying that, "medium-high white noise", is not enough to make you understand. Imagine the world is loud all around and is also loud inside you. Imagine that what you actually want to hear (nothing. the forest. her voice.) is too quiet, just out of reach. Imagine that your brain is an ouroboros, that you are the sound and the sound is you, that your mind is in a panic and chasing its own tail.

Last night, wakeful agony. The sound not of me, but in me. Together in a terrible, perpetually blossoming moment. And now, this morning, my fretting hands, my strangely lengthening hair.

And still the sound. Now changed to something like high-pitched—though that simplifies its many layers—with a deep thrum anchoring it. I swear if I focus on it I feel it lasering in, straight to the center of my brain. Like it is breaking me, like I am a glass.

I walk to the woods to clear my head, to soothe my hands. My hands touch branches nodding with leaf. The forests have decades left, thanks to warming air and warming soil. Thanks to us. I am siphoning calm from a dying body. As I walk, the sound throbs.

And my hair floats behind me, a sensation I haven't felt since I was younger, since before she was born.

Suddenly a noise—not in me, but behind me. A small animal following. I shoot back around to spot it. As I do, I trip over a sickening mass of hair that has gathered behind me. Has come from my head. My hands were right. This is not my hair.

I begin to run, following the noise, which comes from a shadow that darts through crevice and hollow and pulls the hair with it. In a copse I stumble on a root, fall into a tiny, furred creature. Long limbs pencil-thin. Eyes large as a baby sloth's. Mouth hung open like an ancient god.

Streaming from the mouth, like vomitus, is the hair.

My hands tear at the hair, the hair coming from the creature's mouth, the hair that is locked to my own head.

As I pull, the sound grows, and grows. Blinding pain grips. My hands keep pulling.

My eyes lock with the creature's, energy streaming between us. I can feel my energy distort, lengthen, leave me for it. My hands are finally still.

Looking into its eyes, I speak—why

(I need you)

Its words a sibilant extension of its sound. My hands lessen their grip further; the creature quiets.

—what do you want

(your listening)

—what is this substance

(my sound. takes listening. feeds me)

—where are you from

(the ground. it warmed. I woke)

—the ground warmed

(I woke. I feed)

It woke, it fed. Don't I know how to feed? And don't I owe it that, having helped to call it forth? I ask if I can pick it up. It sighs its assent. Its sound bathes me. I cradle the creature and its sound becomes a rhythmic suckling. We walk through the dying forest, air in my sinuous hair. We listen. The woods are not as quiet as you might think.

As we walk, the creature calms to quiet, for now. My hands find peace around its small body. I hum it to sleep, mother's unwords humming through its bones.

POOR BUTCHER-BIRD

GEMMA FILES

"Down here," he says, and I nod, like it's not obvious. Dip my head like I'm nervous, but a little shakily, too. Like I'm as excited as he is. You have to be careful about these things; he's dumb, sure, but nobody's *that* dumb.

You'd be surprised.

I had to work hard to hook up with this guy, who claims his "name" is Shrike93, just like his email. These Web-handles really crisp my arse-hairs, which I know makes me sound old—old enough to know what a Luddite actually was, any rate. The main good part about having once been a factory girl is, it keeps me small and weak-looking. Not a threat, supposedly, 'specially when stood next to some bro like the Shrike, all swole up with hormone-saturated meat and childhood vaccines. Nothing like. That, and I know not to sound how I think, either, when I speak out loud. Worked hard on that over the years. So much so, it holds pretty well, except when I get riled up; lucky how none of this posturing is quite enough to rile me, though. Not as yet.

He always picks two, and one of 'em doesn't tend to come back—that's the rumour. That's why I wasn't surprised I found another potential initiate waiting for him, when I got to our IRL meet-point; made sure to bristle a bit, then waited for the Shrike to step in once it got truly heated. Can't waste that precious red, now, can we? And he was quick enough to make his move, the minute this other wee pixie-haircut bitch pulled a flick-knife out. Which was just as well ... for her.

She thinks she'll be the one gets picked, all right. But I *know* I will, and that's the difference.

Experience always wins, that's my motto.

So down we go, the three of us, the Shrike leading the way, with me and Pixie-Cut trailing after. It's almost always down, with these sorts. The house is an abandoned two-story box on a high-fenced lot somewhere in the Annex, thick inside with cobwebs and mouse shit and dust, except for the lane these slags have cleared between the kitchen's back entrance and the door to the basement. And at the bottom of those stairs there's another door—brand-new, very fancy, normal on the outside but heavier than it looks, with a neat little combination smart-lock built into its knob that has to be keyed from the Shrike's iPhone, using his thumbprint. He undoes it on one side, then does it back up on the other.

Note to self: Need to get hold of that thumb.

Inside, another stubby flight of stairs, going down half a story to some sort of sub-basement; might have been meant as a wine-cellar, maybe, or a bomb shelter. There's lit candles stuck in bottles everywhere, half-melted into wax stalagmites, and the air heavy with incense like it's 1969. Whole floor's paved with bare mattresses slicked in dark plastic on either side of a clear area, three feet wide by thirty long from the door on inwards, mosaic-tiled in red and gold—a ritual path to that joke of a shrine they've set up along the back wall. And there, at last, is that big red lacquer cabinet, inside which I can only assume they've got the thing—the person—I want.

The rest of the cult are all lined up on either side of it, too, not that they probably think of themselves as such: Twenty of 'em, all told, unless somebody else is hiding in the bog somewhere. Not that they seem to *have* a bog down here, that I can see.

They've all got names he insists on telling me, which I forget almost immediately, 'cause it makes it easier. Instead, I file 'em under characteristics: Blue Hair; (too much) Face-Metal; Green Highlights; Snatched Brows (with scarification); Needs More T. Not to mention Bare Midriff, Assless Chaps, and straight-up Topless (girl *and* boy), plus a variety of other mock-Goth costum-ing: leather, studs and vinyl, too-large hoodies paired with artfully ripped fishnets. There's even one in the back seems to be wearing a blood-stained fake fur-suit, bright pink, splotched all over like some naff bunny-leopard hybrid. Think I'll call him Anime Chimera, if and when it comes to it.

This is church night for them, I reckon. Get together with like-minded individuals, share something meaningful, go through the ritual celebration that gives their dull little weeks a goal—all dressed up with something to pray to, not to mention somebody to kill over it. And so blessed, blessed sure, in their black little hearts, how no one else ever does the same. Bloody children.

Still, kids can be tricky, 'specially when they're high and armed. As I know from hard experience.

They're passing 'round bottles now, probably scarfed from parents' liquor cabinets: tequila, scotch, bourbon, vodka, red wine. I take a swallow or two, enough to make sure my breath smells like theirs, and mime the rest, while Pixie-Cut gleefully chugs whatever she's handed. By the time the Shrike stands up by the cabinet and loudly claps his hands, she's well and truly plastered.

"Brothers and sisters!" he shouts. "The moon's gone 'round again. It's that time!" Yells and cheers and hoots. "Time to renew ourselves, once more. Time to be *more*." More noise. I clench my jaw, holding my cardboard smile still. "Anyone have a story to share?"

A beat.

"I did it!" Green Highlights yells abruptly. "I found my boss. Told him I'd changed my mind, and when we were alone, I broke his nose and I knocked out his teeth—" this gets more cheers "—and then I carved PERV into his forehead, and I whammied him so hard he's never gonna know who did it! *Ever!*"

Howls of triumph fill the room; people hug Green Highlights, slap her back, hoist her hands into the air like she's won a boxing match. She's actually crying now I look close enough, poor cow. Still, I'm sure it feels good, while it lasts.

Up by the cabinet, Shrike's grinning like a preacher tallying up donations in his head. Calls for other stories, and gets them: All much the same, though none quite as righteously vindictive as Green Highlights'. Petty grudges, gleeful sadism, conquest-notches; the sort of selfish tat people dream about in bed or in front of a bathroom mirror, through clenched teeth, tears, or panting, between the short strokes. The *I Deserve This* rag, I call it—high on their own drama, the sweet bile backwash.

"This is church night for them, I reckon. All dressed up with something to pray to, not to mention somebody to kill over it."

Pixie-Cut looks pretty much like she's already halfway to getting off herself at the spectacle, what with those big eyes and that flushed face, rapid-breathing through her nose. Me, I make sure to keep on trembling, just in case. Not that anybody's really looking.

Finally, Shrike calms the crowd down with a gesture and beckons me and Pixie-Cut closer, both of us shouldering past each other down the red-gold road to Paradise. Because tonight's the climax, right? The end of a months-long seduction waged over every form of social media available, led down a trail of whispers about transformation, transfiguration, apotheosis, *power*. Some new kind of kick, or—just maybe—a very, very old one, all dressed up in post-Millennial drag.

"Other people talk about confidence, or love, or tapping enneagrams," he tells us. "But we're not like that. Our shit isn't bullshit, it's *real*. Gotta be ready to handle it, though … to show how you're willing to pay the price. That you can *stand* knowing this sort of secret."

The crowd's stepped back by this point, clustered to hide exactly what's happening with the cabinet's slick red doors. Behind them, I can hear a couple of flunkies wrestling with the gilded handles, grunting in effort as they heave it open and pull out *something* heavy enough to scrape the floor beneath. The ones in front grin a bit to themselves, eyes studying our faces. Oh, they want a reaction, can't wait to see it, that first moment when—whatever it is we're gonna end up looking at—registers. Not that Pixie-Cut even seems to notice, her gaze still riveted to the Shrike's own, chest heaving pornographically.

"No rituals," Shrike goes on, smiling even wider. "All you need to do is see it. 'Cause when you do, I'll look at you, and I'll just *know*. That simple."

I nod, slightly. Pixie-Cut swallows, quick and dry enough I know she's going to ask, which means I don't have to. Blurting out, a second later: "Know *what?*"

"If you're one of us, of course."

He turns, smoothly, like he's rehearsed it. Steps aside to show what's standing there: a triangle of tarnished brass, three coiled legs topped with a wide, flat metal bowl big enough to wash in, and who knows, maybe that's what it was originally meant for. There's a half-mirror set above it, after all, fanned out like a glass ruff behind the thing that sits inside, haloing its awful-ness in sullen, splintered light.

A gasp, from Pixie-Cut. While from everyone else—even the Shrike—comes a long, slow breath, drawn out rather than in. Half religious awe, half physical pleasure, admixed with just a hint of happy recognition: So *beautiful*, this artifact, this thing we serve and own. This thing that owns *us*.

It's really hard not to laugh, watching the other girl's face change. Watching her suddenly grasp that this isn't a joke or a piece of ego-boo, simple playacting. That when they crow about violence wreaked on anyone who pisses them off, they actually *mean* it, and the only right move for any still-halfway sane and moral person who finds themselves in this particular situation is to scream and run forever.

Neither of which she has the brains to do, of course. Instead—

"That's a *head*," she blurts out; can't stop herself from doing it, poor bint. Like she genuinely thinks maybe someone in here just hasn't noticed yet, and needs to know.

"It is," the Shrike agrees.

"A head ..."

"Yes."

"You guys ... *killed* somebody ..."

The Shrike smiles, slightly. "Not exactly," he replies.

Which is when the head opens its eyes and blinks at us, blearily. Like we just woke it up. Like it's *pissed*.

Around us, the crowd whoops and claps. One of them gives this weird crooning laugh, a baby's crow of pure delight. The head opens its mouth, lips drawing back in a snarl, the corners slightly torn—think it'd be hissing, if it only still had a voice-box instead of that ragged bit of gristle and skin where the neck's been sliced through right underneath the jaw. The slightly uneven mixture of bone, tendon, and sluggish black grue prevents it from standing straight up like it's on a pedestal, so it has to sit cocked sidelong instead, off-kilter.

Pixie-Cut is shocked silent now, for which I don't blame her. The head in the bowl rolls bloodshot, ice-coloured eyes up at us, lids flickering spasmodically—I see its pupils narrow horizontally, u-shaped, cephalopodal. Its filthy mat of hair is snarled to the point I can't tell its original colour, let alone whether it's supposed to be curly or straight. The face, both gaunt and flat, has skin like black volcanic beach-sand, cheekbones like napped flint. The teeth are stained brown, serrated edges sharp enough to glint in the candlelight. Its jaws work up and down, trying to bite at empty air. Its nostrils flare, eyes snapping back and forth between me and Pixie-Cut, who's started to make a noise like a balloon deflating. I raise my eyebrows.

"Someone's not too good with surprises, is she?" I ask the Shrike, as his cult explodes in laughter around us. He doesn't reply, though; only sighs, like he's seen this before. Then he glances at me—I try to look thrilled, or not disgusted, at the very least—before nodding to the others.

They're on Pixie-Cut before she's even finished taking her first step backwards, one on each arm, one behind her; Green Highlights yanks her head back and cuts her throat with a big kitchen knife, while the other two shove her hard, backwards, into the cast-iron clawfoot bathtub they dragged up behind us during the Shrike's little speech. She trips over the edge, hands still trying to staunch her wound, quick enough her head slams into the tub's metal floor, ending her struggles instantly. And then there's only the sound of liquid, hot enough to steam a bit, glugging into the tub.

There's an odd little beat of silence, as if even the Shrike's startled how fast she went down. It sets me back a moment myself, truth told. Can't feel too much sympathy for Pixie-Cut; she wanted what these gobshites are selling, after all ... just couldn't reckon the real price, not 'til it was too late. But it still hits hard sometimes, seeing life end like that: so sharp, so sudden, a blank face on a mound of cooling meat. Meat which used to be a person.

I'll probably go the same, one day—too fast to see it coming, let alone feel it happening.

The Shrike recovers himself, with a little shiver. He leans down and grabs Pixie-Cut's belt, hauling at the corpse 'til he folds her into one end of the tub, making room for her blood to pool at the other. Then he turns and reaches up, carefully, to lift the head from its dish. Hooks his fingers through knots of hair over its ears and makes sure to stay well shy of the teeth—slow and steady, same way a smith uses tongs to carry a casting cup full of molten metal. Gasps and whispers ripple through the crowd; they back away as he brings it within sight of the tub, which sets its jaws working even faster; the teeth grind against each other, making an eerie sort of *zizzz*, so much like flint striking I almost expect to see sparks fly from the mouth. But all that comes out is a slice of tongue, liver-coloured, torn where hunger's made it chew at itself.

"Who drinks first?" the Shrike asks, that same hyper, cultish, too-happy tone back in his voice. To which all the rest of 'em yell back, pretty much as one—

"*She* does!"

"That's right. Her first, then us. Blood in and blood out, blood come 'round and back again like every full moon, every time, forever." Turning to me, then, with a return of that oh-so-charming smile, of his: "And you drink too, of course, if you want to. Because ... you *do* want to, don't you?"

And me, I don't even spare Pixie-Cut a blink, since that'd put me in the tub right along with her, most likely. Just hold his gaze instead, coolly, and reply, as I do—

"Wouldn't have come here in the first place if I didn't."

"Smart girl," he says, approvingly. And lowers the head into the blood.

The moment he withdraws his hand, they all surge forwards, gathering 'round with avid eyes and panting mouths. I let the crowd carry me, let *my* mouth hang open too, trying not to breathe too deep; can't let the scent get to me. Not just yet.

The change starts the instant the head sets down. Swollen threads of reddish-purple tissue crack their way through the sand-black skin, spiralling up jawline and cheekbones like time-lapse footage of vines growing, inflating out of nowhere. The eyes widen, their slotted pupils rippling, blooming circular; irises darken, sclera flushing abruptly clear—alert, aware, *human*. The lips plump out, tongue soft instead of shrivelled, blushing from purple back to pink the way jerky soaks up water. Beneath the black outer crust, smooth brown skin wells up, splitting it apart and shedding it in a rain of dark flakes; dust powders off the teeth, bleaching to old ivory, new ivory, salt-white. Even the hair thickens, darker and sleeker under its entangling slick of dirt.

All of a sudden, the thing in the tub is a living woman's head, face distorted with rage, eyes flashing around to glare at all of them, mouth shaping curses none of them would understand even if they could lip-read. The sight only makes them laugh, and applaud; Metal-Face actually leans down and mouths a version of her own words exaggeratedly back at her, like he's imitating a bad kung-fu movie dub. That just gets *more* laughs, making me sigh in disgust, if only on the inside. These bloody kids. No respect for anything, them. Not even themselves.

"Is that safe?" I distract Metal-Face by asking, when I can't stand to watch any more. "I mean ... you're not supposed to look 'em in the eyes, right?"

He makes a raspberry noise, scoffing. "Nah, bitch can't tell you to do shit, not without lungs—just glowers at you, way she's doin' now. It's kind of a turn-on, actually." He grins at me, confidentially. I make myself grin back, choking down the spiky knot of fury in my gut. "'Sides which, sometimes if you get close enough, you can even kinda tell what she's thinking ... you know, like all the stuff she wants to do to us for cuttin' her up in the first place, and yadda yadda. Like sharing somebody else's dream, and you're starrin' in it. Know what I mean?"

"I think so."

"You'll find out soon enough. It's trippy as hell."

The Shrike grabs the head by her hair again, lifting it high. The throat's ragged, severed edges having lengthened, strands of tissue twining down the way an avocado grows tendrils if you stick it in a glass of water, still soaking up red drops. I can see the white of bone amongst raw flesh—half a new vertebra straining to form itself, maybe—and the twin holes of trachea and esophagus. It's fascinating, if queasily so. The Shrike holds her above his face and shakes the drops into his open mouth, gulping them down, shuddering like it burns him good. Blood like scotch, like tequila, like mescal. Like Black Death vodka. Then he brings the head back down and smiles, right into her raging, champing face.

Next to him, Mr. Anime Chimera hands over yet another knife; no ripped-off cooking tool, this one, but a big, ugly thing with an ulna-length blade and a handle made from antler, fit to gut a wild boar with. The Shrike takes it, spins it like some hibachi grill chef at a teppanyaki restaurant. The head snarls at the sight.

"Open up, baby," he tells her—practically purrs it—before he jams the blade in between her jaws, stabbing through tongue and soft palate alike with a squelch, then slicing back and forth out through both cheeks with a flourish deft enough I know the son of a bitch must actually have *practiced*. Her mouth rips open in a soundless scream, tearing the wounds wider; I can see the helpless agony in her eyes before the Shrike drops the knife, forces the lower jaw shut and slams his mouth against her ruined lips, sucking up the spurting blood the way one of my old factory-floor mates might've slurped up the froth off the all-sorts keg's spigot when no one was looking—that hideous mixture of dregs sold for whatever pittance got offered at the local boozer's, right between the rat-fighting pit and the hanging meat. The bottom half of his face is a crimson mask by the time he's done, white eyes glaring through the spatters above it.

He raises the head high. His teeth are sharper. His nails have sprouted into claws. He howls, and his flunkies all howl back at him. For the first time, there's a note in their voices sends ice over my skin. They're stupid petty slags, these infants, but they're still monsters. Can't go forgetting that.

Shrike-boy turns the head so the mouth is facing away and holds it out, like an Aztec might show off a fresh-cut heart before throwing it into the flames. These blood-junkies all scramble up to it in a line, each one gulping down as much as they can before the rush knocks them crazy-eyed and reeling, stumbling away to make room for the next. Every few drinks there's a pause as the Shrike reopens the gaping wounds in her face, which keep trying to close. And then it's my turn, right at the last. Bastards actually start chanting, like it's a frat party, while Shrikey lifts the head towards my face.

I tip my head forward, touching foreheads with the thing like we're old friends. Through slitted eyes I see the head's nostrils flare; it can't breathe, but this close, my scent's got to be in its nose all the same. Any luck, that'll be enough.

I'm sorry, I think, trying to will the words inside her skull. *You've suffered so much, taken so much insult, such ... indignity. But this is the last time, I promise.*

(*We promise.*)

I press my mouth to the hot, sodden, shredded lips and smear my own with the run-off, forcing dry-swallow after dry-swallow to make as if I'm drinking. Trying not to think about how, if the Shrike relaxes his grip an instant, she could take my nose and lips off with one bite; *probably* won't, if she's recognized whose spoor lies on me, and yet. At last I pull away, do my best job of screaming at the roof like the rest of them, and then suddenly they're all around me—hugging me, pounding my back, kissing my cheeks and forehead and red, dripping mouth. I grin back and let them kiss me, let the orgy take me, even though I want to puke.

Metal-Face flops onto the mattress beside me, naked and grinning, blood-mask already drying to powder. "Rush, huh?" he sniggers, propping himself up on his elbows. "Like crack and meth and MDMA all together, an' it lasts for weeks. Barely need to sleep, and it never takes more'n five minutes to get it back up again ..."

He rolls over and gestures proudly down at himself, like: see? (Schwing!) I drag my hand over my eyes, trying to look too shagged-out for him, stifling the urge to kick him there as hard as I can. If he senses it, it doesn't bother him.

"Don't worry," he laughs. "You're one of us now. We don't do anything we don't want. That's for them. Out there." He lies back and grins at the ceiling, letting out a long, slow, happy breath. "There are," he tells me, "so ... many ... little bitches out there never got told 'no' in their life, you know that? So many assholes think they own the world. That it owes them." He holds his hands up, drawing his lips back in a silent snarl, flexing the claws on his fingers so they slide in and out. "I live for that moment," he confides. "When I catch them, and they realize it's just me and them. And everything they thought kept them safe, their money, their looks, their family, their guns, some of 'em ... none of it means shit. I look in their eyes, and I know no matter how many pills they take, they're never gonna sleep again without screaming."

"That's why we try not to kill, you know?" he adds, suddenly earnest, in some weird mentoring-big-brother mode. "Like the Shrike says, anybody can kill. That's nothing. Leaving someone alive, and broken, and stuck that way, like a worm on a hook ..." His gaze defocuses; the claws retract. "That's what it's really like."

"What what's really like?"

His eyes snap back to mine, looking almost startled.

"To be God," he says, simply.

Can't think of an answer to this that doesn't involve murder, so I just shut up. Not that I give two shits about God if he's even up there, and my own jury is still very much out on that.

Against the wall where the Shrike flung my jacket after pulling it off me, I can see the alert light flickering on my phone, fallen from pocket to floor.

Finally.

I slip my panties on, quick and quiet. The rest can wait. I step over the Shrike, heading for the cabinet. He blinks after me, clearly taken aback by how fast and steady I'm suddenly moving, but too blood-drunk to quite realize what's going on. And then, before comprehension can hit, I'm back, his big fancy gutting knife in my hand. Down on my knees, free hand slamming his arm down, *whack*. It's a good knife, no denying that. Takes his hand clean off, quick as a guillotine.

Shrike's mouth opens ludicrously wide, his eyes bulging. He grabs his spurting wrist, so choked with shock he can't even get a scream out, only a kind of rattling gasp. The blood dulls pain, but I think it must really just be plain failure to understand what happened—he's gotten far too used to invulnerability. I don't give him time to recover. I grab up his iPhone from where he left it, on a cabinet shelf, then weave deftly through the rest of the junkies to the door. His thumb activates the phone, and the security code's pre-entered on the app.

I shake my head, amused. "Sloppy, sloppy," I murmur, triggering the app as I toss the Shrike's hand over my shoulder.

The door unlocks with an audible clunk. I pull it back.

The woman who stands there is—as ever—the most lovely thing I've ever seen: Angel-tall, her eyes and hair the same shiny black, skin the colour of rose-gold buffed with silk. When she smiles at me I feel dizzy, lit from within, ready once more to beg to be drained to death's point again and again, living forever in that moment just before my heart starts to stutter and my breath to catch, my blood mainly plasma, sucked transparent. I start to kneel, but she lifts me back up, effortlessly.

"Not tonight," she murmurs, and I know it must be true. She always knows best, after all.

"Milady," I agree, instead. And bow my head.

The Shrike's roar cuts through the air, shocking the ghoul-junkies to their feet, turning the post-orgy haze instantly into a cold blast of fear and fury; they're all on their feet, crouching with claws out, sharpened teeth glinting through snarls. He staggers towards us, and I can see that his wrist's already begun healing—give him a couple of weeks and he'll have his hand back, not that he'll ever get to see it. "Who's this bitch—?"

"She's my boss." I grin at him, this time, feeling like I'm washing away a week's worth of sweat. And then I point over their heads, at the cabinet behind them. At the head in the dish. They turn like they can't help themselves, and I finally let myself laugh as they see what I see. They gasp, swear, a couple even shriek.

The head is smiling. And its eyes are wide with joy, even as tears spill down its cheeks, trickling into the rotten grue around its throat.

"My boss," I repeat, "and *her* sister."

Milady smiles, close-mouthed, and shrugs off her cloak; it puddles to the floor, leaving her body nude and shining in the candlelight, like polished wood. Her eyes throw back the candlelight in a yellow-orange glitter. The ghoul-junkies instinctively shrink back, wide-eyed and slack-jawed, looking as much dismayed as terrified—like children about to cry, thinking only *Oh shit, someone caught us they caught us they* caught *us!* And then Milady lets her mouth spring open, and a forest of dripping fangs bursts forth. A long, purple tongue lashes out, whipping back and forth; drops of smoking spittle fly across the room. One hits Green Highlights' face. She screams in flabbergasted agony and staggers back, hand over her cheek. When she takes it away, her smooth pretty skin is a raw patch of oozing lesions, like leprosy gone mad. That *really* freaks the shit out of them.

Except the Shrike. I'll give him this, he must have been the only one with enough brains to think about this possibility. He moves fast enough even I can't follow, scooping up his knife with his remaining hand and flashing across the floor. In the next instant the knife's sliced almost spine deep through Milady's neck, in and out, while his wrist-stump smashes into her stomach and drives her backwards. She grabs her throat, genuinely surprised, as blood slicks her breasts in a crimson flood. I can't repress a gasp. The Shrike pins her against the wall with his stump and poises the knife over her breast, point first.

"Head and heart, bitch," he rasps at her, panting. "Everything else in the stories, it's all bullshit—but the one thing they all agreed on? Head, and heart, and spilling your blood. How do you think I got hold of that thing in the first place?" A jerk of his head, back at the cabinet. Then turns his head, slowly, to glare at me, and asks exactly what I know he's gonna ask:

"... the hell are *you* laughing at?"

It takes a second to master myself. "Well—you, obviously," I finally force out, revelling in being able to use my real voice for the first time since this whole dance began. His eyes narrow. "Regular Van Helsing, you, eh? But I don't suppose it ever occurred to you that some vampires, they come from places *outside* Transylvania."

His flummoxed look only makes me laugh harder. Adding, as I do—

"Yeah, that's right. Like ... *this.*"

An unearthly noise rips through the air, between us: A sickening wet *crunch* like a hundred bones breaking at once, followed by a glutinous, bubbling, drawn-out squelch. Milady lifts her head, seeming to stand up taller and taller and taller yet, even taller still, as her blood-smeared body slips downward out of the Shrike's one-armed wrist pin and thuds to the floor. The torn skin of her sliced-open neck stretches wide, like a sphincter, shitting out a viscous tangle of pink and scarlet, purple and yellow. The acrid sour stink of acid billows into the room, so strong the Shrike stumbles backwards and half a dozen of the cultists double over, retching. Down against the wall like some cast-aside doll with her skull popped off, legs slid out in front of her beneath, an abandoned toy made from flesh. And then ...

Then, Milady floats free, glorious as some bee-orchid floating on the tide, her beautiful head sat proud atop a hovering mass of slimy, shining viscera. Flowers of breast-fat cling to her fluttering lungs, her unshelled heart hammering fast enough to spurt blood with every beat, a thready red halo, jet upon jet upon jet. Her nude spine whipping like a wet glass-snake, a legless lizard, all scale and tail.

Penanggalan, *they named my kind, in my homeland long ago,* she told me, the night we met, laughing at my fumbling attempt to shape my South-wark-flavoured lips 'round the word. Still can't really pronounce it, even now, but she never did make me try again, after that night.

Just the sight's enough to break some of them. Metal-Face is one, exploding into a frantic screaming sprint for the door, face stretched and blind with the terror the vicious little idiot thought a god never needed to feel again. He's not as fast as the Shrike, but he's still faster than a human—and it's not enough. Milady's tongue whiplashes through him like a razor, turning off his scream in a gurgle. He hits the floor in two pieces, body fountaining blood and his piercings clacking as his head rolls away. Howls, wails, and screams drown the room once more; this time, though, there's no triumph, no joy. None but hers.

Milady floats forward as the blood-junkies cower away, sobbing, trying to push themselves back into the walls. I slam the door hard behind me, hearing it lock—should've kept the hand, shouldn't I? Ah, well, spilled milk; find it later, easy enough—and bend down to scoop Milady's abandoned body up by hooking my arms under hers, dragging it after her. The head is still grinning, still crying, as Milady draws up before it and lowers her eyes, her own tears welling up in sympathy.

"*Sister*," she says, voice gurgling like vinegar through old, slimy pipes. "*I am ... so sorry we could not be here sooner.*" Gives a sigh like bagpipes tuning up, and cuts her wet eyes my way. I carry Milady's skin-suit to the cabinet and set it down, seated against the side, empty neck gaping upwards. Then I lift her sister's head—no need to be careful now—and set it onto the hole, positioning it carefully. Within an instant, I feel it jolt and twist in my hands; see the skin rippling as tissue weaves to tissue, sealing fast. The body jerks, hands thrown high, grabbing at the head to make sure it's on tight. A second of startlement, right before she knows she's truly free once more. Then she throws her head back, mouth wide in soundless laughter.

At that, Milady laughs too, a sound like a tar pit swallowing something helpless. Sister turns to me. *Can you still read lips, little one?* she mouths. I nod. Her grin turns savage. *Then tell them this.* She gives me the words, and as she stands, her fangs sliding out, I turn to the cowering crowd, and say:

"You owe this woman a *lot* of blood."

It's a different sort of orgy, after that. Milady lets her sister do most of it, though she joins in when the ghouls start fighting back at last, terror supercharging their strength and fury rather than sending them running; if they knew how to fight, or fight together, even Milady might have trouble with these numbers. But they don't. I go back to the door and stand guard, meanwhile, the Shrike's knife in my hand, making sure none of them escape. Which is why I get a great little surprise bonus when the boy himself comes at me, having managed to grab his iPhone again—I hear the door unlock behind me, as we struggle. Well, I've earned a little fun for myself, haven't I? So I step aside, let him by, watch him use that same blinding speed through the door and up the stairs—

Which is when I show him *my* speed. My strength. Catch him by the ankle just before he reaches the upper door, and with one hand I twist and whip him back down into the subcellar, hard enough to bounce him a yard high off the mattresses when he hits. Then I jump back down onto him and hamstring him in both legs, flourishing the knife the way he did when he carved up Sister's face—not that he'll appreciate that irony, but I do. I flip him over, then sit back down on his stomach, crushing the remaining breath out of him.

Most people when they know they're beat, they just crumple. Credit where credit's due, the Shrike isn't one of them. He glares up at me. "You *bitch*," he rasps, repeating himself. "Go ahead, kill me. I'll still die something you'll never be: *Free*. You work for monsters. I ... made the monsters ... work for *me*."

Believes it, too, even now; well, well. Some prats, they never learn.

So I cup his face in my hands and lean down, suddenly not angry any more. Just tired. "We're all monsters to somebody," I tell him, and twist, *hard*.

Still got enough of Sister's blood in him the broken neck won't kill him, right away. Nor will what I do next, which is to chop off every limb at elbow and knee; his boosted metabolism's sealed up the first amputation before I finish the last. He doesn't feel the pain, but I can see it in his eyes: inside, he's screaming. And he'll scream until Milady and Sister finish him.

I take a deep breath, then, and let myself collapse sideways, finally resting, not moving as warm blood slowly pools 'round me like a comforting bath. Nobody left alive that's capable of running, not any more. And as always, my mind goes back to the past ... my past, long past, a hundred years and more. When I made my choice, the choice *he* thought was such a joke, and why.

Milady wasn't the first monster I ever met, you see. But she was the one that changed me.

On the factory floor, we were all of us just meat to the owners, one mere mistake away from being maimed or killed, lit on fire or sliced apart by machinery gone wrong. I once knew a girl licked matches for a living, ha'penny a week, and called it good; she died with her face gone soft and her teeth rotted out, unable to eat for fear of choking on bits of her own phosphorus-poisoned jaw. Just like the hat-makers who went mad from mercurous nitrate fumes, or the dyers who puked themselves to death turning out yards of arsenic green just because it was that year's most fashionable shade, or the poor Radium Girls in their turn, glowing in the dark while their bones decayed from the inside-out.

But me, I was lucky; Milady took me away from all that. Fed me her blood, and fed on mine, though never enough to turn me. Only enough to bind us together and keep us bound so I could do her daytime work throughout the years, the centuries. 'Til I knew myself older by far than almost any other ghoul in North America, if not the whole world. I never had to give up the sun, or the taste of bread, or anything else most true humans think make their tiny, fragmentary, mirror-shard fragile mockery of a life worth living. I never had to give up nothing I didn't want to, did I? And I never, ever will.

The Shrike thought he'd got it made, breaking the chain like he did: all the perks and none of the labour, none of that hunger to love and serve and be mastered. Bloody child, like I said. But I'm no Renfield, nor is Milady any sort of Dracula. It's far more like being an apprentice than a mere employee. Far more like being someone's adopted child, loved for her dreams as well as her skills, her capacity to love and *be* loved. And no human gets in the way of that, ever.

But I'm something else now—a monster, a god. Servant to a god, sole priestess of She I worship. It's a better life than any I ever hoped to have, back when, or could ever hope to have, in future.

Milady comes—mother-lover, endless fount of knowledge, strength, power. *Eternity.*

Who raises me back up now from where I lie cocooned in these false ghouls' blood, her rescued sister at her side, and kisses my cheek, my forehead, my mouth.

Who licks the excess from me like a cat cleaning her kitten only to take my lower lip between hers and nip it lightly, tattooing it with the sacred symbol of her bite.

Who lifts me high in her cold embrace, her guts twining 'round me like tentacles, digestive acids burning at my skin, and cradles me against her doubly-naked bosom, pumping with stolen blood.

"My little London sparrow, my soot-grimed dockyards orphan," she calls me, knowing how I can't help but shiver with delight at her voice. "My lovely, faithful, poison-hearted little cannibal girl."

"Always, Milady."

Stroking my face, thumbing my eyelids closed, as the ecstasy comes on me —that deep, slackening, satisfied sleep which always comes after true slaughter. These fools thought they knew it, but they didn't know the half; couldn't, could they? No human ever will.

"My sweet, poor little butcher-bird."

I close my eyes and dream, glad yet once more how when death finally did come for me, it had nothing at all to do with industry. And in the dark behind my eyes, I see only red, the same endless hot salt sea that laps inside Milady's skull, the same thing that will surely drown me, eventually—take me down, drag me deep and ingest me, never letting me surface again until my flesh has changed to sharp-edged, quartz-toothed pearl, fit to stand at her side instead of kneeling before her. The same thing which will finally lick the last, sad taste of my humanity from me forever and spit me back out, re-born into darkness.

"Dirt covered, blood smeared, and hungry, he clawed his way back."

CRACK OF THE BAT

T.J. TRANCHELL

Flanagan stumbled into a gas station with a wall calendar behind the counter. His legs had not quite remembered their function, but his arms ached from digging himself out of the ground moments before. As his eyes adjusted to the various lights—the natural sun, which he missed, and the unnatural glowing orbs all around him—he saw the calendar. Ninety years in a hole he'd buried himself in and crawled out of without even thinking about it. No sun, no moon, no stars. No food, no water ... only the grumbling inside him that had pushed him to emerge.

The pain didn't come just from his stomach, but from every inch of him. He focused, thinking it was his heart or his lungs, but his focus revealed neither to be active. He licked his dry lips, searching for hunger spit, and listened to the rustle of his tongue scrape over dead skin.

"Hey, man, no junkies in here, okay?" said the young man from behind the counter. Flanagan could hear the man's nervous breathing but not his own. Behind the man's shoulder was the calendar proclaiming the year to be 2023. "If you yark on the floor, I have to clean it up. If you pass out, I have to call the cops."

Avoiding eye contact with Flanagan, the man—Gill, according to a tag on his shirt that Flanagan could see clear as day from ten yards away—held up a glowing rectangle, wielding it as if it were important. In what seemed like one step, Flanagan closed the gap, knocked the object from the clerk's hand, and fastened his teeth on the man's throat. A heartbeat later, Flanagan tore the man's larynx away and drank the spurting blood like he'd drank water from a pump as a child. The breathing and beating heart sounds from the man ceased and Flanagan was left with the incessant buzzing of the store's lights, the cars zooming by outside, and voices nearing the door he had entered only moments before.

As he ran, he remembered. He remembered running for joy and glory. He remembered running with fear. As he used muscles that had lain dormant for nearly a century, he could hear the door of the gas station open and the screams that followed. One scream chased him from inside his own mind.

Flanagan hung from a low limb, his broken bat beneath his swaying feet. The blood vessels in his eyes began to burst, filling his vision with red. Looking, as much as he could, to the left, he saw the men who'd beaten him with his own bat before hanging him, running east back toward town. To the west, into the sunset, ran Padgett. Running wasn't quite right; plodding quickly was more accurate. Padgett's legs—thunderous legs that earlier in the day had driven Padgett to three stolen bases and four hits including a triple—had taken Flanagan's bat multiple times before the men turned the ashwood onto its owner.

Run, Flanagan thought. Whether he was happy about his friend getting away alive or that the bastards who'd picked a fight were heading the other way, he couldn't be sure.

Feet swinging in the air, Flanagan died.

Flanagan and Padgett had formed a rare combination that year. Flanagan turned pink every summer, his Irish skin not meant for the constant sunshine of playing second base. Padgett told Flanagan that he got sunburnt, too, but he and the other colored players on the Bismarck Flames hid it better than their white teammates. Padgett and Flanagan converted fifty-six double plays before their midsummer break in 1933. If the North Dakota league they played in had an all-star team, they'd have been on it.

Taking the team south for two weeks of exhibition games proved to be an error.

Flanagan hailed from Utah, a second-generation Mormon immigrant who'd never seen a black man until he signed on with the Flames. Like his new northern plains neighbors, he didn't think he held anything against the colored, but his ignorance caught up to him. Flanagan offered to bunk with Padgett, seeing as how they'd form the middle infield together. The team was integrated, but the whites and the blacks hadn't shared rooms before. Flanagan didn't know any better.

He grew to know, and seeing as how his parents taught him to love his neighbor as himself, befriending Padgett and his other colored teammates came naturally. The folks down in Kansas didn't see it that way.

"Hey, Cupid, how much they pay you to play with the monkeys," a large man said as pink-skinned Flanagan stepped up for his first at-bat. "You a zookeeper instead of a ballplayer?"

Flanagan had heard worse, but at the Flames home field, rabble-rousers like that were tossed and never came back. Here, that zookeeper taunt earned the man a round of applause. The insults continued throughout the game, which the Flames won 7-2.

The next-to-last batter for the opposing team hit a one-bouncer right at Flanagan. He snapped the ball out of the dirt and turned to throw to first. Before launching the ball, he winked at his first baseman and threw the ball into the stands. Reynolds, the white first baseman, turned to see it hit the zookeeper heckler square in the mouth. The umpire called a throwing error, but the man on first got picked off trying to steal second, ending the game. Flanagan put the final tag on the runner's shoulder and quietly headed for the dugout.

———

Suspended from the tree, eyes closed and dead, Flanagan first refused to acknowledge the bite on his neck and the impact of the ground as he fell.

He never saw whoever had sliced through the rope and he spent an eternity wondering how long he had hung there.

As the sun rose, Flanagan had instinctually buried himself in the ground, the soft earth giving way as if he were a dog hiding a bone.

Now, under the cover of dark—dirt-covered, blood-smeared, and hungry —he clawed his way back to the surface. The night sky loomed above him. Bright lights from buildings spotted what had been empty plains. The tree he'd died from was a stump, and a sign with its own lights proclaimed the spot to be the future home of something called a mall. Only one of the lights glowed and the sign looked almost as beat up as Flanagan felt.

He turned, looking for his destroyed bat, saw no sign of it, tried to spit on the could but could muster no saliva, and walked away.

The heckler and his friends caught Padgett and Flanagan near the hotel bar. Finn Stevenson, the owner of the Flames, put them up in the nicest hotel they'd ever had, which wasn't saying much. Flanagan had heard the beds were better than straw-filled mattresses, but nothing to write home about. He and Padgett never found out. Flanagan had hoped to bring Padgett a real drink from the bar, but caught the younger man running from the colored section into the whites' section, followed by the heckler and three others from the game. Flanagan followed them all out and into the field near the large tree. On the way, he'd grabbed his ashwood bat from the equipment bag by the door.

He saw one end of the rope in the smallest man's hands and the other, tied into a noose, in the big heckler's hands. The other two men held Padgett, bleeding from his nose, one eye already swelling. Padgett tried to shoo Flanagan away, but Flanagan gripped his bat tighter and closed in.

The first swing connected with the large man's neck. The noose end fell to the ground.

The men holding Padgett let go and charged Flanagan, who had cocked his arms, ready for the next pitch. One went high and one went low. Flanagan had always been a sucker for the low and outside meatballs and smashed the barrel right into the low man's crotch. The high man caught Flanagan's backswing on the jaw, rattling him but not knocking him down.

As he prepared to swing again, Flanagan felt the rope around his ankles and then his face hit the ground.

The small man, smarter than he looked, had managed to trip up Flanagan while he wasn't looking. The big heckler, recovered enough from the blow to the neck, now had Flanagan's bat.

"Well, lookee here, boys," the heckler said. "The zookeeper came to rescue his chimp."

"Fu—" Flanagan started, then felt his bat crash into his teeth. He absorbed a few more strikes as the rope was loosened from his feet and the noose put around his neck.

Padgett stayed a safe distance away, as he'd tried to warn Flanagan to do. Once Flanagan could see his friend, he did his best to mouth *run.*

Then his feet disconnected from the earth and the four men took turns hitting him with his own bat until it broke. They pulled together on the rope, finding a smaller tree to tie the other end to, and left Flanagan to die.

Nothing seemed familiar. The tumultuous world crashed against Flanagan's ears, but he didn't stop running. His belly felt full for only a brief time and that driving hunger returned. The pangs propelled him, would not let him stop.

Ahead, he saw a clearing that at first he thought was a meadow. As he neared, he saw the meadow was black and filled with what looked like motor cars from the comics some of the ballplayers passed around in the clubhouse.

Ninety years, he thought. *I was ... gone ... for ninety years.*

The black meadow ended at a large brick façade. Slowing his pace, Flanagan turned and saw photographs of baseballs and bats, and what must be the players in this futuristic date. And then he saw Padgett.

The statue loomed over Flanagan. Padgett, bronzed and twice his normal size, in full stride toward the next base. Flanagan stopped, thinking he'd need to catch his breath, but found he didn't need to breathe. Slowly, he approached the bronze vision of his old friend. The memorial plaque filled him in.

THEODORE ABRAHAM PADGETT
1912-1999

Player-Coach-Owner
A Kansas Baseball Legend

Flanagan stared at the plaque and the statue, then down at himself. His shredded clothes looked like the uniform the bronze Padgett wore. He ran his hands down his legs, across his chest, and around his neck. There, he felt a knot of skin and muscle, the scar left by the rope he'd hung from. Nearer his shoulder, another lump of scar had formed, but the surrounding edges resembled a ring of teeth, rather than a loop of rope. He closed his eyes and fell to the ground.

Only darkness. No heartbeat, no blood pulsing through his veins, no feeling of the air between the ground and his feet. Flanagan's eyes opened and he felt teeth—some sharp and pointed, others meant to grind meat into nutrition—just below the noose around his neck. He wanted to kick and flail, but whatever bit into him had its arms around his arms and its legs pinning his together. The teeth gnawed at his skin. He expected to feel the blood rush out and into the mouth of this unseen creature. Instead, Flanagan felt only emptiness. He gave himself up to the void and prayed for a return to the dark.

I don't know if you will remain dead or come back, Flanagan felt a voice say. *If you do return, feed.*

The mouth let go with a final guzzling noise that was quickly followed by the snap of the rope breaking. Flanagan fell atop his broken bat but registered only its presence, not pain. *Dig,* he heard the voice say and so he did.

On the opposite side of the plaque memorializing Padgett was another smaller inscription. Reading it, Flanagan began to sense the emptiness inside him again.

For My Friend Flanagan
Wherever You Are

He Fought For Me
Against the Worst of You
T.A.P.

Flanagan wanted to smile but could not. The emptiness turned to hunger. The command from the voice filled his mind. *FEED.*

"Hey, Buddy, you okay?" said a new voice. "We don't play games during Halloween, friend. You should get out of that costume." The hand reached out toward Flanagan's shoulder and he felt it before it could touch him.

He spun, grabbing the man's arms and pulled its owner next to him. Flanagan was sure he could hear the man's next—and last—thought. *You smell like something outta the zoo,* and that was all Flanagan needed to hear.

A slight adjustment of his grip allowed Flanagan to tear the arm from its socket. The rest of the body flopped to the ground.

Other people, so many in baseball jerseys like the one he had been so proud to wear, rushed toward the two men.

Flanagan swung the severed arm around like a bat at anyone who closed the gap, spraying what blood remained in the limb across white home jerseys and their gray road counterparts. He lifted the biceps area to his mouth and tore a piece from it, feeling his own teeth become more accustomed to rending flesh as he did so. He chewed as the jeers and taunts increased.

"Somebody stop him!"

"He's some kind of animal."

"Are you sure it's human?"

"Where are the cops?"

"If I'd had my gun, I'd put it down."

Flanagan sought that voice, the most threatening of them. The stocky man reminded him of someone from before: the heckler from his final game.

Flanagan bull-rushed the man, never giving him a chance to get his guard up. Wrapping his arms around the man, Flanagan buried his face in the man's neck, biting and tearing, all while squeezing the air out of him. They fell, Flanagan atop the man akin to the one who'd orchestrated Flanagan's first death. Flanagan continued to chomp and slurp, filling his stomach and impervious the gathered crowd around him.

Then came a familiar and oddly comforting whistle: a bat slicing through the air at its target. The target, however, was not a white, leather-covered baseball. Rather, the bat lined up square with the back of Flanagan's skull. Flanagan had lived for that sound: the solid wood crash against the hurled orb. The crack of the bat and the cheers of the crowd brought a smile to his bloodied face. He was sure they cheered for him.

Hands grabbed at him and whatever lived in his stomach begged him to gnash at the fingers, but he could not. The hands flipped him so that he stared into the sky. He heard the voices—*like some kind of animal ... you can still smell him ... where did he come from ... some gas station clerk down the road ... not a zoo for miles ... institute*—but didn't care. He felt something like a large finger then an entire hand pushing and entering his back. He looked down and saw one of Padgett's exaggerated feet. Turning one way then the other, he could see parts of each inscription.

"I'm here, friend," he whispered. "I'm here." The quiet came next, then the darkness. Then nothing.

A CLEAN KILL

JUSTIN GULESERIAN

iane watched moonlight shimmer on the buck's pelt. Black blood dried around two bullet-sized holes. One in the shoulder. The second in the throat. Lashed to the hood of the station wagon, the young whitetail looked smaller than it had when they carried it from camp. The road needed repair, and Greg sped. The deer's head bobbled.

"Slow down, Dad," Diane said.

"We're feeling the road more because of the extra weight. Don't worry, sweetie. We'll get home all right."

She kept her gaze on the whitetail, on the ropes digging into its fur. But she felt her father's eyes, his concerned expression, fall on her.

"It was your first time out," he said. "A four-pointer is nothing to be ashamed of."

"I shouldn't have taken the shot."

"If it was any bigger, we might not've been able to carry it out. Would've had to butcher it at camp."

"You've carried out bigger."

Greg chuckled. "I was a younger man once."

"How old do you think *he* was?"

"It's hard to say. Two. Maybe three years."

"Only two years?"

"Maybe three. Listen, sweetheart, we have to eat every ounce of your kill. And once we start, you're going to be very glad he's not a tough, grizzled old buck like me."

"It wasn't even a clean kill."

"Cleaner'n he might've got."

Diane recalled the rippling of muscle as the buck tensed, the way it staggered before regaining enough balance to bolt off into the woods. Two days of tracking blood, hoof prints, and scat. She'd spent weary hours staring into the fire, waiting for Greg to turn in, and still longer hours of waiting in the darkness of their tent for restless sleep to come.

Thump-thump! Bang! The station wagon hit a bump in the road, and the buck's head slammed off the passenger side-panel.

"Goddammit," Greg swore.

"Would you slow down, please?"

"We're fine. Just worried about the paint. Should've tied the head down tighter."

Sweat prickled Diane's scalp. She took off her hunting cap and shook out her shoulder-length hair. Headlights shone on the edges of the forest. Far ahead, the silhouette of pine tops on a hill turned its serrated edge on the evening sky. She pondered her father's words.

"Dad, what'd you mean by that? 'Cleaner than what he might've got.'"

"Well, you like reading about nature and such in your classes at the high school, right? Don't they teach you about death in the wild? Creatures in the wild don't die like Uncle Bill in his bed, all warm and cozy, with a full belly. It doesn't work that way. Death in the wild isn't—"

She caught a mere glimpse of an animal that darted across the road. Its hindquarters shone for an instant in the headlights before Greg swerved. Sleek black fur and a long bushy tail.

An elm rushed up to meet them. The station wagon coughed out its windshield, wrapped its fender around the trunk, greeting it like a long-lost friend. The buck burst free of its ties and landed at odd angles on the crumpled hood. Its tongue lolled on the windshield.

Father and daughter staggered to the road. Their phones showed no signals, so the pair tottered on, looking for some sign of help. Greg gripped his shoulder and groaned. Diane, who had hit her head against the window, felt dizzy and nauseated. Blood seeped from her right temple. Her neck throbbed.

They hadn't gone far before spotting little lights twinkling nearby, among the trees, and found the dirt path into the woods. It led to a wind-swept clearing, carpeted by a lawn of wild grasses in front of a cottage. Warm lights flickered from inside its windows. This was miles from anything resembling a town and there hadn't been another car on the road for the past two hours. Still, something gave Diane pause.

"There's no driveway," she said.

"Maybe they don't own a car," Greg said. "Christ, I hope they're not hermits. Hermits don't have doctors and don't keep painkillers."

A short wooden fence surrounded the cottage. Inside the gate, a narrow cobblestone path covered the few paces to the austere cottage of gray brick and plaster. Each round window, quartered by mullions, resembled a ship's portal and made the cottage appear to be adrift in a sea of windblown grass. A low roof of weatherworn shingles blanketed the cottage. Smoke billowed from a thin chimney.

One more glance at her father's wincing expression and Diane resolved to knock. They passed through the gate and approached the doorstep. Greg stood up as straight as his tired back and throbbing shoulder would allow. Diane tried to smooth her tousled hair and knocked at the door.

No sound came from within. Greg groaned in pain, cradling his arm. Diane grew impatient and tried the latch. It escaped her hand, and the door swung open, seeming almost weightless on its hinges. Greg called inside and was answered by a crackling of a fire and the smell of food.

Diane tugged at her father, and the two entered.

The cottage stood empty but showed every sign of recent occupation. A stone hearth was set into the far wall, with a trio of blazing logs in the fireplace. Two chairs and a bearskin rug lay before the hearth. Beside the hearth, there was a doorway that had been bricked off. A table stood in the center of the room, spread with breads, cheeses, wine, and a mason jar filled with clear liquid. A small oil lamp sat at one corner of the table and cast a soft, steady glow over the repast. On the left lay a single bed and cushions. On the right, a side door.

"Hello!" Diane called.

"Our host is probably out back," Greg said. "Maybe getting more wood for the fire. Let's have a look."

The pair shuffled toward the windows neighboring the side door. There was no one. The moon rose over the darkening trees and cast a spectral light into the clearing. Only the chirping and buzzing of insects could be heard from outside. Greg sighed and staggered to the table, eyeing its bountiful spread. With his good arm, he reached for the jar of clear liquid.

"Dad, what are you doing?"

Greg sniffed the contents of the jar.

"It's corn. I'd rather have pain pills. But any port in a storm, right?"

He managed a weak smile and took a drink. The smile faded and his face went slack.

"Wow," he said. The glass slipped from his fingers and shattered at his feet. He slumped to the floor and lay still.

Diane rushed to her father, thankful that his head had landed on his injured shoulder and not the stone floor. She stooped and shook him but couldn't rouse him. She felt his throat and found a pulse. His breath was shallow but steady.

She glanced at the puddle and shards of glass on the stone floor. She wondered how her father, a heavyweight when it came to liquor, could black out from a single sip of moonshine. It was the wreck, she decided, a delayed response to his injury. Yet she suspected it would be better to get outside until they could find their host. If nothing else, she could rouse him faster with fresh air.

Diane grabbed her father's arms and tugged. He was a heavy man, and her slight frame strained to drag him toward the door. She shuffled three tiny steps back before one of the floor's stones sank beneath her foot. A faint click came from somewhere below, followed by a shrill grating sound. The front door slammed shut and black iron bars slid down from the solid oak lintel. Diane let her father's arms fall, and she turned, feeling a surge of adrenaline that cleared her dizziness instantly.

"We meant no harm!" she called. "We're injured. We saw the lights of your cottage. Please help us!"

Wood popped in the fireplace.

In a panic, Diane ran to the small side door and tried the bronze knob. It wouldn't turn, and she discovered that her hand was now stuck to the knob, held by some transparent gum. On instinct, she yanked back her hand. As she pulled, the doorknob slid out from the door on a steel rod. She heard another faint click, followed by a sharp clack. She lost her balance and fell to the ground as a scythe whistled past her, coming within inches of her head. The blade sank into the solid wood of the door.

She gasped and reached up with her free hand, testing the blade with her thumb. It was razor sharp and oiled. The scythe's long handle led to a groove in the ceiling. She looked down to see a lock of hair, cleanly shorn from her head.

Easing to her feet, she tugged at her glued thumb, pulling harder until her thumb came free. Soon she was able to pull her palm free. Thinning strings of gum stretched between her hand and the doorknob. She brought trembling fingers to her nose. The scent was pungent but organic, maybe a sap of some kind. Rubbing her palms together, she turned to look at her father. He lay where she had left him, not stirring.

Looking for a means of possible escape, searching for any hint of another trap, Diane surveyed the cottage with new eyes. She could extinguish the fire and attempt to climb up the chimney, but it had, she realized, looked too narrow at the top for even her slender body to squeeze through it. She could try to force the side door, but its thickness was likely too great for someone of her size to break down. Then she saw the windows. They were small, too small for her father's bulk, but if she could break out the frame, they might have a chance of escape.

She reached over and tugged at the scythe. Whatever hidden joint attached it to the ceiling was holding it fast. Even the blade was sunk too far into the door for her to extract it.

A fire poker rested on the hearth. Suppressing the urge to run to it, she tiptoed to the fireplace. Every flagstone was suspect, and she tested each one with her sandaled toes before placing her full weight on it. Soon, she had made her way past the table and reached the two fireside chairs.

She was about to slide between the chairs when, from the corner of her eye, she spied something glinting at her ankles. Firelight reflected off a thin steel tripwire, stretched between the two chairs. Her breath caught as she took cautious steps over the wire and placed her foot on the bearskin rug. As she shifted her weight onto the rug, she heard a faint click, followed by a dull squeaking. A plate, hidden beneath the rug, sank beneath her feet.

The fireplace spewed gouts of flame, and Diane dove to one side. The paint on the chairs blistered and peeled, revealing glowing red iron beneath. Caution turned to mute terror, as she realized the truth of their situation. This wasn't a home set with protective traps. It was a trap, made to resemble a home.

She stood, aching, and picked up the fire poker. On a hunch, she threw it at one of the windows. The poker spun through the air, top over tail, then struck the nearest window. Behind the sound of breaking glass, another sound rang out, like hammer on anvil. The window's mullions were neither wood nor even soft lead, but tempered black iron.

The fresh oil on the scythe and the painted iron chairs told of careful maintenance and upkeep. Diane doubled over and cried. She feared she couldn't find a means of escape before whatever trapper built this cottage returned to check and clean his traps. The trapper who hunted people would enter the cottage and, slinking about the place with expert steps, would repaint the chairs, replace the broken glass, and ...

"He'll reset the traps!" Diane hissed. The mechanics of so many traps set into the floor would require a crawlspace beneath the cottage to house all the works. She reached out and tore the bearskin rug from its place before the fire.

Beneath the rug, a thin steel plate was set into the floor. Because the plate was meant to be covered by the rug, the trapper hadn't bothered to make it resemble part of the floor, and its fit among the flagstones wasn't entirely snug. A thin gap showed between the plate and the surrounding stones, perhaps just wide enough for the sharp end of a fire poker to be wedged between them.

She carefully retrieved the poker, then retraced her steps to the hearth, crouched, and pried at the plate's lip. She leaned in, using every available ounce of her weight to drive the poker farther in. When she had pushed the makeshift crowbar as far as it would go, she lifted her leg and stomped her sandaled foot on the poker's handle. The plate sprang into the air and came crashing down beside her. Diane shut her eyes until certain the falling plate hadn't triggered anymore traps.

She was safe, for the moment. Reaching with the fire poker, she lifted the oil lamp off the table and lowered it into the hole she had uncovered. She knelt and peered in. The scent of machine oil assaulted her nostrils, but it was the sight that made her gasp.

There was, as she had hoped, a narrow crawlspace between the floor and the ground, but the space was choked with the clockwork mechanics of traps. Floor plates led to jointed levers and pulleys, which in turn led to untold numbers of wheels, cogs, springs, oiled chains, and billows. The machinery formed a kind of maze, through which only the trapper could maneuver with any surety. And the task would be made all the more difficult when dragging her father in tow.

Diane held stock-still and eyed the floor, plotting her course over the floor to reach Greg, trying to recall which of the floor stones she had tested. A grinding sound came from behind her.

"But I haven't moved."

The bricked-up doorway next to the fireplace cottage divided. Something behind the wall gibbered in a hushed tone. Diane hesitated, reluctant to leave her father in the clutches of whatever chattering devil waited behind the bricks. She knew, however, that even if she could drag his body to the hole without springing a dozen traps, she would never be able to get him into the crawlspace in time. Shutting her eyes against the sight of her unconscious father, she turned and jumped down into the crawlspace.

Diane snatched the steel plate from where it lay on the floor, and slid the plate over her head, back into place. With one hand, she covered her mouth to muffle the sound of her own frantic breath. With the other, she extinguished the oil lamp. She waited and listened.

The bowels of the cottage sprang to life with busy clockwork machination. A clanking, puffing, squeaking symphony of cacophonic phrases played in every direction. Diane's eyes widened, adjusting to the dark. She could discern a faint spot of moonlight shining through a grate in the foundation. She crawled as fast as she dared toward the light, leaving the oil lamp behind, using the fire poker as a kind of antenna, to avoid being snagged by any of the works.

Above, she heard not two, but dozens of padded feet shuffling over the floor, moving in every direction. The uttering of a single voice became the gibbering of a throng. She whimpered. These weren't human voices. Her dizziness returned at the thought of her father lying helpless among those unnamable hosts.

She fought the dizziness by quickening her pace from a crawl to a scramble, bruising her face, shoulders, and hips against the cruel machinery.

Diane heard something behind her lift the plate she had pried from the floor. The sound of the gibbering grew louder as the plate was removed, and Diane could hear panting. She froze.

After what seemed an eternity, a wrench clanked against a lever as the unseen enemy began repairs on the trap. Diane scrambled forward and soon reached the grate on the edge of the foundation. She sat with her back against the cold brick and waited, calmed by the scent of wild grass through the grate.

The steel floor plate snapped back into place, muffling the sounds above. Diane rammed the fire poker into the grate and began prying.

Stubborn, the grate held. She repositioned herself, bracing her feet against a nearby pulley. She gripped the iron rod with both hands and threw her weight backward. The grate sprang free.

Frantically, she pulled herself through the small opening onto the ground outside—a wounded deer, springing into the relative safety of the woods. The night air cooled her, drying the sweat on her face. But her father. With a deep breath, she raised herself up and crept to one of the windows, the fire poker still in hand. Diane gasped and shuddered at the sight.

Separated from her by only a thin pane of glass, a writhing and inhuman drama played out. Several creatures, the size of small men, busied about the cottage. They had the elongated bodies of weasels, with sleek black fur and long bushy tails. They bore the eyes of thieves, intelligent and cunning. Dual slits, flaring with quick breath, served in place of noses. Dozens of saw-like teeth lined their wide mouths. Long black hair hung from their heads, and several wore it bound up in a single braid. On their wrists and ankles, they wore the mismatched jewelry and watches from half a dozen eras. Silver and gold rings hung from the creatures' pointed ears.

The creatures bent and twisted in their labor, alternating between twos and fours, walking and crawling. The top of the bed had been lifted, revealing a false bottom, from which the creatures pulled supplies. Each member of the throng had its own job. One repainted the scorched metal chairs. One sharpened and replaced the scythe. One swept up broken glass and replaced it with freshly poisoned drink. One, after a fruitless search for the lantern, took a candle from the bedside and placed it on the table. A stout and mangy thing lifted the bars from the front door by means of a lever, hidden beneath the bed. Finally, the repairs finished, the beasts crowded around the sleeping Greg, binding his wrists and ankles.

Diane felt pins and needles pricking their way from the base of her skull down her back and arms.

Six clawed hands gripped her father by the wrists and pulled toward the brick doorway. One held a large butcher's knife in its mouth. Another ran a flat tongue over its thin lips. The abduction was unbearable to watch and impossible to ignore. Diane took a sharp breath. The scream escaped her before she knew what she was doing. Beady eyes and furrowed brows shot up to the window.

Fear numbed her senses, her nerves singing, her vision clouded. She ran, half-blind, to the front of the house and burst through the front door. The smell of musk nearly overpowered her. Black beasts turned every twinkling eye upon the doorway. Lurching forward, she brought iron down on the first creature in reach. The thing's brittle skull caved beneath the blow. In an explosion of foul musk, the creatures sprang in every direction. They bounced off the walls and each other in a mad dash to their secret door. But the three who held Greg would not release their prey.

Gripping him by the shoulders, the beasts dragged Greg on his back in a hurried zigzag toward the brick door. Diane hopped and strode after them, stepping only where her father's body had passed over the flagstones. The beasts were practiced in their escape and were almost to the brick door.

Tossing away the iron poker, she dove, landing hard on her ribs. Ignoring the new agony in her side, she shot out both hands and managed to reach her father's ankles, holding on with every ounce of strength she could summon.

It was perhaps the pain in Greg's shoulder, aggravated by the tug-of-war, that roused him back to consciousness. He stirred and groaned. Diane pulled herself onto the small of her back and yanked again at his ankles.

"Let him go! Let him go! Let my father *go*!"

As if in answer to Greg's groaning or Diane's pleas, one of the creatures took the knife from his sibling's jaw. The butcher suspended his knife point above Greg's temple like a clock's stilled pendulum. The other two crouched low, pulling at his arms, stretching their prey taut. Greg's slack mouth closed to form gritting teeth. His closed eyelids clenched tight. Diane hadn't even time to scream before the butcher buried his blade in Greg's temple with a sickening *schlunk*.

As quickly as that, an unbreakable bond, a friendship between a father and daughter, was snuffed out.

Diane's shriek—so wild, so despairing—poured out of her. But the monsters didn't care. Feet shuffled forward. Heavy and lifeless, the body was dragged across stones. Then, the whir of cogs and grating bricks; the brick door slamming shut.

There was not one drop of Greg's blood on the floor to match the tears that fell as Diane sobbed. When she wiped away her tears, it was only to see and remember the safe path back to the bed and its false bottom. Once there, she took oil and matches. From there it was a careful trek to the front door and outside. She splashed oil on the shingles.

"The floor may be stone," she said. "The chairs may be iron. But the goddamn roof will burn."

She lit matches and volleyed them onto the roof until the oil ignited. Her mind reeled as she wondered from what Stygian pocket of evolution these monsters had erupted. And from what warren beneath the cottage? The tiny spare room couldn't house them all. They had come from below. How deep did the tunnels plumb, and for how many miles in every direction did they stretch? How many trap-houses lay in wait?

The roof burned. The walls burned. The warren would remain.

The words of a father echoed in his daughter's ears: *Death in the wild isn't—*

"You're wrong, Daddy. I'm sorry but you were wrong."

She stood with white knuckles. Her eyes blazed with the spreading flame.

"Sometimes it's clean."

THE FINGERNAIL MAN

JOHNATHON MAST

"I'm doing a report on the Fingernail Man," Marcus answered.

The classroom stopped. Light rain pattered against the windows, sounding almost like someone tapping at the glass. A few of the students snickered. A few grasped the edges of their desks. Mindy started crying.

Mrs. Malm shook her head. "No." She took a deep breath, her eyes darting over the rest of the classroom, counting her students. Her eyes lingered on one of the empty desks a moment longer than necessary. Her hands clutched at each other.

"But you said we could do the report on anything," Marcus sulked. His fists clenched, but he released them quick. Threatening, even pretending to threaten, was naughty. There were enough naughty people not in the world anymore; he didn't want to join them. He just wanted to say something to the Fingernail Man. Just one thing. That was all.

Really.

"I did say you could report on any current event, yes." Her voice was light and fast. "Marcus, good little boys and girls don't write reports about the Fingernail Man. You're a good boy, right?"

He didn't answer what he was thinking. "I just want to know why he takes who he takes."

"Marcus, you know everything you need to know."

Marcus gave one of his fake smiles. The same one he used to give his mom, back before the Fingernail Man took her. "I'm a good boy, Mrs. Malm."

"Well, good. Just like all of us, right class?"

The entire class answered, "Yes, Mrs. Malm," in strained unison. Mindy sniffled loudly.

Mrs. Malm took a deep, deep breath. "Marcus, many people are curious about the man who makes us all be good, but it's better if we don't talk about him, all right? Just. Just leave him be." She went to go comfort Mindy.

When they went to the school library to do research, he joined the protests of many of the other students. Why learn to look in books at all? Everything was online. But no, they had to go to the old library. Whatever. They tromped down the stairs and past the posters with young men and women smiling, holding babies, and declaring, "Good boys and girls become good moms and dads!" or "Help the world! Have kids!" A few of the guys sniggered, the way they always did when they looked at those posters.

Marcus stared at the one proclaiming that good boys and girls become good moms and dads. He unclenched his fists again, prying his fingers out from his fists.

Something clicked right behind his ear.

Fingernails.

Marcus spun, jumped back, let out a startled squawk.

David burst out laughing. "Geez. Come on, kid. If you want to learn about him, you better get used to the sound. He'll come and take you away, just like your mom."

Marcus's hands were fists again.

Mrs. Malm stepped between them. "David, are you being naughty?"

"No ma'am." He scrambled away down the hall toward the library.

Mrs. Malm put on her sad face and turned a sad smile toward Marcus. "I know you're having a hard time. And our class has been hit hard this year besides. Three children taken. But don't worry, Marcus. You're a good boy. Come on. Let's go to the library. Doing research should distract you a little."

Marcus was not a good boy. He knew how to behave, sure. That wasn't the same thing. It didn't help that what he wanted wasn't good. He asked Mr. Paliphos, the librarian, "Where can I find books about the Fingernail Man?"

The thin man's eyes darted around, one hand covering the other, hiding the tips of his fingers. "We don't have any books about that subject," he stuttered. "Why don't you look up something on the reforestation of Chicago, or something like that?"

Marcus pressed his lips together, annoyed at another adult getting in his way. "I don't care about reforestation. I want to know about the Fingernail Man!"

"You already know everything you have to." He gulped. "Young man, you should know. People who ask about the Fingernail Man usually are taken by him. Don't research this." Mr. Paliphos scuttled away and found someone else to assist.

Marcus checked out some books about depopulation, but they were only the symptom. Everyone knew about that. Everyone knew that the Fingernail Man took away anyone who was naughty, and when he started his work, there were so, so many naughty people. Marcus didn't care about that. He wanted to know more about the man himself.

That evening, Dad made his usual pancakes. They ate and talked at the old beat-up dining room table under a yellow buzzing bulb. Dad asked how his day went. Marcus gave minimal answers. Dad had been repairing cars all day and was tired. He went to go watch some analysis of a movie he hadn't seen yet. Marcus went to the computer and pulled up a search engine. "Fingernail Man," he typed.

Yep. Way too many entries. Just like last time. Got to narrow it down some.

He found the poem right away, but that was useless.

> *Don't be bad or he'll nibble your fingers.*
> *Don't be mean and, no, don't linger.*
> *Don't be naughty—a lot or some.*
> *The Fingernail Man will come.*

They all knew the warnings. When half his kindergarten class had been taken for skipping nap time, well, it's hard to forget.

But Marcus had to know. Why did the Fingernail Man patrol the whole world? Why did he take Marcus's mom?

Why didn't he take her sooner?

He typed, "Meeting Fingernail Man." His finger hovered over enter. Do it? He knew the warnings. He didn't need the stupid librarian telling him that. That's why he didn't search earlier.

But he had to know.

Enter.

Lots of entries. Lots of little blogs all over. Nothing that looked official. He clicked the third link down. What it said made sense. Just invite him in with what he craved.

Stupid. Simple. Something a kid would come up with.

"Bedtime," Dad called.

Marcus turned off the computer without arguing. He was not naughty. He might not be a good boy, but he was not naughty. Even if the Fingernail Man took him away for trying to find out more. Even if he took him away for just saying what he had to say. He got ready for bed and tucked himself in, keeping his hands inside the railing of the bed. Didn't want to give anyone the chance to nibble anything, right?

Dad bent down to kiss him goodnight.

"Dad?"

"Yeah, Murky?"

"Why did the Fingernail Man take Mom?"

Dad was quiet. "You already know. You can't get out of bedtime that way."

Marcus's voice got very, very quiet. "I'm not trying to get out of bedtime. I just. Tell me again."

Dad put his head down and rubbed his eyes. "Mom didn't want any more children. She was happy with you. And the council said we had to have more. Too many children were disappearing. She said you'd never disappear. You were too perfect." Dad put his hand against Marcus' cheek. Marcus flinched away, but then let Dad touch him. Dad continued, "She was naughty, I guess. The Fingernail Man came and took her away. I never even felt her leave the bed."

"When are you getting together with someone else for more babies?"

Dad sighed. "I still have a couple of months before I have to. And since Mom ... well, I just don't want to be with anyone else. I don't think I'm good enough for anyone else, really." He got up. "And besides. I love you. And that's enough." He bent over to kiss Marcus again and stepped out into the hallway, closing the door halfway behind him.

Marcus watched to make sure Dad was gone and stuck a clenched fist out between the rails. He darted his hand back. He closed his eyes.

Really? This was what he was going to do?

Well, it was the only way of maybe bringing the Fingernail Man here without just being naughty. If it worked. It might be the only chance Marcus got. And it might mean he got taken. One more empty desk for Mrs. Malm.

He stuck his hand out again. He forced himself to let the fingers drop down, one by one. A clenched fist is naughty. An open hand is not.

And he waited.

He remembered the night. He'd been crying in bed, the way he usually did. Mom banged around in the kitchen, fighting with Dad. Probably about the empty bed in the next room. Marcus didn't even remember Cathy, but his parents always fought about her. About having more. About not giving more children to "that monster." Marcus always hid when they fought. He always hid when Mom got angry. And that night, he heard the sound of fingernails tapping together, fingernails sliding along the hardwood floor of the hall, fingers squeaking against the hard surface, hundreds of fingers worming their way down the hall, the clicking of someone chewing on a fingernail, and then more clacking, and then … nothing.

And the next morning, Dad bawling over another empty bed.

Marcus took a deep breath, keeping his hand out. Holding it steady. Not shaking. Mom had been gone less than a week.

Now Marcus was going to meet the man who took her.

About an hour later the hall light clicked off, and he heard his father close the master bedroom door. Darkness settled in the room. The house shifted. Wind pushed up against the window. The red digits on his clock illuminated his desk.

A sound. A clicking, like two fingernails tacking up against each other. And then more ticking. And more. It scraped down the hallway, worming down the hardwood floor, stopping in front of his room. It scraped into his room. Skin rubbed up against the wood. The clicking stopped. He felt something scratch at his fingernails.

He snatched his hand back. "Fingernail Man!" he whispered with ferocity. His heart was really, really loud.

No answer.

"Fingernail Man?" he asked the darkness.

Words rose out of black, whispered and elegant, each syllable weighted and savored by the speaker. "Come come, naughty boy. You baited me? Not good. Not good at all. Only a naughty boy would do that. I shall nibble your fingernails off and take you to my home so I may feast from you the rest of my life. A delectable feast."

Marcus shivered. Don't let your voice shake. You're not being naughty. Don't let him see that you're naughty. He felt something leaning over him, some darkness, something ready to snatch him away and nibble off his fingers, something that knew what he was thinking, that knew how bad it was, but he had to say it. He had to let it out. It burst from his lips, loud and defensive: "Thank you!"

The presence stopped. Marcus kept his eyes squeezed shut, waiting. He breathed. He waited. He whispered, "I just wanted to say thank you. It's naughty to not say thank you."

The blackness was quiet again. The presence seemed to step back, fingernails rattling on the floor. "Thank you?"

"For taking Mom."

Fingers rubbed against the floor as the thing seemed to shift. It was so, so dark. "This is a curiosity, is it not? A child thankful for the Fingernail Man. Never before have I witnessed it. No one has ever expressed gratitude. Fear. Anger. Threatening retribution, but never, ever thanks. Tell me, child, tell me, little Marcus Denver, why are you so grateful for the absence of your mother that you would risk your fingers—your tiny, savory, crunchy fingers, and your life after them—to simply express that gratitude?"

His fingers curled into fists. "She hit me. A lot. She just. Her fists. All the time. And now she can't. I wanted to hate you. I did. But. But I'm glad. I'm glad she's gone." Marcus was breathing hard, trying not to cry. He was telling the truth, wasn't he? Wasn't he glad his mom was gone?

He knew he should be. He knew he shouldn't be.

He was a bad boy.

But he wasn't naughty. He wouldn't lie.

He screwed up the courage to ask another question. "Where did you take her?"

"To a place she will never hit you again. I carried her to a naughty, naughty place."

Marcus fought back a sob.

He missed her. He hated her.

"Fingernail Man?" He waited. "Will you take care of me?"

Silence answered. "Child. I roam the world at night. I watch every home, every school, every business, every park. I watch for the naughty, and I take them away. I punish. I do not love. It is not in me. I am the monster that every child fears, made real. I cannot care for you."

"But you rescued me."

"No. I punished, child. Tonight, you are not naughty. I came in error. Sleep tonight. Behave in the light. And the Fingernail Man will be watching."

"Liar!" Marcus screamed. "Liar! She hit me for years! She wanted to make sure I was a good boy, but she was naughty! She hit me and hit me and hit me! You weren't watching! You didn't take her away! She was naughty, but you didn't care!"

A thump sounded from his father's room. Stomping feet.

The darkness didn't answer.

The hall light clicked on, and illumination flooded Marcus's room. A man made of fingers stood before his bed, tall, so tall, but there were no arms or legs or eyes. Just fingers. Long fingers and stubby fingers and gnarled fingers and white fingers and black fingers and burned fingers and whole fingers clinging to each other in the form of a man, each one with long, long fingernails.

"It is very naughty to trick me," it threatened.

Dad shoved the door open and saw the nightmare. He fell back, a strangled cry in his throat.

"It's naughty to pretend to punish people and not do it!" Marcus screamed. He sat up on the bed, kneeling on his knees, shouting, screaming, tears running down his face, hands balled up at his sides. "You didn't punish my mom! You're naughty! You're naughty! I hate you!"

"Ah. There it is. The truth at last. You summoned me to vent your rage because I took your mother who deserved to be taken. Are you naughty, too,

Marcus Denver? I give you a choice. Choose wisely. I have never offered the choice before you, and I will not offer again. Are you naughty?"

If he was naughty, he could be with his mom. His mom who hit him sometimes. His mom who scared him. But his mom. The only one who loved him. The only one who cared for him. And the Fingernail Man was offering him the choice? To be with Mom ... or to stay here.

Was he a bad boy?

"I hate my mom."

In the hall, his dad tried to stand, fell as his legs gave out, stood again. His eyes darted. They landed on a bat inside of Marcus's room.

"Fingernail Man, is it wrong to hate someone you love? Does that make me naughty?"

The fingers all seemed to flex around the thing's body.

Dad slipped into the room, clinging to the wall, staying away from the monster. He took stuttering steps toward the bat in a far corner. "Murky," he squeaked out. "Murky, I hated her, too. And I loved her." He let out a choked sob. "You're not naughty. You're not. She was."

The mass of fingers turned toward Dad. "You were not invited to this discussion, Timothy Denver."

Marcus grasped at the words Dad said. Words he had never said before. Words that said that he and Dad were alike. And Dad still wanted to protect him. Dad still wanted to save him, even though he was a bad boy. But Dad said. Dad said.

Dad snarled, "You're trying to steal my son the way you stole my daughter and my wife, you—"

"Dad. Fingernail Man." Marcus took a deep breath. "I'm not naughty." Did he believe it?

It didn't matter if he believed it. Dad said it. It was true.

The Fingernail Man stood still. The light of the hallway outlined it. Dad reached the bat. He wrapped his fingers around it, hefted it.

The monster nodded. "Very good, Marcus Denver. I will not savor your fingers tonight. Behave in the light. And the Fingernail Man will be watching." The mass fell apart, the fingers clattering to the floor, squiggling away like worms, crawling into all the shadowy places of the room, clacking against the wood, squeaking against the hard surface. Then they were gone.

Dad dropped the bat and gasped for breath. He fell to the ground and crawled to Marcus's bed. The two embraced, held each other close, clung to each other. They sobbed, over and over.

"Dad?"

"Murky?" Dad choked out between sobs.

"I wish the Fingernail Man had come sooner."

There was quiet, and then, "Me too, son. Me too."

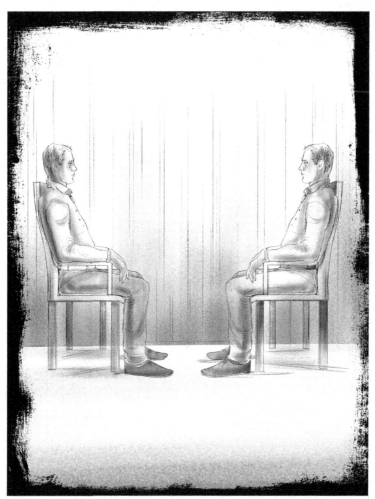

"Carl Turner—one of us, anyway—had to go."

MEA TULPA

GORDON LINZNER

Tis is how the end began.

The where: my third-floor apartment in a pre-World War I walkup building on Manhattan's Lower East Side. Correction: our apartment. As a freelance copyeditor I'd, we'd, spent the morning going over my, our, final corrections to the manuscript of a private detective novel, the latest in a long-running franchise. Its author had felt rushed, or burned out, or both.

The when: less than fifteen minutes after placing our usual lunch delivery order with the café on the corner.

The who, what, and how:

Three former colleagues from the Oxmyer Psychic Research Group entered his, our apartment. Carl—the other Carl—having skipped breakfast, impatiently and absent-mindedly opened the door without first looking through the peephole. The building had no doorman to vet visitors or alert us.

We had, on some level, been expecting, and dreading, this visitation, ever since we'd broken off all contact with Oxmyer a month earlier. The trio's purpose was beyond obvious. Carl Turner—one of us, anyway—had to go.

Eye contact was made. I moved away from the computer. The program was set to automatically save the file on which I'd, we'd, been working, to the Cloud every few minutes—a lesson we'd learned the hard way. Neither I nor my other self felt compelled to speak. Any confrontation would be completely the responsibility of the invaders.

A long, awkward silence followed.

Finally:

"There's no easy way to say this, Carl." Yuriko Martinez, acting as spokesperson, buried her hands deep in the pockets of her tan trench coat. That was one of her more prominent tells, and never a good sign. "You need to put an end to your tulpa. It's been around too long, developed a life of its own. They always turn on their creators, eventually. You know that. You've seen it happen." Her tone conveyed more resignation than threat, but the threat was nonetheless there.

"You do realize, Yuriko, that Carl, my other Carl, is standing right next to me, don't you? That he can hear every word you're saying?"

I waved in the direction of my friend and partner. My smile was more than a little forced.

Martinez' eyes rolled behind her tinted glasses. "That's the issue, Carl. It's not just the most sensitive and astrally aware members of Oxmyer that can see your Other now. Ordinary people, those who have no idea what a tulpa is, or that one's mental energies can create such a thoughtform, have been observed interacting with it. When they become this corporeal..."

I exchanged a familiar glance with my other Carl. When he first manifested, we rarely looked at each other. It had felt disturbingly like looking into a living mirror. We were long past that stage, though.

"Not happening, Yuriko. Carl has not shown the slightest interest in undermining my life. He's displayed none of the petty bickering, cruel trickery, or deliberate sabotage that some of you complained about with your own tulpae. The very opposite, in fact. I've been able to double my workload. Carl's insight and attention to detail over the past few months has been invaluable."

Martinez shook her head. "You're describing your own skills, Carl. You created this mental copy of yourself to help hone those skills, as well as have an understanding ear to bend. This thoughtform was intended to be a reflection of yourself, not a separate entity. You took it a step too far, even gave him your name and appearance!"

"The decision to adopt my name was his choice. That's how closely we bonded, after he materialized."

Eric Mueller, standing left of Martinez, removed his fedora, bowing slightly before speaking. "We've all been where you are, Carl. Remember my situation? I'd practically become a hermit before I realized Jonah was ruining my life by making himself, itself, the sole focus. It required all my will power to banish the selfish creature."

Allison Dawa, who towered over the other two by at least a foot, even without her beehive hairdo, agreed. "I wasted a full week mourning the breakup with my girlfriend before I discovered it was all Paddy's doing. I still imagine hearing that miserable leprechaun's laughter from time to time. I'll never let that little bastard back into my life."

"Carl's not like that."

"Not yet," Alicia muttered. "Wait."

"We're your friends, Carl." Martinez softened her tone, stepping closer. "We're trying to help you."

I responded with a sharp laugh, echoed by my other Carl.

"Oxmyer's idea of helping is the reason I left the group. What's the point of being enlightened if others control your enlightenment?"

Martinez sighed. "A gradual phasing out would be less traumatic. Unfortunately, we know from experience how rarely that works." Her right hand slid free of her coat pocket. Her fingers could not wholly conceal the hypodermic needle's tip.

I'd observed such interventions in others, without protest, to my shame. The propofol in the syringe was strong enough to knock out a unicorn, and more than powerful enough to disable a pair of Carl Turners. Oxmyer's leaders would follow up with forced hypnotic sessions. After that . . .

But, as noted, we'd been expecting this. My other Carl was halfway through the open window behind our desk before Martinez could take another step. I followed, so closely I almost crashed into him. The automatic window latch clicked into place as we slammed down the rail. That should delay the three while we clambered down the rickety fire escape, giving us time to elude them.

For now.

The next few hours were nerve-wracking. Perhaps because we hadn't wanted to think too much about the consequences of such a confrontation, we had never planned further than fleeing, beyond a vague idea of leaving the city in favor of a distant, less populous area. We wandered streets at random. At one point I acquired a sandwich from a street vendor and handed it to Carl, who was clearly tiring. He offered me half, which I turned down. That gesture, however, provided my first unwelcome hint of what needed to be done.

We couldn't return to the apartment; Oxmyer would have that covered. Outside temperatures were dropping, and we hadn't brought extra layers. Sometime after midnight, we decided to spend the rest of the night riding the subway. Carl could sleep while I took guard shift.

"They won't stop," he said morosely. We stood on a local platform, waiting for the next train. An express had just rumbled through along the center track. Aside from a lone homeless woman, snoring loudly and slumped on a bench thirty feet from us surrounded by a tower of plastic bags, the station was empty.

"I know." I stared down the tunnel, reluctant to meet his eyes.

"All of Oxmyer will be searching for us, plus their own tulpas. They might even call up some nirmitas."

Those emanation bodies could travel anywhere, sense anyone. "They will find us," I agreed glumly. "Our will is strong, but their techniques are highly effective."

"We need a real plan."

Feeling the other Carl's desperation, I placed a comforting hand on his shoulder. "We'll sort it out, Carl."

Rumbling echoed from the south tunnel. "Is that our train?"

I squinted. "Not sure. I only see the lights reflecting off the walls. Can't even tell which track it's on."

"Let me try." He leaned over the edge of the platform.

As I expected.

I could no longer endure seeing my other self so distraught. The Oxmyer Group was right. I had no other options.

My right hand still gripped his shoulder. Placing my left against his back, I spun Carl around. His eyes widened as I thrust him onto the tracks.

Train brakes squealed. Too late.

Much too late.

I'm not proud of what I did. Even as I made the move, I knew it was an act of cowardly betrayal, its only purpose to ensure my own survival. A thought-form such as a tulpa cannot be done away with so easily, of course, but the attempt would make it feel angry and betrayed. The tulpa would seek vengeance, or, if the relationship with its human was as close as ours, simply move on, refusing to ever interact with its creator again.

A living human, on the other hand, would be crushed beneath the train's metal wheels, killed instantly.

Which is exactly what happened to the original Carl Tucker.

My guilt was only slightly alleviated by the fact that Carl would never suffer the burden of having to make such a dark decision himself.

I backed away from the edge of the platform, moving quickly to the stairs, though none of the emergency responders would have been aware of my presence unless I wished it. If the motorman of the train had spotted me, his description would match that of dead Carl and be dismissed. The remaining Carl Tucker, me, needed to re-establish himself in another city, perhaps a small town, and in any case as far from the Oxmyer Group as possible. The Tucker name was a common one; if I kept a low profile and made sure my work was not publicly credited, I should remain under their radar.

Confession is good for the soul, however, even an artificial soul. Hence this missive. I will save the only copy on a USB, which I plan to keep with me as a constant reminder that even I, as much as any human, may end up regretting my actions, however necessary they appeared to be.

This is the end of my new beginning.

"She had no idea how to communicate with something so old, so other."

IN THE HOUSE OF THE ELEMENTALS

LISA MORTON

No one noticed the Elemental walking along Broadway in downtown Los Angeles.

The hurrying crowds hid it, as did the ill-fitting tattered clothing. If anyone had taken more than a casual glance at the face visible beneath the baseball cap, they might have noticed that the skin seemed too smooth, hairless; the eyes unblinking. The body was straight and genderless; it moved mechanically, as if unused to joints.

But those rushing along the sidewalks, on their way to work or school or home or nowhere, unconsciously avoided it. They gave it a wide berth, didn't raise their eyes to it. A few might have wondered why their phones were abruptly drained, went dead. Some who passed it would awaken in the middle of the night from a half-remembered terrible dream. Someone who brushed against it would find their hand suddenly cold and unresponsive.

For its part, the Elemental was searching, unsure of exactly what it sought. It was a thing of ancient instinct and reflex; it trusted that it would know when it found what was needed.

"Your future looks good, Mrs. Garcia." Maria smiled as she gathered up the tarot cards, and she saw relief on her client's face.

"Thank you," the aging widow said, as she rose painfully, reached for her purse, and produced bills she handed to Maria.

After she left, Maria allowed herself a moment of contemplation. The truth was, Mrs. Garcia's cards *hadn't* looked so good, but Maria felt such affection for the woman that she'd fudged the revelation. Maria's usual guardian spirits had given only vague clues today, and she intuited that it was less a bad outlook for only one person than for *everyone*. She'd felt stirrings for weeks now, but they were multiplied today.

"Tell me what's going on," she called out, but she received no reply. Her spirit guides either weren't listening, or weren't answering.

Maria's own future hadn't looked too good for a long time. Although she had a list of regulars who appreciated her skills, she could barely afford the taxes on the house she'd inherited from her parents; it needed work, like a new roof, that she couldn't pay for. She was alone, without a husband or parents; her nearest sibling was an alcoholic who she hadn't spoken to in some time.

Given what she could do, and how well she could usually do it, her life should have been better.

She watched the paranormal television shows sometime, marveling at the obvious fakery. She could *really* do what they could only play-act: talk to spirits, ask them to reveal the future, help those who had run afoul of something inhuman.

"I wish," she muttered aloud, to anything that might be listening, "that you could just help *me* a little, please."

But there was no answer except that throb of dark energy she'd been feeling. It consumed the usual voices that spoke to her, yet she couldn't tell exactly where or what it was. Her sleep had become an uncomfortable nightly journey into half-remembered dreams of apocalypse.

Something bad was coming, something unspeakably old and powerful.

Whatever it was, it was getting closer.

There ...

As the Elemental trudged along the sidewalk, downtown left behind, to the west now, something impinged on the borders of its awareness, something near—

It followed the trail for several miles, moving past an industrial area of warehouses and train-yards, the feeling of power in what it sought growing stronger. Finally it stood outside a small house in a rundown residential area; it didn't understand letters, and so didn't know that the hand-painted wooden sign stuck in the yellowing lawn read "PSYCHIC."

It was momentarily befuddled by a simple gate latch before comprehending how it worked. Once past the splintered wooden gate, it marched up to the open front door and entered a room hung with heavy draperies and artwork of angels, where a middle-aged woman with long hair, dyed violet, and tired eyes looked up from her phone, her face automatically creasing in a welcoming smile. "Welcome, friend. My name is Maria. Would you like a—"

Her expression went dead as the Elemental waited passively.

"Oh my God," she said, crossing herself, "what are you?" Maria staggered back, fear filling the void she'd first felt as the thing before her had entered her house.

This ... this is what I've been sensing ...

But even as she thought that, it didn't feel right. This thing, with its unwrinkled face like a blank canvas and its stiff movements, wasn't human, but it didn't exude the inchoate *rage* that had assaulted her.

It opened its mouth to speak, but what came out was a rusty groan, a sound only those who had encountered spirits in the wild might have recognized, although they thought it was wind grinding metal against tree trunks, or animals howling in mortal agony.

It gave up on speech and simply inserted itself into Maria's mind. *Please do not fear; I seek your help.*

Maria repeated, "What *are* you?"

Your kind has given me many different names: god, angel, demon, spirit. The term that best fits, though, is Elemental.

"Elemental? Like ... a powerful ghost?"

I am not a ghost because I've never been human and I've never died.

We were born with this planet, and have been here since. When your kind rose to dominance, we retreated, mostly to the wild places.

Her heart calming now, Maria tried thinking her question: *How many of you are there?*

Thousands, came the answer.

Maria realized now: what she'd felt for the last month hadn't been the thing that stood before her, but another one like it, one that was *not* inclined to benevolence towards humanity.

Yes, the Elemental answered her thoughts, *I am ... concerned about one of my kin. I can no longer sense its intentions, but I can feel its presence. It moves along the fault lines of this place. I believe it has gone mad.*

Maria barked a bitter laugh before thinking, *That can happen?*

We are aligned with the planet, which your kind has plundered and tampered with and violated, and some of us have responded. They have taken residence in hidden places and hurled their fury at those of you who have come near.

Maria thought back to a ghost-hunting show she'd once watched in which the team had been investigating an abandoned, half-ruined, once-great resort hotel that dated back 150 years. There were rumors that the hotel had failed because guests had been too frightened to stay there, and now the team fled, the camera following as they jogged back to their vans. Maria had empathized with their fear, thought it was probably one of the most genuine moments she'd ever seen on any of these shows, and she'd never forgotten the one man who was still shaking as he said, "I think that was an Elemental."

And you're trying to find one of those who are ... angry?

I am, because of what its anger can do.

Abruptly chilled, Maria blurted out, "Because it's near the fault lines, like the San Andreas."

Yes. Our anger can be a powerful thing. If it lashes out ...

She knew immediately, just as everyone who'd grown up in Southern California knew: the Big One, the legendary moment when tectonic plates gave way to pressure, slid along the San Andreas fault line, and resulted in an earthquake of unimaginable size, causing equally unimaginable devastation. "Millions of us could die ..."

And the planet will suffer.

With a small, bitter smile, Maria thought, *You don't care about us, do you?*

I care about this place that I was born with, and you are part of that as well.

Maria lowered herself into a chair, struggling to process, aware that *it* knew every perplexity and wonderment and terror that cascaded through her mind. After a few seconds she looked up at her steadfast visitor and asked, "So why are you here to see me?"

You have abilities others of your kind do not, abilities you may not even fully comprehend. I cannot communicate with my kin ... but perhaps you can.

"I ..." Maria had been about to say, "I can't do that," but then she remembered being eight years old, on a family picnic at a park up in the hills, and her Tia Rosa (who she later realized also shared her gifts) had told her the land was haunted. Maria wandered off at one point, leaving her brother and cousins shrieking as they played games she had no interest in. Instead, she felt something there, and in a quiet dim glade five hundred feet from the rest, she'd encountered *it*. At first she saw nothing except a thicker darkness, but then *it* became aware of her, and hurled something she could only call a psychic bolt. It had filled her with indefinable terror, had weakened her, and she'd staggered back to her Tia, crying, clinging to her skirts as Rosa told her about being careful seeking the old things in the earth. It had taken her many nights to stop dreaming of it.

Yes, said the Elemental standing in her visiting room, *you will be in danger. If I can protect you, I will.*

So, she thought, *how do we communicate with it?*

I can direct us to where it will be close. From there, you should feel it strongly, more than you have recently.

Maria rose, paced a few feet. *If I don't ... I might die anyway, when it upsets the faults and the earthquake comes. Is that right?*

No word formed in her head, but she sensed agreement and realized there was no choice.

An hour later they were in Maria's ancient Toyota, heading east on the 10 freeway. It was mid-afternoon and traffic was light, rush hour still in the future. The Elemental sat in the passenger seat, looking at nothing.

"Tell me," Maria said, before remembering that she needn't speak aloud, *Tell me more about Elementals. You've been here since the beginning of things?*

Since the beginning of this planet, yes. We dwelt here alone for billions of year; then when pools of organic compounds began to form, we offered our essence.

Maria swerved the car in shock before blurting out, "You created life?"

Yes. And we were pleased with it for a long time. We delighted in the processes of evolution, the flow of new forms. When the first humans appeared, we found their intelligence intriguing ... but as civilization spread, we retreated before it. It has been but a cosmic second for us since we felt the first rumblings as humans reshaped the earth, but it's been a second that has changed us.

"Are you ..." Maria broke off, shaping her thoughts. *Are some of you the bad spirits that haunt old buildings and ancient places, frightening us?*

For the first time she sensed discomfort in her guest. *Yes. But most of us wish you no harm.*

They continued east, older suburbs replacing lower-middle-class neighborhoods, which in turn gave way to desert. As they drove, Maria felt the indefinable prickling in her mind and her gut increase, like an odor that grows stronger as the source comes closer. Her passenger occasionally offered directions—*we'll go north soon*—but she needed little assistance. They stopped for gas once, leaving Maria to pay for a tank she hadn't planned on, but she knew the Elemental likely didn't even know what money was.

Just past Palm Springs, they turned off the 10 freeway onto a deserted two-lane blacktop that led into the desert, and Maria's senses told her they were above ancient plates overlapping, fault lines forever in infinitely slow motion. They drove further, past a landscape dotted with yucca and Joshua tree until even that hardy growth stopped, replaced by rocky tiers and low scrub. The Elemental was silent as Maria's instinct, roaring now with sensations she couldn't name or describe, led them to a point in the foothills where paved road gave way to dirt. She drove until even that ended, at a small grouping of long-abandoned industrial tanks and scaffolds. She parked there, hoping her car wouldn't just become one more rusting metal hulk forgotten in the wastelands after she disappeared.

The sun was painting the western skyline in vibrant gold and rose as they hiked along a hillside trail, Maria's feet sliding on pebbles. A breeze picked up, sweeping across the floor of the valley below them and creating small dust devils that caused the coyotes to howl. With each step, Maria felt increasingly as if she was walking through water, going deeper, the pressure around her increasing. At last she could no longer bear it and she dropped onto a boulder, gasping.

Here ...

The Elemental stood a few yards away, pointing at something below a rock outcropping. Maria rose wearily to join it, saw an opening into the earth framed between rotting wooden boards.

"I'm supposed to go in *there?*"

Agreement flowed from the Elemental.

"It doesn't look safe."

We must get closer.

Maria walked down to the mine opening, pulled out her phone and used the flashlight to peer in. The floor was sandy and sloped slightly downward; the boards around her creaked, but held. Taking a deep breath for courage and offering a prayer to her spirit guardians, she entered.

She'd only taken a few steps when the Elemental appeared in front of her, impossibly—it couldn't have gone around her in the narrow mine shaft. *I will lead you.* She was glad, because she'd come to trust it, despite its sheer alienness.

They skirted cobwebs and collapsed side caves, continuing along the main shaft, which was clear and continuing to descend. Maria found herself wondering who'd worked at this mine, how long ago that had been, what they'd found ... how many had died here. There was no doubt that ghosts dwelt here, but she was thankful they left her alone, didn't assault her with questions and demands. She wondered if the Elemental was responsible for that.

Or maybe it was the sensation building in her head, the consciousness so strong it would permit no other to approach. The air hummed with it, until finally Maria fell to her knees, closing her eyes, her head a maelstrom of colliding sensations: confusion, grief, but mostly *rage*.

She cried out. One arm involuntarily shot out, encountering something that felt like little more than heavy air, but which nonetheless offered support —*her* Elemental.

"*It's* here," she gasped out. "Below ..."

She realized now that she had no idea how to communicate with something so old, so huge, so *other*. She pulled her legs in under her, crossed them, tried to calm her breathing, to reach out in silent invocation.

The mine rumbled, a rain of fine dust falling onto her.

Maria opened her eyes in fear, but the rumbling faded. She felt the reassurance of her Elemental guide: *yes, you've reached my kin.*

She looked up at the dispassionate face and thought-asked, *What should I say?*

Tell it the others are concerned. Tell it that it will harm the planet irreversibly if it continues.

Nodding, Maria closed her eyes again and let that message play through her thoughts.

The answer was an outraged explosion of dark energy that instantly corrupted the delicate circuits in her phone, casting her into utter darkness. The earth trembled. In the distance, Maria heard wood snapping and rocks cascading down. She felt her own panic rise; she tried to stand, but the rolling ground made it nearly impossible.

She was going to die here, buried beneath tons of rubble, forgotten ... but this side of the world might well die with her.

NO.

That was not her voice, but the Elemental's. She felt it, then, moving past her at the speed of thought, down into the earth, following the release of energy. Her consciousness was there as it found its kin, and though they didn't need language to communicate, she followed their exchange. They shared images, of a ravaged earth that first heated and shifted, then buckled and collapsed. She felt argument, fury, soothing ... and finally reconciliation and agreement.

The earth's shaking stopped. The mine grew quiet.

A glow appeared in the air; Maria realized it was *her* Elemental.

We were successful, it thought to her. *I will now show you the way out.*

Numb, she followed the glow as it painted the shaft walls in blue shimmer. She realized the Elemental had abandoned all pretense at human form now, but she understood that it was no longer necessary.

At last she felt a cool evening breeze on her face, and there was moonlight overhead, rough scrabble beneath her feet. The glow led her all the way to her car.

Once there, it began to fade.

"Wait," Maria called out to it, reluctant to bid it farewell.

We are finished.

I know, but ... let me see your true form.

You ARE seeing it.

The glow expanded, filling most of Maria's vision. It was only the outer edges that glistened with the color of sea waves beneath a cloudless sky; the heart was as black as the space between stars.

In another instant, it winked out. Maria's consciousness knew it was gone; she felt emptiness where it had been. She was suddenly bone-weary and melancholy and hopeful.

She unlocked her car and fell into the driver's seat, then started it up. The everyday sound of an engine was somehow reassuring, as were the distant lights of civilization that glowed on the western horizon. She considered sleeping in the car before the drive back, but she wanted the comfort of her home, with its leaky roof and yellowing front lawn. She had clients due in the morning, and she wanted to be there to meet them.

She couldn't tell them that she'd just saved the world, but maybe she could save a small part of the world just for them.

The Elemental was glad to shake off the cumbersome human illusion, even as insubstantial as it had been. In its true form, it was free again.

It experienced a moment of emotion that surprised it: regret at leaving the human so abruptly. Perhaps it would visit her again in the future. It thought it might find her changed.

In the meantime, it had a very large house to tend to.

"What do other people see? Can they tell, instantly, by looking?"

PASSED ON

DIE BOOTH

I'm not in love. It's not like that. There's just something about Ali that calls to me. Something *right*. And I'm by rights the type of guy he shouldn't want to give the time of day to, but he must see something in me, too. I just wish I knew what it is.

Some people might say he's a cliché, but I've got no time for that. OK, so he's skinny and he's pale and he's got the long dark hair and the black clothes going on. But he's not a dick about it. He's not *obvious*. He's got good style, he really has, and I'm pretty sure his hair colour is natural as well. He dresses plain, good shirts and smart pants, clean lines. I tried it out, once: ordered a shirt and trousers online like he'd wear, just to see, but I looked lumpy and weird even though I was wearing a binder, so I've stuck with my jeans and hoodies since. At least they're black, too: it's a good colour for disguising your shape, which is what I'm trying to do right now. I stretch out my t-shirt and tug the waistband of my jeans lower. I turn to the side, appraising. I smile with my lips sealed. I hate mirrors. When I look at my reflection I can't reconcile who I am with what I am. What do other people see? Can they tell, instantly, by looking? My cheeks are annoyingly smooth: I always need ID for booze. It's a curse, like being trapped in time—you get older, but everyone else still just sees a kid. I stare at my face, study it. Do I pass? Why do I care? He's going to be here in a minute. I throw a sweatshirt on over my tee.

When he arrives and we're installed in my room with beers, I say, "Ali? Tell me about vampires again?"

He chuckles, low and soft. *Melodious.* It's a sound I couldn't hope to replicate, never mind produce unconsciously, but he doesn't even appreciate he's doing it. "Why don't *you* tell *me*?"

That makes me smile. I love it when he gives a damn about my opinion: it doesn't happen often. I mean, it's not like he's a wanker or anything, he can't help the way nature made him, right? "They don't need to feed often." I study him for signs of approval, like this is a test. Maybe it is. His eyes look bright. Almost amused. I'm not sure how to feel about that. "But it needs to be regular. A little bit, taken here and there. Different donors. They don't have any trouble finding people willing to give blood, because they can be very charming when they want to be."

His almost-smile flickers, minutely. He takes a swallow of beer and his white throat pulses. I carry on.

"Taking a little from a lot of people is safer for the donors, but not for the vampire. Like, the more people you tell, the more risk you run of being outed. But you could always pretend it was some kink thing or something, I guess. I mean, to make it easier for other people." He gives a slight, tight nod. Encouraging. "So that way, nobody has to die. Unless ..." I hesitate, thinking how to word it. He's staring at me. It makes my mouth tingle. "Unless you want to pass it on. The sickness."

"The gift." He says. I can see both of us, reflected side by side in the mirror. The films all say that vampires can't be reflected in mirrors, too: it's easy to get the facts wrong when all you've got to go off is the media. I never like to see my own face, but especially not next to one like his. The lights wash me out, sickly. He looks like porcelain. My eyes are brown. His are a blue as delicate as snowflakes, and just as cold.

I say, "If you want to pass the *gift* on, you have to drain them completely. Then they become the vampire, and you're cured. I mean——I don't mean *cured*, as in, not that there's anything wrong with being ... I mean, you're not the vampire any more. They are instead."

"What movies have you been watching?" He stretches his legs out across the bed where we're sitting. He looks elegant and strong. "I haven't heard that interpretation before. If you want to pass the gift on, then you seek the companion you desire and you drain them of their blood. Then, just at their point of death, you feed them the lifeblood from your own veins and thus sire a dark protégé to accompany you through the lonely mists of undeath."

Now, he looks kind of like he's trying not to laugh. I think he might be mocking me a bit, but I don't care. I like seeing him happy, it makes him look kinder. "You'll still be a vampire too, though. There's no going back. Not in any mythology, not even the ones about flying severed heads or blood-sucking pumpkins. You either stay undead, or you're dead."

It doesn't sound very nice, I think. Not much of a choice at all. Although, no scenario where you're different from everyone else, unable to move on, is pleasant when you really examine it. I wonder why anyone would ever choose that. Perhaps that's why nobody does; it chooses us. "So what you're saying," I say, carefully, "is, once a vampire, always a vampire?"

"Uh-huh."

I look at my hands. My short, square nails. "Maybe some people are always destined to become vampires. Predestined. Like, they kind of already were vampires, even from the moment they were born?" I glance across at him. His fingers are elegant, long nails filed to rounded points.

He raises a wry eyebrow. "Maybe, yeah."

I feel like my throat is closing up. "Would you, if you could?"

"Become a vampire?"

Make the decision to change forever, to become the person you always should have been. I nod.

He laughs his soft, exhaling laugh. His irises look almost colourless in this light. "In a heartbeat."

There's my answer. *Heartbeats.* I can hear his, quickening to a canter as I slide closer. Nobody chooses it; it's already there. I never thought I'd pass this Hell onto anyone, but maybe it won't *be* Hell for him. Maybe if he can change in the way he wants to, then I can change in the way I do, too. All these years, I've always been too scared to go to the doctors and ask about transitioning. I thought that if they tested my blood, they'd find out what I am: something I wouldn't wish on anyone, something I've never been able to bring myself to pass on. Except ... he's so right for it. *It's* chosen *him*. *I've* chosen him.

His eyelids flicker as I close the final distance, my lips against his skin. I feel his gasp as my gums retract and I sheath my teeth in his throat.

Ali, you're everything I should have been.

I have a gift for you.

THE BLANCH

DOMINICK CANCILLA

I'm going to tell you what happened to your baby. It has to do with blanch. If you could pay attention, it would be for the best.

You don't know about blanch because you believe your eyes. That's a mistake most people make, and sometimes it gets them killed. Here's what you've been missing.

Blanch is both singular and plural, like deer or sheep, but there's almost never just one blanch. They work together and travel together. It's a survival mechanism. The blanch evolved to survive.

Evolution has a way of preserving features that help creatures live long enough to reproduce, even when those features have unintended consequences. For example, humans have a built-in bias for detecting faces. Faces are so important to human interactions that being able to spot them without thinking has a big evolutionary advantage.

But that advantage comes with a disadvantage. People sometimes think they see faces where there are none. It can be a demon's face in the charred wood of a fire, a deity's face in the darkened surface of a piece of toast, or just someone staring down at you in bed from the visual noise in a stucco ceiling.

Seeing things like this when they aren't there is called pareidolia. It's a flaw in the brain's optical processing system, just like the flaws that make optical illusions work. Because those flaws are minor compared to the benefits they are a side effect of, evolution lets them persist.

Evolution has a way of hunting down and exploiting this kind of flaw in the enemies of a species. If an insect has some quality that takes advantage of a flaw in a predator's visual system so that to the predator the insect appears like an unappetizing stick or leaf, evolution tends to preserve that quality. The more you look like garbage, the less you get eaten, the happier evolution is.

Blanch are insects, almost as big as a house cat, that have followed such an evolutionary path. Just as humans have a flaw that allows them to see faces where there are none, they have a flaw that stops them from recognizing certain combinations of color and shape as being worthy of notice. The combination is so bizarre that it nearly never comes up, and when it does, people don't notice because—well, their not noticing is exactly the point. This flaw is a side effect of human visual processing, and the evolutionary advantage of that processing more than outweighs the disadvantage of the flaw.

Blanch have evolved to take advantage of this loophole in human vision. They aren't invisible, don't have coloration that blends with their surroundings, but even if they're right there in the room with you, you won't notice them. You can't. Your brain isn't programmed to.

Optimally, blanch must remain absolutely motionless for their defensive appearance to work. This means that they need to be intensely aware of their surroundings, which is why they have evolved multiple omnidirectional eyes, exceptional hearing, and the brain power to quickly process and react to copious environmental data. They are, by far, the most intelligent insects on the planet.

You're going to object that even if blanch can't be seen with the eye, they would still appear on film, set off motion detectors, and the like. That's true. They do appear on film. You just don't notice any more than you notice when they're perching on a roof or dresser. They do set off motion detectors, but so do other random things that people write off as glitches. More importantly, blanch have learned what cameras and detectors look like and avoid them, just to be safe. Like I said, they are very intelligent.

That doesn't mean they can't be perceived at all. You ever get the feeling that you are being watched, but then you turn around and it looks like nothing is there? Yeah, that.

Blanch also dispose of their dead. A corpse might give the whole game away if a human found it, but a corpse is also an excellent source of protein. There have, I'm sure, been cases where a human has found a blanch that was hit by a car, or what have you, and not devoured by its companions before being discovered, but if the corpse is mangled to the point a human might notice it, then it's not likely to be recognized for what it is. Anyone saying otherwise would be written off as a nut.

As a side effect of their intelligence and social nature, blanch have language. Sound is so easily detected that any blanch that make noise don't survive long, and over time the species evolved completely visual communication. By using bioluminescence at the far end of infrared, blanch can communicate with any other blanch in line of sight, even with humans about, even while remaining perfectly still. It's a marvel of nature, absolutely unique in the animal kingdom.

Even though so much of blanch biology has evolved to avoid human notice, humans remain the biggest threat to their survival. You can imagine the reaction if their existence became known. It would be genocide, or maybe xenocide, depending on how speciesist you are.

To preserve their advantage, blanch jealously guard the secret of their existence.

Two of a blanch's main appendages are quite sharp at the end. They can easily be driven into a neck, an eye, a chest. But when that is done, humans ask questions. They involve authorities. The risk of discovery, however small, is real.

Blanch kill in this way only as a last resort, when someone stumbles on something not easily explained, or when someone delusional inadvertently skirts the truth. This is rare, though. The real danger is that humans will evolve.

Blanch watch for any sign that a human lacks the flaw that keeps blanch safe. It's why they are so interested in human babies. If an infant's eyes follow a blanch, if it smiles when a blanch climbs a wall or perches cribside, the blanch takes note.

That is why babies are smothered.

A blanch is large enough to restrict a baby's breathing, let it pass away peacefully in its sleep, take the danger it represents out of the gene pool.

It's a matter of survival. A necessity. It doesn't mean blanch kill children the same way a person might kill a chicken or swat a fly. We have children, too. We feel pain when they are lost.

And that's why I'm saying I'm sorry, now, as you sit there reading, even though you can't know I'm doing it. I'm sorry for what I had to do. I'm sorry for what you will find in the morning. So, so sorry.

MY FRIEND NESSIE

J.H. MONCRIEFF

~ Chapter One ~

"Y ou're stupid!"
"Am not!
"Are too!"
"Am not!"

The screaming made Beth McGrew feel like her head would crack open. Why had she ever thought teaching ten-year-olds was a good idea? For once, her mother had been right—she should have been a pediatrician. At least then her interactions with children would have been mercifully brief. "Okay, that's enough. Please," she said, trying to sound commanding and not like she was pleading. Children could smell fear. "What's going on?"

Maggie's face was streaked with tears. Beth's heart sank. She'd taken too long to notice what was happening. A cluster of boys circled the crying girl, their faces flushed with merriment. *Bastards.* Why couldn't they leave her alone? Maggie was always getting picked on.

She was a lovely girl, but she was a ginger with a face full of freckles. Was that it? Was that all it took? As Beth touched the child's shoulder, it trembled under her hand. *Bastards*, she thought again.

Maggie looked up at her, blue eyes overflowing. "Th-they called me stupid, Miss McGrew."

"You *are* stupid," bellowed Frank, an obnoxiously outspoken fellow. Frank's shirts never appeared to fit quite right, and were forever riding up, exposing a bulge of snow-white belly. It was a wonder *he* was never the target of the bullies. But it's hard to be the target when you're the head bully. He was two years older than the others, which unfortunately made him the natural leader.

"That's enough," Beth repeated, her voice taking on more of an edge than she'd meant, but she couldn't help it. She loathed Frank. He was always hurting the other children, likely causing irrevocable damage to their frail psyches. "You apologize to Maggie right this minute, Frank Sturrock."

That rotten lad crossed his arms in front of his considerable chest and scowled at her. "Why should I apologize? It's true. She *is* stupid."

Maggie's lower lip quivered along with the pounding in Beth's head.

Great, some role model she was. She was only making it worse. "How can you stand there and say such terrible things? None of my students are stupid, not a single one."

"*She* is. She actually believes in the Loch Ness monster!"

Oh no. Oh dear. The other children were laughing now, that terrible, shrill kind of laughter that meant not all of them found it funny, but they desperately wanted to avoid being the target. "That's no excuse for saying what you said. Apologize now, or I'll have to send you to the headmistress's office."

"Fine by me." Tugging on his shirt, Frank spun on his heels and left the playground. *Shit.* He was the third student she'd sent to Julia that week. Julia had been top notch so far, but she'd start to have doubts about Beth's ability to control a classroom. Any headmistress would.

But there was no time to worry about that now. Stunned into silence by Frank's dramatic exit, the other children watched her, waiting for her next move. Beth cleared her throat. "Back to class, all of you! Recess is over."

"B-but Miss, we still have ten—" Another student, a shy fellow named Patrick, attempted to reason with her, but one look cut him short.

"Perhaps you'll remember that before you torment another classmate."

"But I didn't ..."

"*Inside.*" She pointed in the direction of the school, a dramatic gesture that had the necessary impact. Patrick hurried after his friends, his ears crimson. She shouldn't have yelled at him, he was such a sensitive soul, but she wasn't in the mood to reason with him right now.

Once her students were all heading in the right general direction, she kneeled in front of Maggie. "Do you need a tissue?"

"No thank you, Miss McGrew. I have a handkerchief from my Da'."

"That's alright, then. Do you feel up to joining the class? If not, I can call your folks, ask them to come fetch you."

The girl's eyes widened, and she shook her head almost violently, her fiery curls bouncing on her shoulders. "No, Miss. Please don't."

Beth didn't miss the fear on the girl's face, and it wasn't the first time she had seen it. Poor little wraith. She touched Maggie's arm. "Everything okay, Mags? Everything alright at home?"

Maggie was a pale child already, but at Beth's question, the little color she did have drained from her face. "Yes," she said, barely above a whisper. "Everything's jus' fine."

It wasn't; Beth knew it wasn't. But what could she do? If Maggie wasn't willing to confide in her, she couldn't force it. All she could do was make herself available.

"Good." She forced herself to sound cheerier than she felt. "Let's go join the others, shall we?"

She felt a slight tug on her sleeve. Maggie hadn't moved, and stared up at her, her tear-streaked face earnest and frightened. "You won't tell my Da' what I said, will you?"

Something wrapped itself around Beth's heart and squeezed. "Of course not. What *did* you say?"

The girl looked down and kicked a stone. "The truth, that's all. Shoulda known they wouldn't understand."

"Understand what?"

She took so long to respond that Beth had about given up. She looked at her classroom windows, half expecting to see children hanging from the rafters by now. They'd been left alone too long. She was about to urge Maggie back to class when the girl finally spoke.

"Do you believe in Nessie, Miss McGrew?"

Oh no. Not this again. For some reason, Maggie persisted in talking about the mythical monster, no matter how much the other children teased her. "Nessie is a myth, Maggie," she said as gently as she could, but the words weren't out of her mouth before the girl was shaking her head again.

"She's not, she's *isn't*. I've seen her!"

Not for the first time, Beth wondered if she should have a word with the school psychologist. All children had vivid imaginations, but Maggie's obsession with the Loch Ness monster struck her as abnormal.

What if the child was having hallucinations? What if there was something seriously wrong, something that required medication?

Even in Scotland, teachers weren't trained on how to deal with children who insisted Nessie was real. Should she humor her, or tell her the truth? And if she opted for the truth, would Maggie believe her? She was so insistent.

"What does Nessie look like?"

Looking delighted to have someone take her seriously at last, Maggie couldn't get the words out fast enough. "Well, I've never seen her body, but she has a smallish head on a really long neck. Her eyes are huge, and they're so gentle, but she does have big teeth. I've seen 'em. Her skin looks black at first, but that's just because it's wet. It's really dark green. Dark *dark* green!"

Hmm ... nothing new there. That was pretty much everyone's idea of what Nessie looked like. The girl had clearly been influenced by all the souvenirs and other Loch Ness Monster paraphernalia. For those living in Inverness, it was impossible to escape.

"How did you feel when you saw her? You must have been scared," Beth said, playing along.

"The first time I seen her, I was, but not anymore." There was a hint of pride in the girl's voice.

"The first time? How many times have you seen her?" This could be even worse than she'd thought. Maggie was clearly delusional.

"Oh, hundreds and thousands," the girl said, waving the question away. "Too many to count, really. I've been seeing her since I was little."

Beth bit her lip to hide a smile, but then was reminded of how serious this was. She'd have to make a point of talking to the psychologist as soon as she was able to slip away. "We should get back to class now." She held out her hand, and was relieved when Maggie took it this time.

"Everyone has it all wrong, and it makes me mad," the girl said.

"For some reason, Maggie persisted in talking about the mythical monster, no matter how much the other children teased her."

"What's that? What does everyone have wrong?"

"Nessie isn't a monster, Miss McGrew. She's my friend."

She didn't hear him coming until it was too late. His hand grabbed her hair and pulled her to her feet, making her squeal.

"I thot I'd find you here. Yer late."

"Please Da'," Maggie pleaded, standing on her tiptoes to ease the terrible pain radiating from her head. "Please don' hit me."

"What have I told you about coming down here by yerself? You could slip into the loch and drown, breaking yer mother's heart. Did you ever think of that? Ever think of anyone but yer goddamn self?"

"Nessie wouldn't let me drown," she said between gasps, struggling to loosen his grip, but it was hopeless. She was no match for him. He would drag her home by her hair, and he would beat her. Her mother couldn't stop him, because she was scared of him too.

"Nessie wouldn't let yer drown? *Nessie* wouldn't let yer drown? Yer crazy, ya know that, Maggie? Plumb mad, thas wut ya are. Thinking the Loch Ness monster is real! No wonder ye have no friends."

When her dad beat her, it hurt, but not as much as his words. Somehow, he invariably knew the thing to say in order to cause her the most pain. "I have friends."

"Me mate Jack's son is in yer class, and he says the other kids are always picking on ya, account of ya saying crazy shit like this. Why don' ya stop, Mags? Why can't ya be normal for once?"

"Because it's not crazy," she whispered, her words barely audible.

"Wut's tha? Ya got somethink to say, let's hear it." Another sharp tug on her hair, but this time, she bit back the scream. Something gave her the strength—or maybe it was the stupidity—to look her dad in the eye.

"I said, it's not crazy."

They stared each other down. It was quiet, too quiet, which meant the tourists were on their way to dinner. How often she's wished she could go with them, keep them company while they ate and hear about the fascinating places they were from. They probably ate wonderful things for supper, nothing like the watered-down soup her ma made from vegetables that were past their prime. The thought of the soup was enough to make her stomach turn, but she'd learned better than to turn up her nose. If her dad caught her wasting food, he'd beat her so badly she wouldn't be able to sit for a week. He'd threatened her often enough.

Without warning, he backhanded her across the face. Pain exploded under her eye, and she cried out.

"Why can't you be like other lasses? Why do ya have to embarrass me in front of my mates?"

This time he used a closed fist, hitting her square in the mouth. She tasted her own blood. Through eyes blurry with tears, she could see him drawing back to hit her again. "No, Da! Please don't!"

She squeezed her eyes shut and braced herself for the next blow, but it didn't come. Shivering with cold and pain, she waited. Knowing her dad, he wanted her to see it coming, to anticipate how much it would hurt. Maybe if she never opened her eyes, he'd get tired of waiting and go back to the pub.

Maggie might have stood there blind for another hour if she hadn't realized the pain from her scalp was gone. He wasn't pulling her hair anymore. Slowly, she opened her eyes to a squint, but didn't see him. She whirled around, thinking he was readying himself to hit her from behind. It wouldn't have been the first time. She wouldn't have been surprised if he'd pushed her into the loch, either.

There had been days she'd considered falling in. It seemed preferable to going home. But Nessie wouldn't let her.

Nessie.

She understood then what had happened to her father. Crouching at the water's edge, she saw the smallest spots of blood on the pebbles and guided the loch to rinse them away. After washing the blood from her face, she headed home.

For the first time in her life, it might not be so terrible.

She whistled as she walked.

~ Chapter Two ~

It was fair to say Maggie's father wasn't missed.

Once her mother realized he was truly gone, she'd phoned the bobbies and reported it, as any good wife should do. The constabulary did pop by to ask some questions, but once they got a glimpse of Maggie's split lip and her mother's black eye, they appeared to lose their enthusiasm.

"So you have no idea where he got off to, then?"

Her mother had shrugged her thin shoulders. "How should I know? He hardly answers to me. Usually he spends his days in the pub, and sometimes he goes by the loch to collect Maggie, but she hasn't seen 'im."

The bobbie knelt so he could look her in the eye. "Is that true, lass? You didn't see him yesterday evening?"

She shook her head. "No."

"That looks pretty sore, your lip. Who did that to you?"

"Some kids at school." The lie escaped so easily that for a moment, she felt like someone else. But she couldn't tell anyone what had really happened to her dad, not even her ma. She couldn't bear it if anything happened to Nessie, her only friend in the world.

Maggie saw their situation through the bobbie's eyes—he didn't believe her. She didn't understand how he knew, but he did. He knew it had been her dad who hurt her. She waited, silently begging him to let them go. All she'd done was lie about seeing her dad. She wasn't the one responsible for him going missing.

He'd done that to himself.

The man straightened. "Do you have a photo of him, then?"

"Nothing recent." Her ma flipped through an old album and removed a picture. "Here's one of us at Christmas."

He examined it with a skeptical expression. "How long ago was this taken?"

"About four years ago."

"You don't have anything more recent?"

"Paddy didn't like to have his photo taken," her ma explained.

The cop sighed and gave Ma his card, said he'd call if there were any news. Once he'd left, everything felt lighter.

Ma put an arm around her shoulders. "You didn't see 'im, did you, Maggie?"

"No, Ma. I didn't see him." This lie was easier, because she could tell her mother didn't want to know the truth.

If she'd thought losing her dad would earn her sympathy from the kids at school, she was wrong. They still teased her, bad as ever. As usual, Frank was the worst.

"Heard your da ran out on your ma," he bellowed, his face jiggling as he laughed. "Heard he's got a brand-new woman tucked away somewhere."

Maggie scowled. The rumor bothered her even though she knew it wasn't true. She understood how much it would pain her ma to hear this. People would say she was a failure as a wife, would blame her for running him off. "That's a lie."

"I bet it's true. Look how red you're getting." He pointed at her face, and she was tempted to bite off his finger. "You're as red as your hair!"

"You better stop it right now, Frank Sturrock."

"Or what?" His eyes danced. It was obvious how much he was enjoying this, how much he always enjoyed making her life miserable. It was his favorite hobby. "What are you going to do, make me disappear too?"

"That's enough, Frank," Miss McGrew said, sounding more weary than usual. "How many times do I have to remind you not to tease Maggie about her father? This is tough enough for her."

But it *wasn't* tough. The truth—and the thing she could never say at school—was that it was brilliant. Without the constant threat of her dad coming home drunk and causing a scene, Maggie had been able to sleep through the night, until her ma woke her for school. She'd never slept that soundly before. Before her dad went missing, some violent outburst was guaranteed to startle her awake.

They could eat what they wanted for dinner. Some days it was something from the forbidden aisle of the store, the place where frozen pizzas and ice cream lurked. Sometimes it was a big bowl of popcorn.

Once her mother accepted that Da wasn't coming back, she laughed more. Her bruises healed, and the years fell away. She looked and acted much younger. Even though nothing had gotten better at school—if anything, the teasing was worse— Maggie laughed more often too. She counted the minutes until school was over and she could rush home again. She didn't need to dawdle by the loch so much anymore, but she still stopped there every single day. When no one was nearby or paying any attention to her, she gave silent thanks and placed a flower on the water.

She hadn't seen her friend since the day her dad disappeared, but Maggie knew she was there. Nessie was always there, if you understood how and where to look for her.

───────

Then it happened.

For the rest of her life, Maggie would tell herself she'd done everything she could to prevent it.

Every day brought a new change in her mother. Bit by bit, Ma was becoming the parent and friend Maggie had always hoped she'd be. That morning, Ma had surprised her with a puzzle. One of the really tough versions that has a gazillion pieces. Maggie didn't know if she liked puzzles, but her Ma was so excited, her smile so big as she unveiled the gift and said it would be something for them to do after supper, that she was eager to find out.

So eager that she didn't hear the footsteps behind her until it was too late.

A hard shove in the middle of her back made her lose her balance. She tripped and fell, hitting the earth hard, palms first. "Ow!"

"Still searching for the Loch Ness monster, are we?" Frank said, leering at her. Her heart sank as she saw he'd brought a few of his pals with him. "You really are stupid."

"She's not a monster!" Maggie defended her friend before she could think better of it. She hated it when people referred to Nessie as a monster. As far as she was concerned, *people* were the monsters. Especially people like Frank. And her dad.

"You're right, she's not. For her to be anything, she'd have to exist."

"She *does* exist. I told you, you better not say that stuff around here." The boys were closing a circle around her, and Maggie struggled to her feet. Frank shoved her again, harder, but this time she managed to keep her footing.

"Why don't you leave me alone? I've done nothing to you."

"But we're here to help you, Mags," Frank said in a sickeningly sweet voice she didn't trust for a second. "We're your friends."

"You're not my friends." She took a step back, frantically searching for someone who would help her. But none of the visitors were close enough, and the ones who could have seen something bad was about to happen were averting their eyes. It was the same as it had been when Dad was alive—no one cared about her. She would have to find her own way out of this.

"Sure, we are. We even have a gift for you."

The other boys were grinning now, watching her the way a cat watches a lame bird. Maggie knew this wasn't a gift she wanted, but she also understood she wouldn't be given a choice. Still, she tried. "Please, please leave me alone. I've done nothing to you," she repeated.

"Aw, don't you even want to know what our gift is?"

She shook her head, but of course it didn't matter. She could have said no a million times, screamed it until the word echoed over the loch, and still they would have gone ahead with their evil plan.

Frank took a threatening step toward her. "We're going to give you a swimming lesson."

Maggie backed up even faster, but bumped into one of Frank's friends, who'd circled around behind her. The loch was freezing at any time of year. It was cold enough to steal the life from your bones. And it was deep too, so deep that often the best swimmers drowned in its depths. "Please don't, Frank."

"Oh, don't worry. We're not going to make you swim in *that*. You'd sink to the bottom, overdressed that way." Frank smirked, and cold horror chilled her as she realized what he meant. She struggled in the other boy's arms, but he was much too strong for her. He held her fast.

"Cover me," Frank ordered his friends. "Lay her down on the bank. Go on, now."

"This has gone far enough, don't ya think?" one of the boys asked. "You said we were just to scare her."

"I'll decide when it's gone far enough!" Frank's cheeks turned the color of beets. "Carry her to the water *now*."

Maggie tried to scream, but one of the boys pushed his hand over her mouth, mashing her lips against her teeth. She kicked and flailed her arms, but they carried her to the water like her efforts meant nothing. She was a butterfly in a net, a dragonfly trapped in a jar.

When they had her pinned on the banks, Frank forced himself between her legs and knelt there. She felt his horrible hands on her bare skin and thrashed with more desperation than before. The boy who was keeping her quiet loosened his pressure slightly and she sank her teeth into his flesh with every ounce of strength she had. He shrieked and ran off, shaking his hand. Maggie was gratified by the taste of blood.

"You stupid bitch. You're nothing but a whore like your ma." Frank sneered at her. "Forget swimming. I'm going to teach you another lesson, and it's gonna be one you'll never forget."

"D-don't you touch me." Her voice wavered, but she wasn't scared anymore. She was by the water, which had always been her refuge, her sanctuary. Even Frank Sturrock couldn't ruin that. "I swear to you, it'll be the last thing you ever do."

"I'll take that chance." He lunged for her, and she closed her eyes. She heard the other boys scream. When she risked a look, she saw that Frank's head was missing, but before she could feel sick, the rest of him was gone too.

There was a flash of something black and glistening, something that cast a large shadow. The slightest rippling sound from the water behind her. And then it was over, and so was Frank.

His friends were scrambling up the bank as quickly as they could, their shoes slipping on the grass. But that was okay.

She knew they'd never bother her again.

~ Chapter Three ~

"Gosh, I'm really sorry this happened to ye, Maggie."

It was the same bobbie who'd questioned her the day her dad went missing, but this time Miss McGrew was with her, so she felt better. Safer. The teacher squeezed her hand.

"The boys told me what that lad did—what he was about to do—and I assure you, they won't get off easy for it."

She nodded. She'd heard it all before. Adults were forever saying that the bullies would pay, but kids realized that they never, ever did.

Frank had paid, though. Her dad had paid. And that also made her feel better. Safer. Maggie squeezed Miss McGrew's hand in return.

"They, er—have a bit of a crazy story, I'm afraid. They said they saw something down at the loch. They claim you saw it as well." The man's face colored, as if he was embarrassed to mention it.

"What do they say they saw?" Miss McGraw asked, not sounding the least bit intimidated by the bobbie in her office.

"Well, uh, I'd rather ask Maggie what she saw first, if I may."

"Go ahead."

He leaned forward. "Maggie, did you see anything unusual down at the loch yesterday?"

"Not unless you mean those boys, no." It was a relief not to have to lie this time. She *hadn't* seen anything unusual. She'd seen exactly what she'd expected to see, what she'd known was there all along.

"Are you certain?"

"Constable, Maggie has been through a lot, as I'm sure you can understand. First the loss of her father, and now this. Those boys were always tormenting her—I've witnessed it myself. If she tells you she didn't see anything unusual, you can trust that she's telling the truth."

The bobbie nodded, and that seemed to close the subject. He rose to leave, but Miss McGrew stopped him. "Wait," she said. "You never did tell us what they claim to have seen."

The man's shoulders slumped, and he sighed. For a minute, Maggie thought he wouldn't answer.

"They say the Loch Ness monster did away with Frank." He paused, looking at her closely. "What do you say to that, Maggie?"

"I say that's crazy. There's no monster in the loch. That's just a silly story."

Her teacher smiled at her, looking so proud. Miss McGrew was cool, but she didn't understand. She never had.

Maggie had always known was no monster in the loch.

Just her friend, Nessie.

*"We would wander for an hour or more before circling back to the tent.
By that time, the next camper would be in his position."*

LAUREL'S FIRST CHASE

CHRISTI NOGLE

My daughter and I came upon a yellow tent in the rocky stretch of Western forest. She might have thought the camper must be somewhere near, about to come upon us—or she might have though he was lying inside. What pleasure, to read in a tent through the last few hours of daylight, to put off the gathering of wood and laze inside!

He *had* done that for a while. He had lain inside on a soft green nylon sleeping bag and read his adventure story, but he was not doing it now. Still, it might have seemed so to Laurel if she could not see the fall he took on his fateful trek for wood.

I saw clearly. I saw the sun at noon in his memories and the sun at three o'clock with my own eyes. I apprehended that his death would not come until dusk. He was close enough I could feel how he'd suffered at noon and how the suffering changed by three o'clock, the richness of it, the almost-ecstasy. I felt how it would sharpen by five and ebb soon after.

If I'd not had Laurel with me, I might have gone to his side. He might have mistaken me—or pretended to mistake me—for a good Samaritan and begged for my help. Or he might have asked me to take a rock to his head. I might have obliged or not, depending.

I wondered, could Laurel feel him at all? I was initially certain that she could not.

I unzipped his tent's flap and we kneeled inside. I watched her face as she talked about how lovely the light was through the tent walls and how pleasurable it might be if we had book *of our own* with us. (She said that with her hand on the bag where the man had tucked his little adventure novel.)

She said we could lie here and read and think about gathering wood, but we would not gather wood. We would lie here and feel the dark coming on and keep reading. We could laze here, dreading the coming cold but keep reading.

So she saw all of this but could not see the rest. Or could she see the rest but not bring herself to say it?

She talked more and more frantically.

I thought it must be true: she saw something but was too afraid or too shy to say what she saw. When I put my hand on hers, she jumped up.

"Let's see more of this place," she said.

We would wander for an hour or more before circling back to the tent. By that time, the next camper would be in his position.

"Once?" she asked.

"Once we had a home here. Once a sort of town stood nearby, a road, a—"

"No," she laughed.

No? I rapped on the boards of a cabin. The cabin was not there, but I saw in her face how the sound came to her.

"We were … homesteaders? Farmers," I said.

"That's ridiculous. There were never any farms here," she said, rushing ahead. "I want to go home soon," she called back.

It was only four or four-thirty in the afternoon, but a campfire took shape up ahead. I walked a long rocky clearing behind my daughter, wondering if she saw the coming fire or anything of the night ahead.

I admired her height, the fine gold threads in her darkening hair. Her gait was still awkward, though she moved swiftly. I felt how aware she was of me behind her, felt her refuse to look back.

She swept her hair to the side and touched her neck. A month ago, it was,

I saw a ball of flesh in that spot while we were finishing yard work. I twisted the skin, and before she could react, pinched it off with my fingernails.

"Ouch," she said. "What the—"

I flung the thing into the grass. "I think it's called a skin tag. I got it for you."

She touched the drop of blood. "Thanks?" she said.

Now she walked across the clearing, fingering that spot on her neck. She would not look back at me. A second Laurel walked beside her for a moment, and this one did look back, but in an instant, it was gone.

I stopped and watched her reach the end of the clearing, saw her walk between two stunted pine trees, shift to the right to move around another. All I caught was the red of her shorts, and then she was gone.

I drifted toward the camper who had just arrived. He was going to be the one to start the fire. I thought at first that he was already walking in a spiral around the camp. I thought he had gone looking for the missing man.

I came closer and saw he was not spinning any spiral. He was only thinking of doing so. He stood beside the other man's cheap yellow tent and looked out into the trees, thinking how a man could move in a tight spiral and find someone who was missing if he cared to do so, then thinking that he would do that very thing soon now, any minute.

I came even closer.

I felt around inside his mind and took out a catalog of numbers and dates. He weighed one-hundred and seventy-eight pounds and held at twelve percent body fat. The numbers for cholesterol and such were good numbers. I knew because they had a prideful reddish glow. He had paid 349,000-some dollars for his home, 36,988 for his latest truck.

He had begun hunting at age eleven, and along with the ages that marked the first of each animal he killed, I found the totaled numbers of kills. Along with the numbers of kills was the sharp white flood of emotion for the first kill. That one was not the only kill that mattered to him, but it was one of a precious few. He thought of these as diamonds.

He was a good man.

He thought of his meaningful kills as diamonds, and the time he passed the diamond to the one who would be his second wife? He thought of that moment as a small flawless pearl. The birth of his boy was a grand and yellow jewel, uncomfortably intense like a direct view of the sun.

The boy was too small to be hunting, but the year in which the man would take him for his first kill was set in a calendar in the man's mind. He was already deciding on the place and imagining how the weather would be on that day. There were dates on the man's calendar for his next truck and other milestones to come such as the forty-fifth birthday and the fiftieth birthday, and the year in which it would be reasonable and necessary to take his wife on a cruise. He dreaded that year.

There were deep, pure emotions coloring all of the tables and dates.

He was sure he was a good man.

I thought for a moment of leaving my daughter to him. How happy would she be if I told her to go to him and say *I'm lost. Can you help me?*

But I knew she saw. And we were mostly in agreement. All that was left was to put my hand on hers and say it was time.

I needed to find her first. I felt her around me but all dispersed, in several places at once, stronger and brighter here and fainter there. A swarm of my sweet Laurel.

I didn't pursue her. *Let her play her games for now*, I thought.

I watched the man pitch his impressive little plum-red tent, watched him take out an ultralight hiker's stove and miniature cooking gear. The price tags and advertising copy seemed to hover over each item as in a catalog, and how inordinately pleased he was to find the large rock with its flat top for meal preparation! I felt a little pang of pity for him then.

In his mind, he spun his web around the camp. He might find and save the weaker man, be a hero, but wasn't he already hero enough in his mind?

He began to bore me. The perfect posture, the wasteless motions of cooking and eating and tidying up. I wandered away.

As I wandered, image-memories came unbidden. A small fierce creature hunting on the forest floor, a ball of flesh the size of an orange in my hand, a girl in an art book with arms swept up growing branches, growing leaves.

"You remind me of her," I told Laurel. She closed the book and never asked why.

I found my daughter curled against the base of a tree, face dirty and leaves in her hair. She'd sighted him, must have.

"If he came upon you now, you'd catch him easy," I said.

"I don't know what you're talking about," she whined.

"It would be cheating to do that—no doubt—but it would work," I said.

"What," she said, not like a question but like the start of some question. Her breath hitched.

"Are you really crying?" I asked, amused. I came closer, and she cringed back against the tree. Tears came all muddy down her cheeks. I wanted to touch her face and feel the heat, but I didn't dare touch her.

We'd gotten too close, was that it? She sensed how good he thought he was.

After a time, she said, "Can we go home?"

"What home?" I said. Did she mean the house up in Bend? Was she missing her little pink room, the garbage I let her keep in it? The constant pretending to be human?

I will not go back there, I thought fiercely and was surprised by the thought.

Dusk was falling, and just across the creek, the weak man was finally ending. We were silent while it happened and shared, I thought, a meaningful look.

She crawled toward me, hoping to feed. I shook my head.

The man wallowed in shame, thinking how he ought to have searched instead of just imagining it. He sat before the yellow tent, called, and checked inside. He stepped inside without his shoes and came out again, reshod himself. He rifled through the other man's bag for a long while and then arranged the items back inside. There was nothing in the bag that surprised him or answered a question he had. He unzipped the tent again and set the bag inside. He rocked back up onto his feet, zipped the tent flap, and began gathering wood.

The shame he felt for not searching and the shame he felt for snooping in the bag were sweet and pure and equal in intensity.

My daughter squatted at the edge of a creek with a stick in her hand when I came upon her. Better. At least she was not crying.

"What doing?" I said.

"I'm hungry," she said.

"Me too," I said.

"I'm trying to catch a fish."

I thought of how I might have caught a fish when I was small—easy, with no second thought. Catch the watery sweetness of it in my mouth and move on to the next with no reflection, no delay.

I'd done her damage, raising her all these years. I'd made her less than she could have been.

She leaned in and poked her stick in the shallow water. She sighed and leaned back.

"Stop watching me," she said.

"Do you see the fire yet?" I asked. It was so bright and beautiful, just a half hour away from starting and a hundred yards south. I was thinking like the man now, and I wanted to tell her how strange it was to be seeing things in his way, in yards and compass points and calendar squares. I tried to show her, but she was closed to me. It seemed she had always been closed.

I said, "The best time will be when he's still at the fire, before he gets sleepy. He'll be strongest then. He'll give you a good chase."

She stared into me.

"Or you could go and tell him you're hungry, but you know that wouldn't be fair."

She scrunched her nose, dropped her stick and rose, crossed her arms.

"I can smell the fire," she said.

"Can you smell the man?" I said.

Laurel nodded. When I approached, she did not shy from me. I took her hand. Her cuticles were raw and red, the nails coming loose.

We watched the fire for a time. The man was still, but the images in his mind were painted in the dark sky above him: bird kills and deer kills and chases after wild, elusive creatures that never existed. The image of a weaker man crept close with all the weight and dread of a ghost, and receded, and went round in a spiral of smoke above the fire.

The man upended his flask above his mouth and then brought out a bottle.

"He drinks to get sleepy," I said.

"I know," said Laurel.

"It's time, or past," I said.

"It's too late now," she said.

"Not necessarily."

She cried again but not for the same reason.

"The things he values are of no value," I said.

She seemed about to open to me, but then the man thought of his little toddling son. The boy seemed to play and coo around the edges of the fire, and she was never more opaque than at that moment.

"Tomorrow?" I said.

"I can't," she said. She walked away again.

The man was a long while at the fire. He expected to sleep there instead of in his tent, but sleep could not come while he sensed me so near him. He went, he lay down comfortably enough in his sleeping bag, but something was wrong. His life began to look terrible to him.

He saw his son growing up without him. All he wanted was to be with his son, but he had come here. It wasn't even hunting season, just a camping trip, self-indulgent. His life nothing but restlessness, aimlessness, and vanity.

He had not even tried to save the man. He felt he had been placed here—in this place, this life—only to save the man, and he had failed to do it.

He knew himself to be a morsel in the center of a web, saved by a spider. He knew his hands would not move, and even if they moved, they would not be able to unzip his tent. He would not be able to try.

I imagined the kill. He imagined it with me. I was that close.

Before a kill, the fingernails loosen from bloody cuticles, the forefinger and middle finger only are needed. The organs my daughter likes to pretend she does not have push out. Long, noodly things. They stretch up and into his nostrils. She takes only what she needs, leaves him empty and beautiful.

I waited for Laurel to return. The man pretended to sleep, and then he did sleep.

He dreamed of taking a new puppy on the playground equipment to desensitize it to new sights and sounds. A montage of happy moments playing on the swings and slides. He walked a playground bridge, the anxious puppy behind whimpering—falling—but when the man looked down at the ground far below, it was no puppy there, but his son. The man shrieked and jumped in his sleep and then was still.

He knew.

He was paralyzed. It was cruel to keep him in stasis, but Laurel was nowhere to be seen or felt. I lay inside the yellow tent for a time. I built up the fire and waited. I slept.

I woke to hard steps on a wooden floor. Laurel stood one foot off the ground, ten or twelve feet from the fire.

"You've found one of the cabins," I said.

She nodded. "He's still here," she said.

"I told you I'm not taking him," I said.

She nodded. She finally believed.

I saw shimmers of firelight on the walls of the cabin and when I squinted, the rough outline of the wood stove and the little iron bed far back. It was the cabin where I'd taken my first family.

The image came of a little rounded seedling coming up from the forest floor, a little animal growing more ravenous as it gorged on small birds and rodents, a troll-like creature stepping onto the front step of a cabin already seeing itself stepping out, days later, a girl.

Laurel thought of it too. It was the most curious, magical thing. I didn't know what had caused it, but there had been a change in her.

"I've never known anyone else like us," I said.

"And who are we?" she said.

Our imaginations played over the sights of the animal hunting in leaves and the book with the sculpture of Apollo and Daphne. Our imaginations spiraled further out among the stars, and that felt true to both of us, but we didn't know which one we came from or why we'd come—or why we'd been flung—down here.

The strands came out of Laurel's fingertips now, not just the first two fingers but all of them. "In the morning," she said, and I felt her hunger.

I felt the man tense in fear. He was exceedingly strong to break that level of stasis. He cried out, just one sharp bark, and Laurel scattered into pieces and ran from me once again.

I released the man into a wholesome, natural sleep and followed.

My daughter and I frolicked those last few hours. That's all I can call it. We laughed for the first time in so long. She let herself go for once, entirely. She unspooled like an anemone, rose like a tree and bended down into the earth. I felt my own body relaxing into the creek and that sweet slack feeling overcome me, like taking off a corset.

I thought of putting on a corset for the first time, and all the other moves I had made toward this life we'd been living. I thought of all the balls of flesh I'd dropped quaking to life on the ground.

We played through the trees, we relaxed, but our minds never wandered far from the man.

He slept. He turned in his sleep. He woke slowly.

"He's strong enough to run now," Laurel said. Her nostrils flared. She smelled him.

"Let him start," I said.

It wasn't long after that I saw him crouching, looking into the trees. I said, "Now."

We followed his frantic movement up and down the dark, steep hills. We stumbled, drunk on the mix of fear and hope that colored the figures in his mind. He didn't think of the weak man or of his son now; he thought only of himself, and I thought that would make things easier for Laurel.

He kept track of sights along the way and estimated from them how much farther to the car. He walked quickly but would soon break into a run as the trees thinned, and when he did run, she would chase in earnest.

Or so I thought. She ran, but she never did catch him. She stopped short and watched him stumble over rocks and sprawl out into the highway.

We watched him rush to his truck, watched the inevitable shaking fumble with the keys. His truck backed out and pulled onto the highway.

"His little boy," she said when I caught up. "I couldn't."

"It was the delay, was all. And he was too old," I said. "It wouldn't have been a challenge." I rubbed her shoulders.

We walked on, a mile and then two. My spirits were low. I thought, *This girl is going to kill me.* I thought how this had been her one chance and that ever after she would want to keep feeding from me, and that we'd have to go back to the sad little house and never be free.

It was just dawn and brighter every moment, but then I saw. We'd move down the road another hour until we sighted a new walker, this a much younger man; too thin with reddish stubble on his head and face, his silver backpack glaring in the sun.

I'd expect her to turn her head and pretend not to see him, but my daughter would brighten.

"This one," she'd say. She'd start at a trot and build speed.

I'd keep my arm around her shoulders until then, feeling so proud. When the time came, I'd watch her chase him on the road and veer back into the forest.

ABOUT THE AUTHORS

Sarah Read is a dark fiction writer in the frozen north of Wisconsin. Her debut novel, *The Bone Weaver's Orchard*, won the Bram Stoker Award for Superior Achievement in a First Novel and the This Is Horror Award for Novel of the Year. You can find her online at Inkwell-Monster.wordpress.com or on Instagram and Twitter.

Michaelbrent Collings is a bestselling novelist, screenwriter, multiple Bram Stoker and Dragon Award finalist, and was recently voted one of the Top 100 Greatest All-Time Horror Writers on a Ranker survey of over 15,000 readers. Find him at WrittenInsomnia.com.

Calvin Cleary is a librarian and writer in central Ohio.

LH Moore's stories, poetry, and essays have appeared in numerous anthologies and publications such as *FIYAH*, *Apex*, and *Fireside*. A historian who loves playing video games and classical guitar, you can find her online at LHMooreCreative.com.

Philip Fracassi's award-winning story collection, *Behold the Void*, won "Best Collection of the Year" from both *This Is Horror* and *Strange Aeons Magazine*. His stories have been published in numerous magazines and anthologies, including *Best Horror of the Year, Nightmare Magazine, Black Static, Dark Discoveries, Cemetery Dance* and others. For more information on his books and screenplays, visit his website at PFracassi.com.

Georgia Cook is an illustrator and writer from London. She is the winner of the LISP 2020 Flash Fiction Prize, has been shortlisted for the Bridport Prize and Reflex Fiction Award, among others. She also writes for the anthology podcasts *Creepy, The Other Stories*, and *The Night's End.* She can be found on Twitter at @georgiacooked and her website at GeorgiaCookWriter.com.

Patrick Barb is a freelance writer and editor from the southern United States, currently living (and trying not to freeze to death) in Saint Paul, Minnesota. Previously, his short fiction has appeared in *Boneyard Soup Magazine, Not One of Us #67*, and Dread Stone Press's *Dose of Dread*, among other publications. For more of his work, visit PatrickBarb.com.

John Langan is the author of two novels and four collections of stories. He has received the Bram Stoker and the This Is Horror Award. He is one of the founders of the Shirley Jackson Awards and serves on its Board of Directors. He lives in New York's Mid-Hudson valley with his wife and younger son. Read more about him at JohnPaulLangan.wordpress.com.

Gabino Iglesias is a writer, editor, literary critic, and professor living in Austin, TX. He's the author of *Zero Saints* and *Coyote Songs* and the editor of *Both Sides* and *Halldark Holidays*. His work has been twice nominated for the Bram Stoker Award, the Locus Award, and he won the Wonderland Book Award for Best Novel in 2019. He teaches creative writing at SNHU's online MFA.

Auston Habershaw's stories have been published in *The Magazine of Fantasy and Science Fiction, Galaxy's Edge, Analog*, and other places. His complete fantasy series, *The Saga of the Redeemed* was published by Harper-Voyager. Find him on his website at AAHabershaw.com.

Corey Farrenkopf lives on Cape Cod with his wife, Gabrielle, and works as a librarian. His fiction has been published in *Tiny Nightmares, The Southwest Review, Wigleaf, Flash Fiction Online, Bourbon Penn, Cemetery Gates Media*, and elsewhere. To learn more, follow him on the web at Corey-Farrenkopf.com.

Leah Claire Kaminski lives in Chicago. Her story in *Humans Are The Problem* is her first published piece of fiction; her next will appear in *Parenting Gone Speculative* from Alternating Current Press. A widely published poet, her newest chapbook *Root* is forthcoming from Milk and Cake Press. Read more at LeahKaminski.com.

Formerly a film critic, journalist, screenwriter, and teacher, **Gemma Files** has been an award-winning horror author since 1999. She has published four collections of short work, three collections of speculative poetry, a Weird Western trilogy, a story-cycle, and a stand-alone novel, *Experimental Film*, which won the 2015 Shirley Jackson Award for Best Novel and the 2016 Sunburst Award for Best Adult Novel.

· · ·

T.J. Tranchell's first published novel, *Cry Down Dark*, (Blysster Press) was picked by the *New York Times Book List* for one of the 50 Scares in 50 States for 2020. He has also published horror short fiction, is at work on his third novel, and was co-editor of *GIVE: An Anthology of Anatomical Entries*, a dark fiction anthology from When the Dead Books. You can see more of his work at TJTranchell.net.

Justin Guleserian is a speculative fiction writer, specializing in horror and dark fantasy. He is also a pen-and-ink illustrator.

Jonathon Mast lives in Kentucky with his wife and an insanity of children. (A group of children is called an insanity. Trust me.) His first novel *The Keeper of Tales* is currently available from Dark Owl Publishing. He can be found at JonathonMastAuthor.com.

Gordon Linzner is founder and former editor of *Space and Time Magazine*, and author of three published novels and dozens of short stories in *Fantasy & Science Fiction, Twilight Zone, Sherlock Holmes Mystery Magazine*, and others. He is a member of the Horror Writers Association and a lifetime member of the Science Fiction & Fantasy Writers of America.

Lisa Morton is a six-time winner of the Bram Stoker Award, and a world-class Halloween expert. Her most recent books are the anthology *Weird Women: Classic Supernatural Fiction by Groundbreaking Female Writers 1852-1923* (co-edited with Leslie S. Klinger) and *Night Terrors & Other Tales*. Lisa lives in the San Fernando Valley and online at LisaMorton.com.

Die Booth likes wild beaches and exploring dark places. You can read his stories in places like *LampLight Magazine, The Fiction Desk*, and *The*

Cheshire Prize for Literature anthologies. His books *My Glass is Runn*, *365 Lies* and *Spirit Houses* are available online and *Making Friends (and other fictions)* is due out soon. You can find out more about his writing at DieBooth.wordpress.com.

Dominick Cancilla has had dozens of short stories and two novels published over the years. The hardcover of his most recent novel, *Tomorrow's Journal*, will be published by Cemetery Dance in late 2021.

J.H. Moncrieff is an award-winning and best-selling author. Her novel, *City of Ghosts*, won the Kindle Book Review award for Best Horror/Suspense. When not writing, she loves exploring haunted places, advocating for animal rights, and summoning her inner ninja in muay thai class.

Christi Nogle's fiction has appeared in publications such as *Pseudopod*, *Vastarien*, *Lady Churchill's Rosebud Wristlet*, and *Three-lobed Burning Eye*. Her debut novel, *Beulah*, is coming in 2022 from Cemetery Gates Media. Follow her at ChristiNogle.com.

EDITORIAL TEAM

Michael Cluff, Editor-in-Chief. Storytelling has always been important to Michael. When he isn't writing his own tales, he's editing for other authors, or planning anthologies. He does post on his site, McCluff.com, when he remembers that it exists.

Willow Becker, Editor. A horror veteran and published science fiction author, Willow has hundreds of published credits in the areas of fiction, the business of writing, and creative nonfiction. Read her work in *Space and Time Magazine* and *Black Fox Literary Magazine*, or her personal nonfiction thoughts at WillowDawnBecker.com.

Jess Lewis, Special Editorial Consultant. Jess (they/them) is a genderqueer and pansexual writer and organizer who hails from the hollers of Western North Carolina. When they're not imagining new creatures or queer utopias, they're facilitating capacity-building workshops and organizing programming for The Outer Dark Symposium on the Greater Weird. You can reach them at QuareFutures.com.

Carl Duzett, Editorial Consultant. Carl Duzett was once both a vampire and a werewolf at the same time, leading to a confusing love triangle with himself. He was able to cure both his vampirism and werewolfism, and now loves himself by writing speculative fiction. Find his half-baked thoughts at CarlDuzett.net, and his quarter-baked thoughts on Twitter at @cduzett.

Christopher Baxter, Editorial Consultant. Christopher Baxter's short stories have appeared in the October 2016 and Spring 2018 volumes of *Deep Magic* e-zine, the *Best of Deep Magic* anthology, and the recently released *Put Your Shoulder to the Wheel: A Mormon Steampunk Anthology.* Chris works as an editor and writer, and you can read his writing tips at StoryPolisher.blogspot.com.

T.J. Tranchell, Editorial Consultant. In addition to his work as a published author, T.J. acts as an editorial consultant and blog master for WLW Press. He was the co-editor of *GIVE: An Anthology of Anatomical Entries,* a dark fiction anthology from When the Dead Books. You can see more of his work at TJTranchell.net.

Abigail Brown, Editorial Assistant. Abigail Brown is an 18-year-old autistic aspiring author from Utah. Her writing focuses on LBGTQ+ and neurodivergent teens as they try to navigate their places in their social groups, the internet, and the world. Find her on twitter at @writerabbieb.

Made in the USA
Middletown, DE
15 October 2021